D0425848

THURSDAY'S CHILD

THURSDAY'S CHILD

TERI WHITE

THE MYSTERIOUS PRESS
New York • Tokyo • Sweden • Milan
Published by Warner Books

 A Time Warner Company

Mysterious Press books are published by
Warner Books, Inc., 666 Fifth Avenue, New York, NY 10103.

A Time Warner Company

The Mysterious Press name and logo are trademarks of
Warner Books, Inc.
Printed in the United States of America

First printing: February 1991

10 9 8 7 6 5 4 3 2 1

Library of Congress Cataloging-in-Publication Data

White, Teri.
    Thursday's child / Teri White.
        p. cm.
    ISBN 0-89296-255-0
    I. Title.
    PS3573.H47495T47   1991
    813'.54—dc20   90-45102
                                            CIP

This one is for my daughter.

Thursday's child has far to go . . .
— Traditional

Don't look back.
Something might be gaining on you.
— Leroy (Satchel) Paige

1

The whole damned city was in a bad mood.

"If you ask me," a shrill female voice on the radio was saying, "I think what they ought to do is take all them rapers out and cut their things right off. Use a pair of rusty pinking shears to do the job. That'll teach 'em."

The call-in show's (male) host gave a theatrical groan of excruciating pain, disconnected the woman, made a wisecrack about how long it had been since *that* broad had been close to any man's "thing," and went to a jingle plugging cat food.

Robert Turchek reached out and switched off the radio impatiently, proving that his mood was no better than anybody else's, at least that of anybody else who was also stuck on the Santa Monica Freeway. It must have been the heat that was making everybody so crazy, he decided, although you would think that by now the residents of southern California should have grown used to the damned inversions that moved in to trap a load of hot, dirty air right over the area. And then just sat there. For days. But apparently they weren't used to it, because everybody and his neighbor was on a real bitch.

Robert realized that he personally was being made even more irritable by the extremely petty nature of the errand he was on. It wasn't any kind of a big deal at all that had him trapped here on this multi-lane parking lot; this was just one of those shitwork tasks that helped to pay the rent. No challenge involved.

It *was* true, of course, that a couple of his business associates were Fortune 500 types, but the guy he was on his way to see this particular afternoon definitely didn't fall into that category. Instead of Beverly Hills, Robert was on his way to East Los Angeles. Real exciting, right? If he ever actually did get there, he would be visiting an exceedingly unlucky—and definitely just plain dumb—horseplayer named Ernesto Gallos. It wasn't the fact that Ernie couldn't pick a winner at the track if his life depended upon it (which it, in fact, did) that had brought Robert into the picture. He was too important to concern himself with the wins and losses of every two-bit racing fan in the state of California.

No, Ernie's sins went far beyond just being unlucky.

Desperation made a dumb man even dumber and Ernie had tried to pay off his markers by stealing money from his own boss. Unfortunately for this hopeless wetback with an uncanny knack for picking equine losers, that boss was not a man who took kindly to such things. All of which explained why

Robert was on the job and why he was stuck in this traffic jam.

Robert finally extricated himself from the horrors of the freeway system and headed for the dismal neighborhood where Ernie lived. At a long red light, he turned the radio on again and punched digital buttons until he found a station that was playing what sounded like Mozart, although he wasn't altogether sure about that. It suited his mood and he jacked the volume way up.

It took him only a few more minutes to reach what was Ernie's most recent address. What a rathole, he thought, parking his pearl-gray Saab directly in front of the run-down residential hotel. Sometimes it made him tired, dealing over and over again with the same kind of people. He honestly tried to help them, going out of his way more times than he could count to make things easier. Even, sometimes, at the risk of irritating those who were paying for his services. But even when he occasionally extended a deadline, it usually didn't do a damned bit of good. A loser was a loser was a goddamned loser.

If Ernie Gallos had the good sense that God gave to a taco, he'd have been back in Mexico by now. But Robert was beyond being surprised by the fact that the jerk was still around. Almost begging for Robert to show up.

Well, now he was here.

This was not a part of town that a smart man would venture into unarmed, even in broad daylight. If the crackheads didn't get you, the street gangs would. Robert checked his shoulder holster automatically, felt the familiar weight of the Magnum he always carried (though he had never actually fired it, except at the range), and was reassured. Then he reached under the seat and took out the cheap gun and homemade silencer stashed there. He put the gun into his jacket pocket.

Damn it, Ernie should have known the way this would go down. Why the hell hadn't he skipped the country? Sure, Robert tried to help the scumbags whenever he could, but if a man allowed himself to turn into some freaking bleeding-heart type, he would end up poor at the very least, and stone dead at the most. Robert had absolutely no intention of letting either one of those things happen to him.

With that thought firmly in mind, he patted the gun in his pocket once more and got out of the car.

He took a moment to lock the door, which didn't mean much these days, of course, not in any neighborhood at all. His only comfort came from the fact that any car thief who was dumb enough to put one little finger on any car *he* was driving would regret it. Sincerely. And the punks seemed to know that somehow. Crooks weren't always as dumb as they seemed to be. Usually, yeah, but not always.

After a quick glance up and down the street—which revealed only a hooker out too early and a couple of hypes for whom it was already much too late—Robert went into the old building.

The janitor who looked after the place was a retired boxer named Sylvester. Too many blows to the head over too many years of an entirely undistinguished fight career meant that Sylvester was several beats off the count most of the time. He paused long enough to peer across the lobby at Robert, his expression one of amiable blankness, then resumed his surprisingly energetic sweeping of the linoleum floor. It seemed like a waste of all that energy, because all he was really doing was pushing the dirt from one spot to another. Sweat had turned his green work shirt black. Somebody probably ought to slow him down before the stupid bastard had a stroke or something. But, after all, it was none of Robert's business, and Sylvester, brain-damaged as he was, still had enough smarts left to realize that whatever Turchek was up to here was none of *his* concern. He just bent over the broom and started whistling tunelessly.

Ernesto's room was on the second floor and, of course, the amenities provided in this building did not include a working elevator. The carpet on the steps was worn thin and stained. This kind of place could really bring a man down, emotionally speaking, if he let it.

Robert was careful not to brush the filthy wall with the sleeve of his new white linen jacket. Belatedly, he realized that it would have been smarter not to wear the jacket on this particular day, but it was too late now. With luck, it wouldn't get messed up during his meeting with Gallos.

The second-floor hallway stank of piss and fast food and several generations of human sweat. Not to mention some other smells that were unrecognizable. Robert tried not to breath too deeply—who the hell knew what you could catch just by sucking up the air in here?

He reached his destination and used his fist to pound on the door of 2D.

"Yeah?" The tentative voice came from the other side of the still-closed door. The caution was no surprise; stupid as Gallos was, he had to know that he was a man about to fall off the edge of the precipice.

"Open up, Ernie," Robert said, not raising his voice at all. Staying calm was one very good way to scare the losers. Robert knew from experience that psychology played a very big role in his business success. After all, facts were facts. He was only five-feet-eleven and while nobody could call him skinny, he wasn't packing nearly enough weight on his frame to intimidate anybody merely by his presence. Even with a gun. People were always getting fooled by his face. The pale skin, with its almost invisible sprinkling of freckles, and the slightly vague-looking green eyes, all topped by a tangle of nearly red curls, frequently caused people to underestimate him. One former girlfriend always claimed that he looked like an Eagle Scout in search of a Norman Rockwell *Saturday Evening Post* cover.

So it all boiled down to a simple technique. Keep it cool, keep it quiet, and you could scare the shit out of the bastards. Attitude mattered.

There was still nothing but silence from behind the door. It was so quiet that he could almost hear Ernesto's shaky thought process as the little worm tried desperately to come up with some way out of what was going to happen. It was lucky (for him, of course, not for Ernie) that they were on the second floor, or the thieving rat would probably be out a window already.

"Open the goddamned door, Ernie." Robert, although he was getting hotter and grouchier by the second, still kept his words soft, almost gentle, as if greasy Gallos were some broad he was trying to sweet-talk into bed.

Finally, apparently deciding that taking a header out of a second-story window onto a cement alley couldn't be much better than facing up to whatever Turchek had in mind for him, Ernesto slid the chain off and opened the door slowly. "Hi, there, Mr. Turchek," he said, flashing a sickly grin. "I didn't know it was you knocking."

Ernesto was a short, plump man with a lot of nervous energy. It was only too bad that he had never learned to apply all of that energy to anything besides picking lead-footed nags. And stealing from the kind of man you should never, ever steal from.

Robert didn't say anything as he stepped into the room and carefully closed the door. In here, it smelled even worse than it had in the hallway. That probably had something to do with the pile of filthy clothes in the corner and the gray, damp sheets tangled in the middle of the bed. How could anybody live like this?

Despite the fact that Gallos was a slob, Robert looked at him with a certain amount of sadness. This was nothing personal; fact was, he sort of liked the fat little man and would miss seeing him around the track. But some people, it seemed, were just born for trouble. It wasn't fair, perhaps, but that's just how it was. Life didn't come with any guarantees. Except the one that said debts always came due. Sooner or later, they all came due. That was the only sure thing in the whole universe, as far as Robert was concerned.

"I'm surprised to find you still here," Robert said at last. "I left word all over the fucking town that I was looking for you."

Ernie licked his lips. "I hadda tip, man, you know? A sure thing, the guy said. And I figured, this paid off, I'd be okay." Ernie grinned again, although it was a pretty safe bet that he wasn't at all amused. The grin was just a nervous habit; a very unpleasant habit, in Robert's opinion. "See, I win that pot, I can pay Mr. LoBianca back. That's what I figured."

Robert could only shake his head. "The nag come in like you thought he would?"

"No," Ernie whispered. His teeth were fuzzy green.

"Well, if it makes you feel any better, Ernie, it wouldn't make any difference if you'd won the fucking state lottery. See, Mr. LoBianca doesn't care so much about getting the money back. He just doesn't want anybody else getting the idea they could take what belongs to him."

"I really needed the bread, man. Times is real rough, you know?"

"Well," Robert said kindly, "at least you don't have to worry about rough times anymore. That's something, isn't it?"

Ernie started to cry even before the handgun was out of Robert's pocket.

Too bad. This kind of thing wasn't fun for anybody. But a man had to learn that if he was going to play the game, he better follow the rules.

2

It was nearly four o'clock that same afternoon when Robert pulled his car into the visitors' parking lot of the Ledgewood Convalescent Home and found an empty niche between a Lincoln and a Porsche. There were no poor visitors here, because there were no poor patients.

What once upon a time had been the luxurious mansion of a forgotten silent film star now housed the wealthy and mostly helplessly ill. The gleaming-white exterior and surrounding lush green grounds gave no indication of what was going on inside.

On a day like today, when he was feeling sort of bad about what he'd had to do to poor Ernie, Robert could cheer himself up considerably by wondering what all the others did. The others who had loved ones in Ledgewood and who also had to come up with the ridiculous monthly charges. Probably there were some who did things that were a lot worse than just ridding the world of one more greasy little hustler. Like the industrialists whose factories polluted the air and made kids sick. Compared to *that*, whacking somebody like Ernie hardly counted at all.

Before getting out of the car, he took the gun from its holster and locked it in the glove compartment. Hard to believe that a place like this would have a metal detector at the entrance, but it did. The device had been installed a couple of years earlier, after a patient's husband walked into the building late one Saturday night, went to his wife's room, and swiftly ended her battle with Lou Gehrig's disease. A single well-placed shot did the job. The woman had been dying anyway and suffering like hell, so Robert didn't really see what all the fuss was about. Apparently, it just didn't look good, PR-wise. So up went the damned detector.

Inside the lobby, the receptionist greeted him with an automatic smile, the guard with an automatic glare. Robert ignored both of them as he went to the elevator and pushed the button for the third floor. The smiling (it must have been a job requirement, except for the guards) nurse on three pushed the visitor's log across the desk toward him. "Everything okay?" he asked, bending to scribble his name.

She removed one chart from the carousel and pretended to read the hen-scratched notes. "The patient remains stable, Mr. Turchek," she said pleasantly.

Stable. Yeah, right. Big surprise.

After nearly three years, what else?

They all went through this same stupid playacting every damned time he came in here. Robert didn't really know why.

He walked down the hall and into room 4.

This was a corner room, which cost extra, and it was still bright with the afternoon sun. Robert was so used to the medicinal smells, the soft beeps of the monitors, and even the sight of the emaciated figure lying curled up in the bed that he just barely noticed any of it by now. He pulled the lone chair over to the side of the bed and sat down. "So, pal, how's it going?"

There was no response, of course.

Robert reached out and lightly tapped his brother on the cheek. "You hear the game last night, didja? Damned Mets trounced us again." He had no way of knowing whether or not the nurses actually turned the radio on for all of the Dodger games the way he told them to. He really hoped so.

Andy Turchek used to be a hell of a pitcher. There had even been talk of a tryout with the Dodgers. That was the dream they had shared for so long. Maybe Robert Turchek was only a wise guy, but his little brother Andy was heading for something much better.

"They sure as hell could use your fastball," Robert said.

Yeah, it was always a beautiful sight watching Andy bullet the ball across the plate. His last year in college, he won every game he started. Quality, real star quality.

Who the hell could have predicted the broken arm? Oh, the bone healed okay, but the arm was never the same again. Andy tried. More than once the kid brought himself to tears as he tried to get the magic back, but it never happened. For a kid who'd thought the whole world was waiting for him, reality was a cold, hard thing to face.

Robert changed the subject; it wasn't healthy to dwell on the past. "You remember me telling you about poor old Ernie?" he said. "I'm afraid he's gone to that big racetrack in the sky. Wouldn't you think that guys like him would learn? They never do, though." He gave a soft laugh, poking his brother in the arm. "Guess we should be glad for that, though, right? Their stupidity keeps me working."

It also kept him able to pay the freight for this place. Otherwise, Andy would be shoved into some state hellhole. Robert would never let that happen, no matter how many punks like Ernie Gallos had to get their brains blown out.

The coma was most probably irreversible; nobody had ever said anything else, even from the very first. And Robert accepted that. He really did, especially when he was sitting there looking at the twisted body that now weighed about ninety pounds. He knew, intellectually, that Andy was never going to come out of this. But still . . .

There was movement that *might* be read as a response. A twitch when a question was asked. Sometimes, even, the eyes would open and it seemed that he was looking right at you, trying desperately to communicate.

Robert unfolded the newspaper he'd brought and read aloud, first the sports page, of course, and then the comics. Usually he read "Dear Abby," too, but the letter this day was all about cancer and dying, which seemed a little too depressing, so he skipped it.

Andy was thirty now, but somehow Robert still thought of him as nineteen, the age he'd been when he last played baseball. God, he was so good. But once the hopes for a career fell apart, Andy could never seem to find himself again. He just bummed around, doing a little of this and a little of that, while Robert tried desperately to keep him out of trouble with the law.

Robert reached into his pocket and took out a cassette. "I brought you a tape, Andy. The new one by Bruce." He stood and walked over to the desk where the radio/tape player was. He couldn't turn the volume up as loud as it should have been for real enjoyment, because the nurse outside would bitch, but he knew that Andy liked hearing the music anyway.

Listening to Springsteen, Robert went to the window and stared down at the lawn. A few patients were out there, resting and probably also getting heatstroke in the ninety-plus afternoon.

It was the feeling of complete helplessness he felt inside this room that Robert hated the most. Outside these walls, Robert Turchek was *somebody*. He controlled things. People respected him and more than a few feared him. But in here, with his brother, there wasn't a damned thing he could do except read the newspaper and play the music.

And think.

He'd sort of thought that Andy was getting his life together at last, up until the night he was the wheelman in an armed robbery where somebody ended up getting killed. Even though Andy didn't have anything to do with actually pulling the trigger, he took a fall anyway.

They never found out who actually started the brawl in the prison shower room, or why. Because of his contacts, Robert *did* know who struck the blow that sent Andy into this coma from which he was never going to emerge. And someday that guy would pay. Someday.

Robert pushed all of that out of his mind before he got mad. Anger like that was useless. He went back to his chair by the bed. He'd stay until the tape was over. Then he had to drive out to Santa Monica and talk to a man about some trouble he was in.

2

Beau Epstein pushed the swinging door open with his shoulder and went into the john. A fast leak before lunch.

There were already three boys gathered in the bathroom. They were perched on the sinks, sharing a joint. None of them spoke to Beau when he came in. He balanced his books on the one available sink and stepped to the urinal.

Beau stared at the graffiti-covered tiles and tried to ignore the snickers from the boys behind him. According to his grandfather, the all-wise and all-powerful Saul Epstein, it just took time for a newcomer like Beau to fit in. Just as it took time for *him*, back in the Paleolithic Era or whenever it was when he came over here from Russia. A poor immigrant boy trying to start a new life.

Beau couldn't see any connection.

Saul was a great one for stories of how hard he had to work to make himself over into the man he was. Beau listened to all the stories, because if you were eating a man's food and sleeping under his roof, you had to be polite. But he didn't bother to tell the old man that he didn't *want* to fit in with the creeps here at Paynor Academy. On the contrary, he was determined to do whatever he could to set himself apart.

One of the ways he did that was to continue dressing pretty much the way he always had, mostly ignoring the designer jeans and trendy shirts that had been purchased for him. Instead, he wore his ragged old khakis and faded, shrunken T-shirts.

Not the usual attire for Paynor Academy, a school that tried to educate the choicest pick of the Beverly Hills-Brentwood crop of adolescents.

Most of the clothes he had came from the American Baptist Mission back home. Along with the wrong way of dressing, his faults included hair that was too long for the neoconservative mood at Paynor these days. Even his shoes did not escape criticism; the handmade leather sandals would have looked more at home at Woodstock.

Behind him, there was more whispering and then a muffled laugh. What had to be his books hit the floor with a loud crash. The sudden noise stopped his heart for one endless moment. Until he realized that no one was firing an American-supplied M-16 in the boys' john.

He zipped his trousers carefully and stepped back to the sink. His books lay scattered on the floor. First he washed his hands and dried them on a coarse paper towel. Then he knelt and started to gather the books.

"Sorry about that," one of the boys said. Beau thought his name was Scott.

Beau didn't say anything.

Scott held out the remains of the joint. "Wanna hit?" he offered.

Beau just shook his head as he finished stacking the books.

All three of them snickered. "What's the matter?" Scott said. "Fucking nature boy doesn't do drugs?"

Beau stood. "It's not that," he said with a shrug. "I'm just not used to the shitty quality of the grass you poor bastards have. Back home, we only smoked the good stuff."

He smiled and left the bathroom.

Beau still wasn't used to being an orphan.

He didn't even like the word very much. *Orphan*. It sounded like something out of a book by Charles Dickens. All he needed was a bowl of gruel.

It just felt so strange. Sort of like having a black hole open up in the pit of his stomach. And it wasn't even that he was a *kid*, for Chrissake. He was fifteen, although sometimes he felt more like ten. Sometimes, he knew, he acted like that, too.

But what the hell; he was an orphan, right? Maybe he was entitled.

No one sat with him in the cafeteria.

Lunch was one of the really bad times of the school day. After having spent almost fourteen years of his life living in a Central American village, the total population of which was about three hundred, this room, filled daily with almost that many teenagers socializing over tofu burgers and Dove Bars, could be pretty overwhelming.

He just tried to eat and get out as quickly as he could.

But sometimes, in the middle of the rushed meal, it would all come back to him in a sudden, sickening flash of memory. He would stop eating and withdraw to a private place deep inside his own mind. The mingled smells of steam-table food and unrestrained youthful hormones were replaced by the far more familiar damp-heat odor of the jungle; the sound of rock music blasting from half a dozen radios was lost in the memory of sudden gunfire and the screams of frightened people.

It had been just an ordinary day. Nothing to make it any different from a thousand other days. The village where they lived was just trying to go on as it always had, despite the increasing troop activity in the countryside. His parents and all the other adults seemed to think that they could ignore the conflict between government and rebels.

Jonathan and Rachel, of course, supported the rebels. They were old-time rebels themselves; why else would they have fled their own country in the sixties and never returned?

They seemed to think that the government was going to let Santa María do as it wanted.

It was stupid to think that way, and such stupidity now left a bitter taste in Beau's mouth. Sometimes he blamed his parents for not telling him what a shitty place the world really was, them and their damned peace-and-love garbage. Maybe that had worked back when *they* were young, but no more. Not today. Could they have really been so dumb? Why the hell hadn't they prepared him for real life?

Beau became aware that someone was staring at him. He looked up, his eyes darting around the room nervously. Two girls at the next table giggled. Beau frowned in their direction, which only made them giggle harder. So he flipped them the finger.

Damn, they wouldn't even let a person eat his lunch in peace. Beau bent over his food again and took a bite.

The tuna sandwich almost gagged him as the memory of that day a few months ago in Santa María returned with sharp-edged clarity.

Just about everybody who lived in and around the village was gathered in the square that hot afternoon. It wasn't, as the government troops thought (or later claimed to think, anyway) a sinister gathering. The main topic under discussion was simply what they might do to avoid getting caught up in the escalating struggle between the nervous authorities and the rebels.

The attack came without warning.

Beau and several other boys had taken refuge from the afternoon sun by lying under a convenient pony cart. Stretched out on their bellies and talking idly about two girls across the way, they had a clear view of the scene as the camouflage-clad troops appeared from nowhere and began to hail machine-gun fire on the crowd. Beau saw both his parents die. Not surprisingly, they were holding on to one another when the bullets struck. It seemed weird that his first thought was one of familiar stabbing jealousy that, once again, Rachel and Jonathan seemed so complete within themselves. He knew, had always known, that while they loved him, they had never really needed him to complete their relationship. Even while dying, they thought of each other, it seemed, not of him.

In the next instant, of course, Beau realized that his parents were *dead*. He was an orphan and the black hole inside his gut appeared for the first time. Beau tried to be brave, so that Jonathan and Rachel would be proud of him. But sometimes he felt like a scared little kid again. A lost and lonely kid.

When he'd caught the first glimpse of the huge mansion on the hill, Beau thought that the stranger he was on his way to meet—to live with—must surely reside in a hotel. But no, the house and the parklike setting that surrounded it all belonged to Saul Epstein.

As did the gigantic black limousine in which a bedraggled Beau arrived from the airport.

It had all been pretty damned scary. And it wasn't much better now.

Beau sat at one end of the vast oak dining table and his grandfather presided at the other. Just the two of them in the huge room. Harold, who worked for the old man, served them dinner. There were candles on the table and the silverware gleamed ferociously as the two of them ate rare roast beef and oven-browned potatoes. The food, as usual, was very good. Also, as usual, there was very little conversation. At least, there wasn't once Saul got past the point of why the hell Beau couldn't put on a damned tie for dinner. Or, at any rate, some goddamned shoes.

It was all just so much noise by now. Beau liked it a lot better on those nights when Saul was out and he could eat in the kitchen with Harold and his wife Ruth. Nobody bitched about what he was wearing then.

Although Beau was not really aware of it, there were very few people in the city of Los Angeles who would dare to defy Saul Epstein over even something as insignificant as proper dinner attire. Saul was about the last of the old-style movie moguls, but he was one who still had power. The studio he had formed decades ago and continued to run with undiluted authority made a profit most years. Not that it mattered much to him. He had enough money already.

Beau poured more gravy over his food. He had

never met his grandfather before that day about four months earlier, had only been vaguely aware that he even existed. Jonathan never liked to talk much about his past. The estrangement between Saul and his only child—caused by politics, a son's rejection of the career his father had chosen for him, and a marriage that was, in the old man's eyes, unsuitable—that estrangement ran deep and never ended.

"Some more beef?" Harold offered.

Beau shook his head. "Thanks anyway." He liked Harold, who had picked him up at the airport and who, with Ruth, tried to make him feel welcome.

What Beau had still not been able to figure out was why his grandfather had sent for him in the first place. Had even, in fact, pulled strings and enlisted the aid of the American Embassy to demand that Beau be immediately dispatched to California. Given the choice, Beau would not have left. He would have done what his friends were doing and joined the rebels. To hell with stupid pacifism. Look where that kind of thinking had got Jonathan and Rachel. But the choice was never offered to him.

After a couple more minutes, Harold cleared away the plates and disappeared into the kitchen to get dessert. Beau tapped the edge of the table and whistled softly.

Saul glared at him and then seemed to struggle for a mild tone when he spoke. "School will be out next week," he said, lifting his wine goblet. He took a tidy sip. "Have you given any thought to what it is you might like to do over the summer?"

Beau frowned, pretending to think about it. He picked up his own goblet and took a swallow. Saul was of the traditional school that believed a young man should learn to drink at home. Therefore, Beau was allowed one glass of wine each night with dinner. He didn't like it as much as the home-brewed beer he and his friends used to sneak back in Santa María. He swallowed more wine and then brightened. "I could travel," he said.

Saul might have been old, but he was no dummy. "No," he said sharply. "You may not go back to that place."

Beau was having a hard time adjusting to life within a dictatorship. Rachel and Jonathan had always run things as a democracy, in which every-body got a vote, even Beau. He drank some more wine. "So why even bother to ask me what I want?" he said. "What I say doesn't seem to matter a damned bit anyway."

Saul sighed. "You're very much like your father, aren't you?" he said. It was practically the first time in all the weeks Beau had been there that Saul had mentioned Jonathan.

Beau toyed with the dessert spoon, sliding it up and down on the white linen tablecloth. "I'm not so much like him," he said softly. "Jonathan was pretty naive. Right up until he died."

Saul's lips thinned.

Harold returned and served them chocolate mousse. Nobody spoke until he was gone from the room again. Saul tasted the mousse. Then he said, "I imagine you must miss them a lot."

"Yeah, I guess." Beau used the curved bottom of his spoon to make canyons in the thick chocolate. It was several minutes before he spoke again. "The thing is," he said carefully, "I feel like I'm all alone. There just isn't anybody out there." He glanced up, but there was no expression that could be read on his grandfather's face. Beau stuck the spoon into his mouth and licked it clean. "What's funny," he went on at last, "is that I've always sort of felt this way. Even before they died. Because they had each other, see? They didn't need me much. But the difference is that I just never had to think about it much before."

Saul looked at him for a moment. "You know, Beau," he said, "I'm here for you. I'm family."

"Yeah, I guess. But it's not the same."

"If we both try, maybe it could be."

Beau stared at him. "How come you hated my mother?"

"I didn't," Saul protested.

"Jonathan said you did. He said that was one reason we never came back here. Because you hated Rachel so much."

Saul shook his head. "I didn't hate her. I didn't like what happened to Jonathan after they met. He dropped out of school, threw away his future. She got him all excited over things that he never cared much about before. Like the war. I didn't hate Rachel. But I hated what she turned my son into."

"Yeah? Well, that's sort of like the same thing, isn't it?"

After a moment, Saul just sighed and shook his head. "That was all a long time ago," he said. "How much can it matter now?"

Beau shrugged. He bent his head over the table and began to eat the mousse quickly.

3

1

It had been a real zero of a day.

Most of his time had been spent chasing around after that bastard in Santa Monica, another man who seemed constitutionally unable to keep his word on a business arrangement. There seemed to be a lot of that going around these days, and while Robert was glad for the work such behavior brought him, it did sometimes make him wonder just a little about the moral climate in the country. Why the hell were people so reluctant to accept responsibility for their own actions?

On a sticky day like this one, when the air quality outside had to rival that which would be found, he imagined, in an equatorial garbage dump, there were a lot of things Robert Turchek would rather have been doing. But because he was a man who believed in doing the job he was being paid to do, he spent hours chasing an irresponsible asshole named Berg through the bars, porn flicks, and fast-food restaurants of Santa Monica and its environs.

His mood after such a day was not good. If he didn't have strict orders from LoBianca about how he wanted Berg handled, Robert would have been very tempted to shoot the bastard on sight.

As soon as Robert walked into the McDonald's, he spotted his prey sitting alone in a rear booth. Instead of going right over to him, however, Robert stopped at the counter and ordered a Quarter-Pounder with cheese and a large Coke. Then he carried his tray back to where Berg was sitting bent over a ledger. Trying to figure his way into the big time, probably. Berg didn't seem to understand that some people were destined for greatness and some for the manure pile.

Berg was definitely headed for deep shit.

If he hadn't been so pissed off about the miserable day that Berg had put him through, Robert might have found the whole thing a little pathetic. But the way he was feeling at the moment, he didn't give a damn if the man had a dying mother and six hungry brats to support.

Berg was a dead man who didn't have the sense to stop breathing.

Robert set the tray down onto the table with a crash. Berg, startled, looked up quickly from his avid study of the figures in the ledger. Although they had never met, a sick sort of look crossed his face when he saw Robert standing there. It was as if he knew immediately that something was up and that it wasn't going to be good. It had probably been a long time since anything good had happened to Berg. Of course, he deserved all the shit, because of being so stupid and trying to play in the same ballpark as the big boys.

Robert didn't say anything. He just sat down

opposite Berg and opened the slightly moist Styrofoam box. He took out the cheeseburger.

Berg set his pencil down carefully. Its end had been
chewed nearly clear through to the lead. There were
tiny flecks of yellow paint around Berg's mouth.

Robert swallowed the first bite of his sandwich and
then took a long gulp of the Coke. It felt good going
down his parched throat. He smiled. "Mr. Berg," he
said then, "you're a very hard man to find."

"I didn't know anybody was looking."

Ah, good. Berg had decided to play it tough. That
made Robert very happy, because a guy who
wanted to show his balls at a time like this was just
asking for trouble. Especially if he couldn't even
hope to back up the belligerent attitude with action.
Robert didn't think that the skinny, balding Berg
could. The only amazing thing was that the dope
had summoned up the chutzpah to try and cross
LoBianca in the first place. "I've been looking," he
said after another bite.

"So who the fuck are you, anyway?" the tough
guy said.

Robert didn't answer right away. He was thinking
that maybe he should have ordered some french
fries, too, but he didn't feel like walking all the way
back to the counter. Which was exactly why he
hated restaurants without waitresses. "My name is
Turchek," he said finally. "Robert Turchek."

Berg blinked. The name obviously meant something to him and that realization pleased Robert in a
way he couldn't really define.

"You know, Berg," he said conversationally, "you
don't look like a complete dope to me. So how come
you've lately been acting like one?"

Berg was playing with the pencil. The look in his
eyes said clearly that he'd like to drive the damned
thing right into Robert's heart. Fat chance. "Hey,

Turchek, this is a free country. Capitalist system and all that shit. Somebody can't stand a little competition, maybe he should get the hell out of the business."

Robert just had to grin at that. "You're talking here about Mr. LoBianca, I guess. Well, see, he doesn't care much about the capitalist system when it starts interfering in his own private business."

"The market is big enough for both of us. Tell that to your boss, why don't you?"

Now he was being treated like nothing but some kind of damned errand boy. Killing Berg—which he would do, sooner or later—was going to be a real pleasure. Robert finished the Quarter-Pounder. He picked up the paper napkin and wiped his mouth carefully. "First of all, Berg, I don't have a god-damned 'boss,' okay?" He crumpled the napkin and tossed it across the table. It fell into Berg's lap. Berg didn't pick it up. "Second of all, your fucking whining about just being part of the free-enterprise system doesn't mean shit to me. Or to the man you're trying to muscle in on. But see, he's giving you a break. Killing you is liable to bring him some compli-cations. Which he'd prefer to avoid, if possible."

A faint look of hope seemed to cross Berg's face.

Robert almost smiled. "So you have twenty-four hours to get your pathetic ass out of this city. Out of the whole fucking state, in fact."

"Or?"

Berg was attempting to sneer, but not quite bring-ing it off.

Robert knew when to talk and when just to look. Now he just looked.

Berg stared at him as if trying hard to read some expression through the sunglasses. They were too dark for that, which was exactly the point. He tried to keep up his hardcase front, but his mouth opened and closed a couple of times with nothing being said. Then the air just seemed to whoosh out of him. "I don't have enough cash on hand," he said in a choked whisper. "And my family is here."

Christ, in another minute the dope would be bawling all over the table. Robert *really* wasn't in the mood for that. He finished his Coke quickly and set the paper cup down. "Twenty-four hours, Berg," he said wearily. "You won't get another warning. Mr. LoBianca is being real generous to let you leave. Most guys, they'd have your balls in the chopper right now." Of course, they both knew that generosity had nothing at all to do with it; LoBianca was just looking out for number one. It made sense to avoid murder whenever possible. Robert didn't think it was going to be avoided here, though. Berg was just too dumb. With a sudden move, Robert snatched the pencil away and, quickly, broke it in two. He dropped the pieces onto the table and started to get up.

Berg reached out and grabbed him by one wrist. "Jesus Christ, man, I got kids. Can't you be a little understanding?"

Robert just looked down at him until Berg released the grip. "Don't ever do that again," he said very softly. "I'll kill you *and* your fucking kids, you ever lay a finger on me again. You got that?"

"Yes," Berg said helplessly. "I get it." He slumped back in the booth, staring at the greasy used napkin that was still in his lap.

Robert left the restaurant. He walked around the parking lot until he found Berg's sea-foam-green Pontiac. After checking to be sure that nobody was being nosy, he took a Swiss Army knife from his pocket. Quickly, methodically, he slashed each tire on the car. Just for good measure, he also broke off the rearview mirror and left it propped on the hood.

Then he headed for his own car. He knew that the vandalism was a sort of petty thing to do, but Berg had really aggravated him. For some people, just killing wasn't enough.

2

Maureen Travers wanted to be an actress.

That was no novelty, of course; not in a town where Robert knew that he could stand on any street corner, spit, and be ensured of hitting not only one or more aspiring thespians, but also a minimum of eight passersby with script ideas to pitch.

It was precisely because of all that competition that Maureen was, temporarily, supporting herself by working as a waitress in a place on Sunset Boulevard. Because it was a first-class establishment and more especially because Maureen was a long-legged blonde who knew how to treat the customers right, she made very good tips.

She was still young enough to be a little bit impressed that her boyfriend (a word that she was also still young enough to use, although it was one that Robert, at thirty-eight, found slightly ridiculous when applied to him) was a sort of mysterious figure. She had no idea what it was he actually *did*, of course, although she had the feeling that it was something not quite, well, legal. Not that he was a real *criminal*, she figured. To her, Robert was just something of a renegade, which seemed to excite her. Robert didn't mind.

What they had going, in Robert's opinion, was a good summertime relationship. Maureen looked terrific in a bathing suit, got a joke when one was told, and was hot in bed, especially when it came to giving a blow-job. What more could he ask?

But there were times when they were out together, like that very night, for example, when she talked all the way through dinner about some damned audition or other, when he had to wonder if it was really worth all the trouble. He was wondering just that as he signaled the waiter for another whiskey.

"Bobby, are you listening to me?" Maureen said suddenly. She was glaring at him.

"Sure, babe," he said, although of course he hadn't been.

"What did I just say?" she challenged him.

Robert tried desperately to think of anything he'd heard in the last ten or twenty minutes. Not one thing came to mind. So he just grinned and shrugged. "Sorry, Mo. It's just that I've got a lot on my mind right now." That wasn't exactly the truth, either. He hadn't been thinking about anything in particular.

"What?" she asked, after a sip of the fancy water she drank all the time.

"What what?" he said innocently.

She sighed. *"What's* on your mind?"

Robert played absently with the small diamond stud in his ear. "Ah, just things."

She almost pouted, although a liberated person like her would surely have denied any such thing. "You never share with me what it is you're really thinking about."

Oh God. It always got to that eventually. But why tonight? And why was it that the fact that two people had a good time together, with some laughs and better-than-average sex, didn't seem to be enough for some women? They always wanted to get inside his head and find out what he was really like. Robert didn't understand this obsession at all; he certainly didn't give a good goddamn about what was going on inside *their* brains.

Meanwhile, she was obviously waiting for some kind of an answer.

Robert was still trying to think of one—he was

really hoping to get laid before the night was over—when the maître d' appeared beside the table. "Excuse me, Mr. Turchek," he said softly.

"Yes?" he answered with considerable relief.

"You have a telephone call, sir."

Saved by Ma Bell. Wonderful.

He got up, giving Maureen an apologetic shrug, and followed the French guy across the room. Only then did it occur to him to wonder who the hell would actually call him there. Although he always gave the answering service a number on evenings like this, everybody knew damned well that he hated being disturbed. When he was alone with the phone, he picked up the receiver and said, "Turchek here," letting whomever it was know by his tone that he wasn't happy.

"This is the Ledgewood Convalescent Home, Mr. Turchek," the crisp female voice said in return. "Dr. Randolph would like you to come over here immediately."

Robert, still half thinking about the upcoming hassle with Maureen, didn't immediately absorb the meaning of the words. "I was there this afternoon as usual," he said irritably. "If Randolph wanted to talk to me, why didn't he do it then?"

"This is a crisis situation."

"What the hell does that mean?"

"It means," she explained carefully but firmly, "that you should get over here as quickly as possible." With that, she hung up.

Robert listened to the dial tone for a few moments, but found there no answers to his unasked questions. Then, as he finally hung up, an unfamiliar sense of panic raced through him. This had never happened before, not in the years that Andy had been a patient at Ledgewood. At last, he moved, practically upending a waiter carrying a fully loaded tray in his hurry back to the table where Maureen was waiting. "I have to go, babe. A family crisis. Can you get a cab home?"

"Sure." She looked bewildered. "But I didn't know you had any family, Bobby."

Robert didn't bother to answer as he threw several crumpled bills down onto the table and headed for the door.

Dr. Alan Randolph, a tall man with a completely bald head, was in Andy's room, along with another doctor whose face was vaguely familiar, but whose name Robert couldn't remember at the moment. A nurse was there, too. None of them seemed to notice when Robert walked in.

His gaze went immediately to the bed. The first thing he saw was that a new machine had been hooked up to his brother. It sent forth an erratic beeping and Robert tried to read some message in the sound, but he could not. He wanted to ask somebody what the hell was happening but hesitated, because the answer would probably be something he didn't want to hear. As always in this room, he felt helpless.

Randolph finally glanced his way. Even under these circumstances, he remained his usual brusque, efficient self. "Your brother's heart has stopped twice in the last hour," he said, skipping any of the polite preliminaries; Robert had always liked that in the doctor. His head gave a nod toward the beeping machine. "Right now, we've got it going again. But our preliminary diagnosis is that extensive and severe damage has been done."

"Which means what, exactly?" Robert asked, matching his voice to the doctor's cool tone.

Randolph shrugged. "Which means that the patient has a very slim chance of survival."

"How much of a chance is that?"

"Slim" was the unsatisfactory reply.

Nobody in the room said anything more for a moment; maybe they were all, like him, just listening to the beeps.

Robert reached up to loosen his green silk tie and ran a couple of fingers around the inside of his collar. "Can't you do something?" he said. "No matter what it costs . . ."

Randolph didn't even bother responding to that remark. Instead, he and the other doctor stepped out into the hallway and bent their heads together over a long computer readout.

Ignoring the nurse who was busily fiddling with various knobs and gauges, Robert moved over to stand next to the bed. "Hey, Andy," he said softly. "What's going on here, buddy?" With one hand, he stroked his brother's arm lightly, taking care to avoid the frightening tubes and needles. "You're not going to crap out on me, are you? No fair, Andy, that's not part of the deal."

Once, a long time ago, Andy Turchek had pitched a perfect game. Robert could still remember every detail of that afternoon as if it had happened just last week, instead of years ago. The hot sun and the cold beer. The crowded bleachers and even the damned hot dogs, which were the best he'd ever eaten.

Andy "The Wizard" Turchek *was* perfect that day. He was in complete control as he stood on the mound, six feet two inches of power and finesse. His white uniform gleamed and his blond hair was like a beacon in the middle of the field. Robert, sitting in his usual place right behind the dugout, washing down hot dog after hot dog with paper cups of cold beer, could hardly contain the love and pride that kept welling up inside him. That was his kid brother out there. Every time the ball went across the plate, he held his breath, proud and fearful at the same time. But Andy never slipped. Twenty-seven batters came and twenty-seven batters went, with nobody even getting close to first base.

When the last man was gone, swinging wildly at a curve ball that seemed to defy every law of physics, Andy turned toward the dugout and saluted Robert with his cap. Then he grinned. Robert never let anybody know about the tears that filled his eyes at that moment.

All Andy ever really wanted to do was pitch for the goddamned Dodgers.

Without any warning, the beeping machine was suddenly making a different noise, a loud, flat sound that brought the doctors back into the room immediately. Robert was unceremoniously pushed aside and obviously forgotten.

He wanted to cry, but this time the tears wouldn't come. Maureen would probably say that he needed to get in touch with his feelings or some kind of shit like that. But he couldn't. The nerve endings were too raw. If he let loose now, things would go to hell very quickly.

Robert went into the hallway. A passing nurse looked at him with what might have been sympathy. He leaned against the wall and closed his eyes.

3

There weren't very many people at the funeral, of course. Robert hadn't even told Maureen anything about when or where the brief service was going to be held. He didn't want her hovering.

It wasn't until he surveyed the small group gathered around the grave that Robert realized something: He had no friends, not really. The sudden realization surprised him a little, because he hadn't felt such a lack in his life. Between work and a parade of women and Andy in the hospital to visit every day, there seemed to be plenty to think about.

Randolph was there, no doubt motivated by some sense of professional obligation. A couple of the nurses and aides who had taken care of Andy showed up, too, and that was okay. The big surprise, as far as Robert was concerned, was that Wayne Brown was there. He must have seen the short obit in the *Times*. Brown, a hefty black man in a three-piece suit, had played on the college team with Andy. He had, in fact, caught that perfect game. Now, as it turned out, he sold insurance, which maybe explained why he read the death notices so carefully.

When the service was over, Brown suggested to him that maybe a drink was in order. It could be sort of a final tribute to Andy. Robert couldn't see anything wrong with that idea, so he followed Brown four blocks to Mike's, a dark, cool tavern that was nearly empty at that time of the day. They both carried boilermakers to a back booth.

"There were some nice flowers at the grave," Brown said when they had settled in.

"Some of the people I do business with sent them," Robert said. He downed the shot in one gulp.

"What business are you in these days?"

"Debt collection," he replied shortly. That was what it said on his income-tax return.

Brown just nodded.

Two youngish women in almost identical gray suits came in and sat at the booth just opposite them. Each carried a leather briefcase and each was drinking white wine. They paid no attention to

Robert and Brown, instead launching directly into a discussion of points and prime rates.

Brown sipped beer carefully. "I was around the majors for a couple years," he said. "And I never saw anybody better than the Wizard. He could have gone all the way, you know that, don't you?"

"I know it."

The women laughed suddenly. Robert wondered what the hell was so funny about interest rates.

Brown sighed. "Let me tell you something, Bob. I'm a religious man, a deacon in the church and all, but sometimes I still can't figure out God's holy plan. Like why things had to go the way they did for somebody like Andy."

Robert smiled a little, not at what Brown had said, exactly, or even at Brown himself, but at the top of the table. "I don't think that God—even if there really is one—had anything to do with this."

Brown obviously wasn't happy with that expression of doubt, but he let it pass without saying anything.

The women weren't talking business anymore. Their new topic of conversation was someone named Edward. Both of them, it seemed, had slept with him. On different occasions.

Robert ordered a second shot; it arrived and he downed it as quickly as he had the first. "I know who's to blame for Andy being dead," he said. "And someday he'll pay."

"Revenge won't bring Andy back."

Robert didn't say anything. Something about the absent Edward's sexual habits ignited another bout of laughter and the women ordered more wine.

"Well," Brown said finally, "it's just sad. Real sad."

Robert raised a hand to summon the bartender again.

* * *

It was very late by the time Robert left the bar. Brown was long gone, having tried but failed to persuade him to go as well.

As he emerged into the still-hot night, Robert realized how drunk he really was. Too drunk to drive, probably, but how the hell else could he get home? So he got behind the wheel and made very sure that he stayed three miles beneath the speed limit the whole way.

The house was dark and quiet, just as always, but, for some reason he couldn't explain, it *seemed* darker and quieter than usual.

He hit the john and took a long piss—too damned much beer—and then walked across the hall to Andy's room. He hardly ever went in there. It was still the way it had been when Andy was first sent to prison. Robert stepped inside the room. The iron band that had been wrapped around his chest for several days now seemed to tighten even more. He picked up the baseball bat that was propped against the bed.

The bat was a real classic, made to Babe Ruth's own specifications.

He ran his hands along the smooth ash. It felt cool to the touch. After a moment, Robert hefted the bat and gave it a trial swing. Felt good. So then he swung it again. The third swing crashed into the trophy case, smashing the glass. Robert turned around and swung again, this time hitting the portable television.

Dimly, he realized that he was crying. Maureen would probably think that was a very good thing. He raised the bat again.

4

Beau didn't even want to be at the damned party.

Unfortunately, in this case, Saul hadn't given him any choice in the matter. Maybe they had lately reached a sort of trucelike state, occasionally even holding a pleasant conversation, but it hadn't taken Beau very long to find out just how far he could go in his rebellions against the old man's wishes. Sometimes, the easiest thing to do was just give in. So here he was. And not only was he appearing at the party, but he was actually wearing the new sports jacket and slacks that had been purchased for the occasion.

Saul, it seemed, gave one party a year, and this was it. A huge red-and-yellow-striped tent had been erected in the backyard and truckloads of catered food were hauled in. Now what seemed like half the population of Los Angeles (the rich and attractive half, of course) was milling around on the lawn, eating, drinking, and, most importantly, being seen. Beau didn't know who most of the guests were, although he did recognize a few kids from school, probably hauled along by parents. On his behalf, no doubt. They shouldn't have bothered. He was pleased that nobody even spoke to him as he walked through the crowd, eating handmade potato chips and drinking Coke secretly spiked with rum.

At one point in his solitary tour of the backyard, he encountered his grandfather, the host, looking expansive and pleased with himself. "Having a good time?" Saul asked him.

Beau finished chewing a chip and then swallowed. "Do you know," he said, "that this is the four-month anniversary of my parents' being killed?"

Saul just looked at him.

Beau didn't know why he'd said that. But once said, it would have been too embarrassing to apologize or anything. So he smiled brightly and walked away.

Fed up with the crowd and the noise, he headed for the farthest perimeter of the vast yard, back where the orange and lemon trees grew. He found a grassy spot that was so shaded it was almost dark and sat on the ground.

Here it was easy to close his eyes and think about the past.

Because his thoughts were so far away, in another time and a much different place, it took Beau several moments to realize that he was no longer alone. He opened his eyes.

A girl in a white dress was standing a few feet away, watching him. "Hi, Beau," she said. "You look kind of lonely out here all by yourself."

"I'm okay." It took him a couple more seconds to recognize her. "You're Kimberly, right?"

She favored him with a brilliantly white smile. "*Right*. Algebra class."

"Yeah, I remember."

"Can I sit here with you?"

Beau just nodded. She looked like all the girls at school—tanned, blond, and casually perfect. Beau felt sweaty and clumsy whenever they looked at him, which wasn't that often, of course. He supposed that his reaction was just hormones, but with so many other things on his mind lately, who had time to think about sex?

Anyway, his actual experience in that area had been limited to solitary jacking off, and even that seemed like too much trouble these days. It probably didn't say much about the quality of his social skills that an occasional wet dream was as close as he could get to an interpersonal relationship.

Kimberly sat down too close to him; apparently the concept of Personal Space, something that his parents had always stressed, was not an idea that she was familiar with. He couldn't help inhaling the cloying scent of her perfume. She gave an expert toss of her head and the golden curls tumbled cheerfully. "You're a real mysterious figure at school, you know?"

"Me?" He wiped at his sweaty face with the sleeve of his new jacket. "Why would anybody think I'm mysterious?"

"Well, you know," she said, smoothing the front of her light cotton dress, "the way you lived all that time in the jungle or whatever. Like Tarzan, sort of."

"It wasn't like that," he said sharply. "I wasn't in fucking Africa swinging from the trees."

"Okay," she agreed willingly. "But it was something like that, right?"

He didn't bother to argue anymore; what the hell did he care what they thought about him anyway? He sipped some of the spiked Coke.

"Well, anyway," she said, "I think you're real cute . . . in a sort of . . . interesting way."

He had absolutely no idea how to respond to that.

She wriggled even closer. "Can I ask you something really, like, personal?"

Her breath was hot against his cheek. "What?" he said warily.

"Have you ever, you know, done it?"

"Done it?" He wished fervently that she would just go away and leave him alone.

But she didn't. Instead, she lifted a hand and touched his hair. "Don't you think I'm pretty? Most boys do."

"You're pretty, yeah." His voice sounded funny to him. He cleared his throat.

Beau wasn't quite sure who kissed whom first, but all of a sudden they were both stretched out on the grass. There was a roaring in his ears. She fumbled with his belt as he, absurdly, worried about grass stains.

When his hand touched the wet warmth between her thighs, the feeling was like an electric shock through his system. The next jolt came when he felt her hand wrap around his growing erection.

A memory shot through him: Jonathan and Rachel and he had always lived in the same small wooden house. A little house with thin walls. The sounds of his parents making love had been a familiar and comfortable part of his childhood. When he was old enough to think about it seriously, he wondered why, at their age, they still bothered. But they did, and what was even more surprising to him, they still seemed to enjoy it.

Even the night before they died, he recalled suddenly, they'd been at it.

Beau tried to put together the sounds he recalled

so clearly—the sighs and laughter and muffled cries—with what was happening here and now to him. Two figures, one sweaty and awkward, the other seemingly cool and only minimally involved, scooted around on the grass silently. The music from the party could be faintly heard, but otherwise they might have been all alone in the world.

Wasn't this supposed to be fun?

He was inside of her for only a few seconds when it was all over; apparently hormones knew what to do even without much cooperation. As he rolled away from her stilled form, Beau found himself hoping that his parents had enjoyed themselves a whole lot more than this on that last night. He zipped his trousers and sat up.

She finished straightening her clothes—nobody had actually removed anything for the occasion— and sat up, reaching for her purse. After a brief search, she found and took out a compact and some lip gloss.

Beau cleared his throat again.

It was then that he heard the giggle. She heard it, too, and looked up with a frown. "Is somebody over there?" Beau asked.

An obvious admission of guilt crossed her face.

Beau reached blindly for his Coke and took a big gulp. "Who's there?"

The only response was a hurried rustling and then it was quiet again.

"Would you please tell me what the hell is going on?" he asked, trying desperately to take control of the situation. Whatever the situation was.

She sighed, looked away, then sighed again. "Have you ever heard of the Bleu Belles?"

He tried to think. *Blue Bells?* What the hell did that have to do with what had just happened here?

Finally, he vaguely remembered seeing signs posted around the school about various activities—none of which interested him at all—sponsored by something called the Bleu Belles. "I guess. That's some club at school, right?"

She snapped the compact closed and looked mildly shocked. "Not just *some* club. It's *the* club. Every girl at school is just dying to get in. But they're very selective."

Beau was getting tired of listening to her. He was tired of *her*. "So what?" he said sharply. "What's the stupid club got to do with me?"

Kimberly was looking at the ground, not at him, as she twisted blades of grass between her fingers. "See, the thing is, it's not easy to get in. Even when you're invited, there's still the initiation. They make you do things. One girl, last year, she had to drive the headmaster's car out of the parking lot and leave it at least ten miles from school."

Beau just nodded.

"So anyway, I was finally invited into the club. And you, well, like I said, you're sort of different. And we were all pretty curious about you. So . . ." She looked up finally and shrugged. "See?"

Yeah, he saw okay. "So this was your initiation."

"Right." She gave him another smile. "Well, nobody got hurt or anything."

Beau just looked at her for a moment, then shook his head. "God, you're really a dumb bitch, aren't you?"

Now she was indignant. "Well, you don't have to get so mad. It was all just a joke."

"Sure. Very fucking funny. And I guess somebody had to watch, just to be sure that you went through with it."

"Uh-huh." Her face turned red for the first time.

"Just the club president and vice-president. And they swore themselves to secrecy." She touched his arm urgently. "You won't tell anybody else, will you?"

He moved away from her. "That's not very likely, is it?"

"Okay, thanks." She jumped up, gave a tug to her dress, and left.

Beau swallowed the very last of his Coke and then wished he hadn't, because his stomach rebelled instantly. For a few seconds, he thought it was all going to come up again.

When nothing happened, though, he got up and walked back to the party. Nobody seemed to have noticed his absence. After a quick search of the yard, he was relieved to realize that Kimberly and her friends were nowhere in sight. Apparently, with their mission accomplished, they had taken off for more exciting places.

He didn't even want to think about having to see any of them when summer school started.

Beau stopped by the buffet table and made himself a sandwich, hoping that some food would settle his stomach. He layered thinly-sliced ham on dark rye bread and slathered it with spicy brown mustard. He had just taken his first bite when someone poked him in the spine.

"You're Saul's grandson, am I right?"

Still chewing, he turned. The man standing there was just past middle age, plump, wearing a white Mexican wedding shirt and several gold chains. Beau nodded, but didn't say anything. He took another bite of the sandwich.

"Great man, your grandfather." The stranger stuck out his hand. "Hank Levy. I'm a producer."

Beau kept eating, ignoring the outstretched hand. "That's nice," he said.

Levy finally took his hand back. "Actually, I'm real glad to finally meet you. I've heard the story, of course, what happened to your folks and all, and I think it would make an awesome film. A powerful story. Politics, romance, death. The people eat that stuff up, you know?" His round face turned solemn. "It goes without saying, of course, that you'd like their story to be told with respect. With *care*."

Beau didn't reply.

Levy, undeterred, plunged on. "I really think it would make an awesome film."

"You want to know what I think?" Beau said finally.

"Of course. Your input would be terrific."

Beau finished the sandwich. He wiped his mouth carefully on one of the little paper napkins that bore the well-known symbol of Saul's company. He stepped closer to Levy and kept his voice low. "I think," he said, "that you're an asshole."

Then he turned and walked away.

Beau was halfway up the stairs when he encountered Saul coming down. "Where are you going?"

"To my room," Beau said softly. "I really don't want to be at this party anymore."

"Not even if I asked you to stay, to talk with people?"

"You talk to them," Beau said. "I'm tired." He pushed past Saul and moved on, not stopping this time until he was in his room.

He stood there for a moment, looking around at everything. None of it seemed to belong to him, to be a part of his life. Then, moving quickly, he stripped off the new clothes and left them in a heap on the floor. He dressed again, this time in his own ragged jeans and a clean white T-shirt. When he was finished, he shoved another change of clothes into his knapsack, added a couple of books, and then a framed photograph of his parents.

For a long moment, he paused, staring down at the faces of Jonathan and Rachel. They almost seemed like strangers to him. Finally, he closed the knapsack.

He waited until the coast was clear and then left the house by the side door, so that no one would see him go.

5

1

There was someone knocking—no, actually, someone was *pounding*—on the door. He had the idea,
vaguely, that the noise had been going on for a very
long time before he actually heard it. Robert Turchek
sat up in bed and groggily reached for his watch on
the nightstand. The room was dark, because all of the
curtains were drawn completely closed, but he figured that the two o'clock illuminated on the watch
face was P.M. and not A.M. Mainly he figured that
because who the hell would come to his door in the
middle of the fucking night? Nobody with any sense,
that was for damned sure.

The pounding hadn't stopped; in fact, whoever it
was out there kept knocking with one hand, while
pressing the doorbell with the other.

"All right," Robert mumbled. "All fucking right."

He pulled on some jeans as he hopped and
staggered into the living room. En route, it did

occur to him that while he knew it was two o'clock, and probably P.M. rather than A.M., he wasn't altogether sure what *day* it was.

For a man who prided himself on being superorganized, this realization was more than a little disconcerting.

He zipped the jeans and then opened the door, blinking rapidly against the sudden and unpleasant invasion of southern California sunshine. Maureen was standing there. "Oh, hi," he said. His voice sounded strange, sort of rusty, and he realized that it had been some time since he'd actually spoken.

"Oh, hi?" she repeated, pushing by him and coming inside without actually being invited to do so. "That's all you have to say? I've been calling for days. What's the matter with you?" She dropped a load of newspapers and mail—which looked like mostly just ads and shit like that—onto the couch. "Why is it so dark in here?" She began yanking the curtains open efficiently. "I was starting to think that you were dead or something."

It all came back to him then.

"No," he said. "I'm not dead."

She trailed him into the kitchen and watched, arms crossed, as he poured himself a large glass of orange juice. "Bobby, I was worried. You call me to say that your brother—who I didn't even know existed, by the way—had died and and so you'd be busy for a couple of days. I certainly understood that. But then, nothing. You wouldn't even answer your phone."

"I'm sorry," he said. The juice was helping his voice return to normal. "Like I said, I've been busy." He tried to remember what it was that he'd actually been doing, but his mind couldn't quite focus yet. "And I think that maybe I had some damned bug. The flu, maybe." When he thought about it, that sounded right. The flu, yeah. That would explain why the last few days were all sort of fogged over in his mind. A high fever could do that. He gulped some more juice. "I'm feeling better now, though."

"Good." With one quick look, she took in his unshaven, rumpled appearance, and then the pile of dirty dishes in the sink. Her attitude softened a little. "It must have been terrible. Your brother dying."

Robert sat at the table and began to search through the debris there for a pack of cigarettes and some matches. The red-and-gold matchbook he finally uncovered was from the bar where he'd had drinks with Brown after Andy's funeral. He held it between two fingers for a moment, then flipped it open. When the Winston was ignited, he looked at Maureen again. "My brother didn't just die, you know. He was murdered."

She gasped. "Murdered? Oh my God, I didn't know that."

He rubbed a hand over his face stubble. "Well, it happened a long time ago."

Now she looked puzzled. "I don't understand."

"I know you don't." He picked up the glass of juice again, but instead of drinking, stared at the glowing tip of his cigarette. "I know you don't understand, Mo, but I'm just too damned tired to explain it all right now."

She opened her mouth and then closed it again without saying anything. After a moment, Maureen went to the sink and turned on the hot water. She squirted lemon-scented liquid soap over the dirty dishes.

Robert shifted a box of Grape-Nuts and threw an empty Ruffles bag to the floor. This place was a mess. He must've really felt crummy the last couple of days, because usually he was a very neat person. After surveying the tabletop with dismay, he got up and went back into the living room. Dropping onto the couch, he started going through the mail with absolutely no interest.

The business-sized manila envelope, with his name neatly typed on it, caught his attention. He ripped it open and found, as expected, a single sheet of paper with another name typed there. Name, address, and an amount of money. The amount was satisfactory, so he carefully folded the paper and put it into his pocket. Probably it was time to get back to work.

Only one other piece of mail interested him at all. The envelope was creased and dirty and it was addressed in block printing. Pencil.

After looking at the envelope for a moment, he carefully opened it and slid out a page ripped from a child's writing tablet. The message was also in pencil, and reading it he had the impression that the act of writing it had been a real effort. The message itself was brief and admirably to the point.

Maybe you want to know that Danny Boyd is out of the joint.

That was all. No signature. Nothing except the simple fact that Danny Boyd was a free man.

Robert crumpled the paper into a small, tight wad. From the kitchen, he could hear the sound of dishes clattering and silverware clinking as Maureen washed them. She wasn't often this domestic; he must really look like hell to have evoked such sympathy.

He leaned back and closed his eyes. It seemed like some kind of a bad joke. Or maybe just pure coincidence. Danny Boyd out walking the streets again. The man who had killed Andy. Sick cosmic joke or just chance, Robert didn't know what the hell he should do about it.

He knew that what he needed was a long, hot shower, a shave, and some clean clothes. But not quite yet. Instead, he lit another cigarette and sat still. There was a lot to think about.

2

The hit on Gary Rydell was one of those easy jobs. Rydell was some kind of hotshot commodities dealer who had decided to triple his income in a hurry by also dealing in a very particular commodity. Nothing wrong with that, as far as it went. The big boys were always looking for salesmen, especially those who could peddle to their rich friends without having to hang out on street corners.

Where Mr. Rydell went wrong, just like so many others, was that he got too greedy. Greed was fine, maybe, in its place, but carried too far, it could be dangerous. Skimming off the profits from the bosses was dangerous and crazy.

Rydell lived in a fancy condo near the beach. The building had a vast underground parking garage. Getting into the garage required a coded magnetic card, but he'd gotten lucky there, because it turned out that one of his clients had a secretary (for which read "mistress") who happened to live in the building. The man was glad to do him a favor, no questions asked, because Robert had gotten him out from under a very nasty blackmail situation a couple of years earlier. Amazing how a couple of strategically placed bullets could dampen the enthusiasm of even the most determined extortionist. You didn't even have to kill him.

The little red sports car pulled into the garage right on time. Rydell parked in his own personal spot and got out, carrying a soft leather briefcase. He was locking the car when Robert stepped out of the shadows.

Rydell peered at him. "Who are you?"

Robert didn't answer; he didn't really believe in chatting with his targets. His only response was to raise the gun and pull the trigger once.

Rydell held on to the briefcase as he fell.

Robert finally tracked down a guy named Pervis, a former cellmate of Danny Boyd. The dope was having a midnight snack at a pizza joint in downtown Los Angeles. Robert leaned on the counter next to him. "Evening, Pervis," he said.

Pervis was a rat-faced man with grease covering his chin and a string of cheese hanging from one corner of his mouth. He hunched farther down over the pizza and didn't even glance at Robert. "We know each other, do we?"

Robert smiled faintly. "Not exactly. We have what you might call a mutual acquaintance."

"Yeah?" He swiped at his chin with the cuff of his shirt. "Who?"

"Old roomie of yours. Danny Boyd."

That got a reaction. Pervis belched and finally looked at Robert. "Boyd? What about him?"

"He's out, I hear."

"You hear more than I do, then. But why do you think I care?"

"Well, gee, I thought maybe you'd be having a reunion. I mean, you two shared a cell for a long time. That makes a couple of guys close."

The pizza was still disappearing. Pervis spoke through a mouthful. "I don't give a flying fuck about Boyd."

"Well, I'd like to find him. Maybe you can tell me where to look."

Pervis snorted; the guy had a variety of disgusting noises he could make. He was probably a real gas at parties. "Why the hell should I tell you anything?"

"Just to be a nice guy?" Robert suggested.

Pervis glanced at him. "Yeah, right."

"How about for fifty bucks?"

"Boyd is a mean son of a bitch. Maybe he doesn't want to be found by you. I tell you where to look, he gets found, and then I find my ass on the line."

"How about a hundred dollars?"

"Hmm," Pervis said.

"That's as high as I go," Robert warned him. "And there's other ways of getting what I want out of you. Ways that won't cost me a fucking cent."

Pervis took him seriously. "I ain't saying for sure, you understand," he said. "But before he got sent up, Boyd had a woman he shacked up with. A hooker named Marnie Dowd. Maybe he might have gone to her when he got out."

"That's it?"

Pervis shrugged. "So where's my hundred?"

Robert took out fifty dollars and dropped it onto the counter. "That's only worth fifty," he said, staring at Pervis. "You got a problem with that?"

After a moment, Pervis shook his head. "No sir," he mumbled. "I got no problem at all."

Robert smiled again and walked away.

6

1

The girl he was looking at couldn't have been more than sixteen years old, if that. She was wearing a yellow halter top that did its best to push her small breasts up and out. The effect made him think, in a melancholy way, of a little girl playing dress-up in her mother's clothes.

Finally she realized that he was watching. Her shoulders, which had started to slump a little from weariness, straightened. The pink tip of her tongue appeared and ran slowly, deliberately, over her already shiny red lips.

He limped over and propped himself against the counter next to her.

She lifted a half-eaten hot dog, took a small bite, and chewed it languidly. Her eyes never left his face during the whole routine. She was damned good. Anybody would have imagined, looking at her looking at him, that this sweet young thing with big blue eyes had the hots for a somewhat over-weight, middle-aged man with weariness etched into his face.

If she ever wanted to give up walking the streets, she could probably have a really good career in the movies. Hell, for all he knew, maybe she had already done her bit on celluloid—or, more likely these days, on video tape.

She was still staring at him.

Gareth Sinclair sighed and reached into the pocket of his rumpled windbreaker. It was too hot by thirty or so degrees for the jacket, but it served very nicely to cover the holster and the gun that he still carried. Too many years as a cop had left him feeling naked without it. He flashed his ID in her direction.

Her expression became one of complete disgust, as if the hot dog had gone suddenly bad in her mouth, and then her face shut down completely. "Cop," she said, spewing both crumbs and contempt into the air between them.

"No," he said. "You didn't look closely enough. I'm private."

Her shrug caused one strap of the hardworking halter to slip from her shoulder. She pushed it back impatiently. "Same fucking thing."

Gar put the ID away. "Not quite. Just for starters, I can't bust you for soliciting."

The girl smiled sweetly; there was a smear of mustard across her pearly whites. Teeth as pretty and as straight as those had visited an orthodontist. Somewhere her parents were probably still making payments on that smile. And wondering if they'd ever see it again, no doubt. "Solicitin'? Why, sir, I don't know what you're talking about. I'm just standing here eating a hot dog. Is there any law against that?"

"No law," he said, although he knew and she knew that no girl—or boy, for that matter—would be standing in this place, at this time of the night, unless she or he was trying very hard to hustle up some cash.

Gar had ordered some coffee. It finally arrived and he stirred it with the skinny plastic stick provided by the sleepy counterman. "Don't worry," he said. "I just want to talk."

"Uh-huh." A sudden light came into her eyes. "Like, how do I know that my parents didn't hire you to find me and drag me back there?"

Before answering, he risked a sip of the coffee, which tasted pretty much the way you would expect coffee at a twenty-four-hour hot-dog stand on Hollywood Boulevard to taste. Luckily, a man who was a cop for nearly twenty years acquired many skills, not the least of which was the ability to swallow any foul brew that called itself coffee. "No," he said. "Your folks didn't hire me."

The light was gone from her eyes as quickly as it had appeared. "Yeah, well, it's a damned good thing, 'cause I wouldn't go anyway. Fuck them, is what I say."

Absurdly, Gar felt as if he should apologize to the girl for the fact that he wasn't looking for her. But such an apology would be pointless, as he knew from painful experience, because it would only piss her off so much that she might not give him any information at all. Assuming that she had any to give, of course, which was a pretty big assumption to make. None of the dozen or so kids he had talked to over the course of what was becoming a very long evening had known anything. Or, if they had, nobody was talking.

She picked up a can of orange soda and drank. As

she set the can down again, her eyes seemed for the first time to notice the black ebony cane at his side. "So, what're you, like a crip or something?"

"Something like that, yeah. I'm looking for a girl named Tammi McClure."

"Don't know her," she said immediately.

Deniability was as important to these street kids as it was to the idiots in the White House. If you made sure not to know what was going on, how could you possibly be blamed for anything? The place to be these days was as far out of the loop as you could get.

Gar reached into another pocket, this time coming out with the photo that Mrs. McClure had given him. "Maybe if you look at this," he suggested. "I heard that maybe she was turning tricks in this neighborhood recently."

"I don't know anything about that." The girl finished her hot dog before reaching out to take the photograph from him. At once, her face brightened. "Hey, you want to hear something really wild?"

Maybe his luck was turning. "What's that?"

"I had this same dress once," she said in a dreamy voice. "The exactly same dress, except that mine was yellow, not pink." She held the picture out at arm's length, tilting it, and pursing her lips critically. "It was much prettier in yellow."

"You must have been a real knockout," Gar said quietly.

"Yeah." She gnawed at her upper lip for a moment and then tossed the photo down onto the counter. "I don't know the bitch."

Gar quickly removed the picture from a puddle of some unknown liquid. The denial didn't ring true for some reason; or maybe he was just naturally suspicious. He took out a ten-spot and fingered it suggestively. "You absolutely sure about that, honey?"

She looked at the bill, then at the photo again. The instinctive desire not to get involved warred with her need for the money, and after a brief struggle, need won out, as it usually did. "Well, it *could* be I've seen her around. She sure doesn't look much like that anymore, though."

Gar didn't bother to tell the girl that with her stringy, greasy hair, druggie's pallor, and hard eyes, she wasn't such a knockout anymore either. She probably already knew it. "Where have you maybe seen her around?"

"Here, like you said." She wanted to take the money, but he moved it out of her reach.

"When was this that you might have seen her around here?"

"I don't know." She sighed. "Not lately. I heard some talk that maybe she split. Went to Venice."

"Venice? Why?"

She shrugged. "Don't ask me. Maybe she fell in love. How the fuck should I know why?"

"Okay. Thanks." He moved the money closer.

She plucked the bill away and shoved it out of sight in a hurry, as if afraid he might change his mind. "When you find her . . ."

He gulped down the rest of his coffee, which wasn't improved much by the fact that it was now cold. Of course, on the upside, it wasn't much worse either. "When I find her what?"

"You going to take her back to her parents?"

"That's the idea, yeah."

"What if she doesn't want to go?"

He crushed the empty Styrofoam cup. "Then she'll probably just take off again."

She shook her head in apparent dismay. "People can be awful stupid sometimes, can't they?"

Gar was tired. He didn't want to look at her face again, to have to see the naked fear and hurt that he knew would be there. Instead, feeling like an asshole, he reached into his pocket one more time and brought out a quarter. He set the coin carefully onto the counter next to the soda can. "You might want to call home sometime," he said. "Put this away and save it for then."

She probably wouldn't do it, of course. But, then again, maybe she would. Maybe.

He gripped his cane and walked away without waiting for her to say anything else.

Sometimes after a day that dragged on much too long, his leg would rebel. That rebellion would come in the form of a throbbing pain, often becoming so intense that he would get nauseous. When things degenerated to that point, he would have no choice but to lean all two-hundred-plus pounds onto the cane and move with aggravating slowness. He would also quietly curse the inept second-story man with the nervous trigger finger, who had put three bullets into him on a rainy night four years earlier.

This was not exactly what Gareth Sinclair had expected to be doing in this, the forty-eighth year of his life. By now, he was supposed to be off the streets, firmly planted behind a desk someplace, elevated to a position within the ranks of the Los Angeles Police Department that would not require him to tramp up and down Hollywood Boulevard in the freaking middle of the night.

Of course, honesty forced him to recognize that when the opportunity for that desk job came along a few years earlier than expected—thanks to the intervention of one Jose Diego, nervous crook—Gar ran the other way as fast as he could. Quit the damned department. Threw it all away so that now, at his advanced age and state of physical deterioration, he was still playing the games that should have been left to a much younger man. One who was not, in the baby whore's word, a crip.

It had all been his choice, yeah, but on nights like this one, Gar sometimes thought that maybe he had made a very big mistake. The absolutely last thing he wanted to do now was drive to Venice and walk some more streets, talking to still more lost children. He was just damned worn out.

But even as he limped back to his car, stuck the cane between the seats and himself behind the steering wheel, Gar knew what he was going to do. It was hell to be conscientious, especially when you were sort of past your prime. Or maybe it wasn't so much that he was conscientious at all; maybe he was just trying to justify his existence.

Whatever.

First things first, though. He took out and swallowed a couple of the tiny pink pills that were supposed to ease the pain. Unfortunately, they didn't work all that well, probably because he never allowed himself to take more than two when he was on the job. They made him groggy and it was hard to work that way.

So, ungroggy and with a leg that still throbbed, he started his car and headed toward Venice.

2

It was late, but on a warm summer night like this one there was still plenty of activity on the boardwalk. Some of what was going on, Gar figured, might have been neither illegal nor immoral. Maybe. The nice thing about being his own boss was that he didn't have to concern himself with anything but the job he was on; it wasn't his responsibility anymore to look out for the whole damned society.

The beach was covered with tents; it wasn't a Boy Scout jamboree, however. This was the new Venice, uneasy refuge for the homeless. Gar thought it was too bad, but he was just a confused liberal Democrat who didn't know what to do anymore.

After walking for a while and talking to a few massively disinterested passersby, Gar bought himself a large lemonade and found an empty bench. Gratefully, he sat.

He hadn't been there long when a boy with a chartreuse Mohawk skated over and dropped heavily down next to him. "Hi," the boy said. "Got any change you're not using?"

Gar handed him a dollar bill.

"All right," the boy said appreciatively.

"Don't spend it on drugs." Gar told all the kids the same thing, not that he imagined it really did any good. But it was something a confused liberal could do.

"Hey, no way. The body is, like, a temple, you know?" The boy grinned suddenly and even with the absurd hair, he managed to look remarkably Tom Sawyerish. "'Sides, what the hell could I get for a buck?"

Gar hid his own smile by taking a swallow of the tart lemonade.

The boy didn't leave with the dollar, but sat where he was, rolling the skates back and forth slowly, whistling a tune that Gar didn't recognize. It

was nice that he didn't seem to mind being seen
sitting with a gray-haired human being.

After a moment, figuring what the hell, Gar took
the McClure photograph from his pocket one more
time. "You strike me as a young man who gets
around," he said.

The kid liked that. "Yeah," he said with a self-
satisfied nod. "I keep on top of things all right."

"So maybe you've seen this girl?"

"You a cop?"

"No."

He seemed to accept that and took the picture.
His fingers were slightly grimy and the nails were
chewed down to the quick, but he held on to the
picture with delicacy. "She does look familiar," he
said after a moment.

"Her name is Tammi," Gar offered. "And probably she doesn't look so much like a prom queen
anymore."

The boy glanced slyly at Gar and smiled again.
"Must be demon drugs, right?"

"Probably."

He gave the photo one more long study, then
nodded firmly. "Yeah, that's her. She hangs out."

"Where, mostly?"

"House. A couple blocks that way. A few blocks."

Gar had the feeling he always got when a search
was about to yield results, a sort of tingle at the back
of his neck. "Show me the house. There's another
buck in it for you."

The boy shrugged. "Sure."

Gar finished the lemonade and threw the cup
toward a trash can that was already overflowing.
"Let's go." He still wasn't moving very quickly, but
the boy, who said his name was Perry, slowed his
skating to Gar's pace. He also talked most of the

way, apparently recounting the plot of a science fiction movie he'd recently seen. The details of the convoluted story escaped Gar completely.

Finally Perry stopped in front of a three-story gingerbread monster that was badly in need of a paint job, as well as a dozen or so new windows. "She lives here, I'm pretty sure."

Gar handed him a five-spot. "Thanks."

"Hey, thank *you*." He grinned once more and held up one hand as if swearing an oath. "No drugs." Then he whipped around and took off like a bullet.

Gar watched him go, then sighed and started toward the front door.

Tammi was not especially happy to be found.

She actually seemed to like living in a filthy room on the second floor of the run-down house in Venice. She shared the room with another hard-eyed young girl, who looked as if her grip on things was slipping even faster than Tammi's. But since Gar hadn't been hired to find *that* girl, he didn't pay much attention to her.

Tammi sat cross-legged on the bare mattress that was the only piece of furniture in the room. She had a can of beer between her knees and a joint in one hand. This particular evening, she wasn't wearing a party dress, either in pink or yellow, but only an old T-shirt with a picture of Tom Petty on the front. Gar wasn't altogether sure that she had anything on below the shirt, so he kept his gaze at eye level.

Her eyes were coldly amused as she studied him, head to toe, and then back again to his face. "You're the best they could do, huh?"

"I guess so," Gar said with a shrug. "But I found you, right?"

She conceded that with a small grimace and then took a long swallow from the can of generic beer. "So what happens next?"

"I'd like to take you home."

"Real fucking polite, aren't you?" Both girls snickered. "What if I prefer not to do that?"

"Well, I won't drag you."

"Good."

He smiled. "But I will have to tell the cops where you are and that you're only sixteen. No matter how much they don't care about one more runaway brat, once they've been officially notified about you, the law will have to step in. After all, your father is a pretty important man."

"Right. Well, fuck you, mister."

Gar dismissed that with another smile. "Everybody has to earn a living."

She took a hit from the joint and then passed it over to her silent friend. "Yeah, man, that's just what I'm trying to do."

"Hey, you're a former honor student, right? A smart girl like you should be able to make her way in life without spreading her legs for the tourists."

She did not respond to that.

He glanced at his Timex. "Getting late, honey."

"So what you're saying here is that I can choose you or the cops."

"That's pretty much it, yeah."

She chose him. Reluctantly, and with a lot of dirty words tossed in his direction.

Gar smoked a cigarette and waited as she gathered together a few things—a pair of jeans, some shorts that she pulled on much to his relief, and another T-shirt. A small leather beaded pouch that probably held her stash. And, with a glance his way, a foil packet of condoms.

At least she practiced safe sex.

Gar just looked bored as she displayed the rubbers, which seemed to disappoint her.

Neither of them spoke again until they were in his car and headed for Brentwood. She leaned against the passenger door and stared at him. "So this is how you earn your daily bread, huh?"

"This is pretty much it."

"Why?"

He just shrugged.

"Doesn't it make you feel bad that everybody thinks you're a real prick?"

"I spent years working as a cop," he replied. "I'm used to that."

"I'll bet," she muttered. "Don't you even care about why a person might have done what she did?"

"Run away, you mean?"

He sped through a yellow light. "I care. Sort of. But, see, I don't allow myself to get all tangled up in heavy philosophical issues like that."

"Sure. You used to be a cop, right?"

He couldn't help smiling a little at that. Sometimes these kids surprised him with how smart they could be. Except, of course, when it came to their own lives. Then they got real dumb.

The conversation seemed to die off at that point, probably from a lack of motivation on either side.

The house in Brentwood was dark, of course. Apparently nobody was sitting up nights worrying about the girl. Gar parked in the circular driveway and they both got out. "This really sucks," Tammi said as they walked to the door.

"I'm sorry," Gar said. "But maybe it'll all work out better this time." He pressed the doorbell.

She snorted in disbelief.

It took several minutes, but finally a light went on

inside, and then the door opened. McClure himself stood there, tying a sash around his midnight-blue silk robe. "Oh, it's you," he said to Gar. Then he spotted Tammi, who was hanging back. "You found her a lot quicker than anybody did before."

"That so?" Gar gave the girl a slight push forward.

"Hello, Tammi," her father said. "Your mother has been worried sick about you."

"I'll bet."

McClure sighed. "Go to your room now. We'll talk about this in the morning."

"Sure. The way we always talk, right?" She turned and looked at Gar one last time. "Prick." Then she ran up the stairs and out of sight.

Gar waited and then, when McClure remained silent, he said, "You'll get a bill."

McClure nodded. "Itemized, of course."

"Of course."

Gar dragged himself back to his car. Another happy family reunited. This work was so god-damned rewarding.

Item: one daughter, returned.

He couldn't wait to get home to his girlfriend and his dog.

7

His dog was waiting for him.

His girlfriend wasn't.

It was just after dawn by the time Gar walked into the house, and the first thing he saw was that the red light was on over the darkroom door. That meant Mickey was still at work developing and printing her pictures from the night before.

They had been living together for almost a year now, he and Mickey Duncan. Mickey was a photographer, one of that oft-cursed breed of ruthless paparazzi who stalked the celebrities of Tinseltown. Their constant hope was to catch one of the beautiful people at a particularly humiliating or salacious moment, capture the instant on film, and then sell the picture for a lot of money. Although he knew absolutely nothing about the business, it hadn't taken Gar very long to realize that Mickey was one of the best in the field. And while he wasn't entirely sure that what she did was a really necessary profession, he did figure that if you were going to do it at all, you might as well be very good.

He gazed glumly at the warning red light for a moment, dismissing his vague notion of grabbing a little early-morning fun in the sack. Even a man his age could, when properly inspired, surprise himself. But today he wasn't going to get the chance. So what to do? He was tired, but hunger won out over weariness. "Come on, Spock," he said to the small Boston terrier waiting expectantly at his feet. "I guess it's just you and me for breakfast."

The dog thought that was just fine, which was one of the main reasons for having him around.

The telephone-message light on his business line was flashing as he walked into the kitchen. After a mere moment of consideration, he decided to ignore the urgent blinking until after he'd eaten.

Instead of breakfast, he opted to have dinner, which he seemed to have missed the night before. A quick search of the refrigerator revealed only a bowl of leftover spaghetti and some tuna fish salad. He tossed a mental coin once and then a couple more times until it finally came up heads for spaghetti. The glass bowl went directly into the microwave. During the three minutes and thirty seconds that it took to heat through, Gar buttered a couple of slices of wheat bread, sprinkled on some garlic salt, and slid them into the toaster oven. All the while, he worked at studiously ignoring the relentlessly blinking message light. A Diet Coke—in a glass bottle, because he hated the taste of plastic or aluminum—completed the meal. Everything went onto a tray, which he carried, one-handed, out to the deck. He liked having a view of the Pacific as he ate.

The house belonged to Mickey, of course. No cop could afford a place like this—if he was honest, anyway. The place was a souvenir of her very early, very brief marriage to a soap-opera star. Once, just after he'd moved in here with Mickey, Gar had tuned in to the afternoon drama, hoping to catch a glimpse of the ex. He looked quite ordinary. Ordinary, at least, for a soap-opera doctor/sex symbol who was suspected of trying to kill his rich wife by poisoning her with a strange South American drug.

As he ate, Gar watched a pair of gulls play tag against the blue sky. Spock sat at his feet, hopefully watching each forkful of spaghetti.

Gareth Sinclair thought of himself as a happy man, at least at moments like this. He could watch the ocean, his leg wasn't hurting too much, and Mickey was working nearby. He pretty much had it all. Or at least as much as a pensioned-off old cop could expect to have.

The main thing was not to question any of this. Don't ask why they had found one another or why Mickey loved him. Don't ask. Just accept it and keep on being happy. After all, what was so hard about being happy?

But even as he finished the spaghetti and garlic toast, feeding an occasional bit to the dog, the flashing light of the answering machine still occupied a corner of his mind. The message that was waiting might have been perfectly innocent, of course. An old buddy from the department who wanted to meet for a beer. Some asshole peddling insurance or aluminum siding. Hell, maybe he'd won the lottery.

None of the idle speculation fooled him at all. He knew damned well what kind of message was waiting on the machine. Somebody had lost a child and they wanted him to find it.

Gar sighed and set the plate down onto the flagstone. There was nothing left on it but a little sauce and some crumbs, but the dog began to lick eagerly anyway.

"No wonder that animal is fat."

He turned and saw Mickey standing in the door-way. It was, as always, a minor revelation. After his wife's death from breast cancer, Gar hadn't really planned on getting into a new relationship. Face it—he wasn't exactly a handsome young stud. No soap-opera star. And although he knew that it was a pretty sexist attitude, Gar was not willing to settle for what he thought he might be able to get: either a plump and kindly widow of his own age, or a too-thin, too-tan, too-desperate tennis-playing di-vorcee. What else could he expect? It simply never occurred to him that a twenty-five-year-old might come into the picture. Especially a beautiful, tal-ented twenty-five-year-old.

"I hate eating alone," he said, justifying sharing his meal with a dog.

"Poor thing. A good woman would be waiting for you when you came home, right?"

"Sure," Gar said. "With a cold drink and a hot meal. And an eager libido."

"*Libido?*" she said. "Have you been reading the dictionary again?"

"Ha-ha."

She smiled quickly and then nodded back toward the kitchen. "Did you see that your message light is flashing?"

"I saw." He picked up the plate and started for the house. As he passed Mickey, she stretched up to plant a quick kiss on his cheek. "I was thinking that maybe I won the lottery, and they're calling to tell me the good news."

"They don't call you, dummy, you have to call them. But I suppose anything is possible," she added doubtfully.

They both went into the kitchen. Gar stuck the

plate, bowl, and fork into the dishwasher. He loved all the gadgets in this house.

Except for the answering machine.

He took the cigarettes out of his pocket and lit one.

Mickey made a face and ostentatiously switched on a small fan. The whirling blades blew smoke right back at him. He didn't mind.

Gar leaned against the counter, smoking and looking at Mickey, admiring her ash-blond hair, which was cut short for practicality, making her look even younger than she was. Especially when, like now, she was wearing an Indiana Jones T-shirt and a pair of baggy shorts.

Mickey started to make a glass of instant iced tea. As she stirred the brown granules into tap water, she frowned at him. "That message has been there all night. You going to check it or not?"

"Anybody ever tell you that you're a slave-driving bitch?" he muttered.

"Dozens of men have said that," she replied, dropping ice cubes into the glass. "They might be right."

Gar gave up. He reached out to punch the "play" button on the answering machine. The kitchen was quiet as they both listened to the voice on the tape. Gar scribbled a phone number on the memo pad, then looked up, frowning. "I should know that name, right?" he said. "It sounds familiar."

She swallowed tea. "Saul Epstein? I should hope it sounds familiar. Vanguard Studios?"

The name clicked into place in his memory. "Oh, right. Movies."

She frowned. "I wonder what he wants."

Gar sucked up cigarette smoke. "What does anybody want with me?" he asked after exhaling. "He must have misplaced a kid."

"Saul Epstein?" she said skeptically. "He must be eighty."

Gar shrugged. "Well, I don't know why the hell else he'd be calling me." There was only one kind of case that he worked on, and everybody knew it. He glanced at the clock. It was too early to call Epstein now. He crushed out the cigarette. "We were talking before about the libido," he said. "Remember?"

"Oh, yeah," she said. "I remember."

He followed her to the bedroom.

The security guard on duty at the front gate of Vanguard Studios took his time looking at Gar's identification. Contrary to the popular image, the sentry was not a kindly white-haired gent named Pop. No way. He was probably all of twenty-two and looked like a walking ad for the Aryan Youth Corps. Blond hair cut too short, piercing blue eyes, square jaw. A squeaky-clean lad, not about to put up with any nonsense.

Gar waited patiently as the guard eyed him. He realized that it was probably some serious flaw in his own character that made him decide he would rather spend time with Perry, even given the chartreuse hair, than with this humorless Dudley Do-Right.

Finally, he was waved through the gate and onto the lot. Not, however, before Dudley had issued explicit instructions as to where he could and could not go, including a specific order not to invade any of the sound stages. Gar could not understand why the guard thought he gave a damn about what was happening in the wonderful world of movies.

Saul Epstein's office was on the third floor of a brick building in the middle of the lot. It wasn't that easy to get to the old man himself, however. The first barrier came in the form of a plump, middle-aged woman in a plain gray suit. She had the air of a person who could have run the whole damned place single-handedly without ruffling a hair. Once he had convinced her that he was indeed who he said, she permitted him to pass on to the third floor.

There, he was greeted by Epstein's private secretary, a slender blonde who, while definitely easier on the eyes, looked not one iota less efficient than the first line of defense down in the lobby. Epstein was obviously no fool when it came to business, which no doubt explained why he'd been around for so long.

Gar was promptly guided to a very comfortable chair, served up some perfectly brewed coffee in a real china cup, and handed the most recent copy of *M*. He browsed through the glossy pages of the good life and surreptitiously watched the secretary as she worked.

Not that he was really interested, of course.

The memory of his recent bedroom gymnastics with Mickey was fresh in his mind. Amazing how his weariness fled the moment they were between the sheets and she was beneath his body. It was a miracle every time. Just as it had been on the first night.

They met at a murder scene, not the most romantic site for a beginning. He had tracked a runaway girl to the house, where she was shacked up with the drummer in a hot new heavy-metal band. The cops were already there when he arrived and the drummer was dead, stabbed in the chest with a dirty steak knife. Kathy, the missing girl, was huddled in the corner of the living room, rocking back and forth and talking to herself.

Gar realized immediately that this was beyond

his meager skills. He called the father, who called a shrink, and they took over.

It was when he walked back out of the house that he first saw Mickey. She was there because the opportunity to snap a picture of the drummer's body being carried out of his Hollywood Hills home was just too good to miss. Pretty tasteless, Gar thought, but when she walked over and started talking to him, he found himself smiling. One thing led to another, and before he knew what was happening, they were at Denny's having coffee.

An hour after *that*, they were necking in his car like a couple of damned kids.

Gar grinned at the memory.

The blond secretary seemed to think that the grin was meant for her. She frowned and swiveled around toward her typewriter.

Epstein didn't keep him waiting much longer, luckily.

The inner office was paneled in oak and furnished like an English men's club. Lots of leather, wood, and polished brass. Epstein sat behind a desk that probably wasn't quite big enough to qualify for statehood. Maybe he really was eighty, as Mickey had said, but he could have passed for a decade or more younger. He was a small man, dressed in a well-cut dark-blue suit, red tie, and French-cuffed white shirt. An unlit cigar was propped in a crystal ashtray next to his hand.

"Thank you for coming so promptly," Epstein said.

Gar nodded. "You have a problem?"

"Yes. My grandson is missing."

"A runaway?"

"I assume so. He apparently packed a few things and simply walked away from the house."

Gar had taken out his notebook, more for appearance's sake than anything else. "He lives with you, then?"

"Yes." Epstein was quiet for a moment, then sighed and continued. "Beau's parents died recently. He has no other family."

"You two get along?" It was a standard question.

There was another pause as Epstein played with the cigar. "I checked you out rather thoroughly," he said, instead of answering the question. "Your reputation is excellent."

"I do my job."

"And you get results."

"Usually." Gar looked up and frowned. "You should understand up front that the results I get are not always what the client would prefer."

That didn't sit well. This was a man used to getting his own way. "My sources tell me that your interest in missing children is personal. Your own daughter disappeared some years ago and was never found."

Gar felt a flush of anger. What gave this old bastard the right to poke into *his* private life? "I was a cop," he said flatly. "One of the things you learn as a cop is to find missing kids. A man has to earn a living."

"I see," Epstein said.

"Anyway, we're here to talk about your grandson. I repeat: Do you two get along?"

He was used to dragging stories out of people. Those who needed to hire him were usually anguished. Sometimes irritated. But it was his opinion that, to a greater or lesser degree, they were also embarrassed. After all, the very fact that they were talking to him at all was an admission of failure. The family was an object of near-worship in this country. Father, mother, children. The system was fondly believed to work, no matter how reality intruded on the myth.

But when you had to invite an outsider in to find one of your children, it was like telling the world that you had somehow messed up.

Gar remembered the feeling with razor-edged sharpness. You were stripped naked in front of others, with all your faults on display. It made a man feel terribly vulnerable. Even when you were a cop yourself and the ones asking the questions were friends of yours. Even then the look in the eyes of the inquisitors judged you and found you lacking somehow. Otherwise, why would your daughter have run away?

He gathered up all those memories and shoved them back where they belonged.

"Until four months ago," Epstein said at last, "I had never seen Beau." He finally picked up the cigar and rolled it between his fingers. "Beau. A ridiculous name, isn't it? My son and his wife were free spirits. And they raised Beau to be the same."

"So you two *don't* get along." He made it a statement this time, not a question.

"It has been difficult. But I thought that we were starting to . . ." Epstein broke off whatever he had been planning to say. His eyes darkened and it looked as if he was now the one caught up in the past. "My son, Jonathan, was difficult, not unlike Beau. We argued over everything from the length of his hair to the war in Vietnam to the weather." He almost seemed to smile. "Jonathan and I started arguing when he was about four and we never stopped. Not until the day he left home." The hint of a smile vanished. "We never spoke again after that day. I kept up on where he was and what he was doing, but we never communicated directly. Rachel wrote me once, when the boy was born."

"So you and Beau argued, too?"

Epstein shook his head. "Not really. He seemed too wrapped up in his own private thoughts. We disagreed, but only about stupid things. Like what was proper attire for dinner. I tried to be patient with him, but it's not easy for a man my age to change the feelings of a lifetime." Epstein grimaced. "Although maybe I would have tried harder if I'd thought this would happen."

Abruptly, he stopped talking and pushed a manila envelope across the desk. "My staff put this together. Two photographs of Beau and the details of his disappearance. Plus whatever other information we thought might be helpful. It will save us both a lot of time. There is also a check for one thousand dollars. Will that be satisfactory as a retainer?"

Gar nodded. "Will you want a daily report?"

Epstein waved that off impatiently. "That seems rather pointless, doesn't it? I shall expect to hear from you whenever there is something firm to report."

Gar stood, tightened his grip on the cane, and started for the door.

"Sinclair?"

He stopped. "Yes, Mr. Epstein?"

"Please find my grandson. I have lost everyone else. This boy is my last chance." Epstein took out a gold lighter and worked for several moments to get the cigar going. "My son ran away and I never saw him again. That mustn't happen with Beau. Whatever it takes, I want him back."

Gar stared at him. Now the old man looked every year of his age. "I'll do my best" was all Gar said. He never promised.

Epstein didn't say anything else and Gar left the office.

8

Robert paused on the sidewalk and lit a cigarette.

When that was accomplished, he glanced at his watch. It was just after midnight, although he felt as if it should have been much later than that.

With no real interest, he stared into the nearest store window. The merchandise on view—through a heavy black steel anti-theft gate—was all just schlock for the tourists. T-shirts with dumb slogans. Mugs and key rings. A lot of cheap (although not inexpensive) crap, made probably in Taiwan or some other Third World hellhole. Why would anybody, even a stupid tourist, buy such junk?

Of course, Robert couldn't understand why any tourist would go there anyway. Maybe Hollywood had once been a glamorous kind of place, but today it wasn't worth walking across the street to see. What the hell would prompt a pharmacist from Des Moines to bring the wife and kiddies here? Unless, of course, he wanted to snap a Polaroid of Junior posing with a transvestite whore. Or unless he wanted to roll the old minicam as Sis watched a junkie pee in the gutter. Not exactly the stuff of video memories or postcards home. The fools would be better off just taking the Universal Studio tour.

As for Robert himself, he was sick and tired of hiking the tackiest streets of Tinseltown in search of a hooker. Not just any hooker, of course—if it were that simple, he could have gotten whatever he wanted (and in Hollywood whatever meant *whatever*) hours ago.

Unfortunately, it was all more complicated than that, because he was looking for a particular whore. Her name was Marnie Dowd and he was looking for her because she was—or had been, anyway—Danny Boyd's girlfriend.

Robert had given this matter a lot of thought; in fact, he'd hardly been able to think about anything else ever since he learned that Boyd, his brother's killer, was out of prison.

After thinking about it so much, he had decided to kill Danny Boyd.

It was all he could do. Until Boyd was whacked, Andy wouldn't be able to rest in peace. And Robert wouldn't get a good night's sleep. But before he could kill Boyd, he had to find him.

The first step, therefore, was to look for Marnie Dowd. And *that* was turning into a real pain in the ass. He'd never really thought about the number of whores in Los Angeles (the day Robert Turchek had to pay for it was the day he'd give up screwing altogether).

Not even his burning need for revenge could keep him from feeling worn out and bored after all these hours looking at whores and talking to bartenders. He sighed; this wasn't getting anything done. Right up the street from the store peddling tourist crap was the Moulin Rouge Lounge. A place that specialized in dancing girls and watered booze. Somebody's idea of a good time, maybe, but not Robert's. Especially when he'd already been in six other places just like it. He dropped the cigarette to the sidewalk and crushed it under his heel firmly. Time to get back to work.

Inside the Moulin Rouge, Prince was blasting over a second-rate sound system as three mostly naked broads danced—sort of—on top of the bar. The action was being observed by forty or so customers jammed into a room that could have held about half that many comfortably. Cigarette smoke formed a thick gray cloud that hung in the air.

Robert sighed and pushed his way to the circular bar in the middle of the room. One of the dancers, a pretty if slightly plump black girl, did her bumps and grinds about thirteen inches from his face.

After a few moments, the bartender wandered over and stood there, looking at him blearily.

Robert ordered a light beer. It was set in front of him still in the can. There was no glass in sight, which suited Robert just fine; he didn't want to put his mouth on anything in this place but the edge of the aluminum can. And he wiped that carefully first.

He swallowed a small sip of the beer and then reached into his pocket for the mug shot of Marnie Dowd; it paid to have connections everywhere, even in the police department. When he had the bartender's attention again, he displayed his fake cop ID and the photo. Actually, the ID wasn't fake at all; it just wasn't, technically, *his*. But since the cop to whom it had actually belonged was dead— through nothing at all that had anything to do with him—Robert didn't see anything wrong with using the thing when he needed to. "She been in here lately?"

The bartender grimaced at the ID, then glanced at the mug shot and shook his head. "Hey, man, one's the same as another to me."

None of the people Robert had spoken to over the course of the evening had really *looked* at him. Not well enough to be able to remember or describe him later, if the subject should ever come up, which Robert doubted very much. There was no reason why it should, even if he had to get rough with the broad. Who cared about a hooker? At best, the tired bartender might recall a man of medium height and weight, wearing glasses and a baseball cap pulled down low over his face. A man to be forgotten as soon as he walked away.

"Her name is Marnie Dowd," he said to the blank stare on the other side of the bar.

"Don't know her."

Somebody yelled for a drink and the bartender wandered off in that direction.

Robert sipped at the beer, which he really didn't want at all, having consumed about seven already, and stared at the dancer. She had edged even closer and he could inhale the faint, musky scent of her body, mingled somewhat improbably with the odor of Johnson's Baby Powder. He knew that smell very well, because the nurses had taught him to put the powder on Andy's useless limbs to help prevent bedsores.

Suddenly he became aware that the asshole sitting next to him was jacking off under the bar. That was sort of the final straw, as far as Robert was concerned. This night had gone on long enough. He left the beer still three-quarters full and got out of the Moulin Rouge as quickly as he could.

Maybe the air of downtown Hollywood didn't smell so terrific, especially on a steamy night like this, but it was still an improvement over what he'd inhaled inside the bar. Robert paused on the sidewalk and took a couple of deep gulps of air into his lungs. It was time to go home. His encounter with Marnie Dowd would have to wait at least one more night.

After taking a moment to orient himself, he decided that the shortest route back to his car led through an alley that ran between a magazine store and a blood bank. Robert was not stupid; he would never even consider taking a route like that at this hour without the Magnum that was tucked under his arm.

He was about halfway through the alley, absently contemplating the horrors of receiving a transfusion from a place that bought blood from the kinds of people he'd been seeing all evening, when he realized that something was going on in the darkness just ahead.

He stopped to listen. A fight, obviously.

Damn. As tired as he was, almost the last thing he was in the mood for was some freaks in a brawl. The only thing he wanted to face even less was having to backtrack and take the long route to his car. To hell with it. Whatever was going on, he'd just pass right by. Not get involved. He stuck one hand under the jacket, resting it on the gun, and kept walking.

What he finally saw ahead of him couldn't really be called a fight. It was more like a gang assault. There had to be at least six young guys beating up one victim. The odds offended him. Punks offended him. Immediately, he forgot his intention just to pass by. "Hey," he said mildly. "Knock it off."

They ignored him, of course.

"Hey," he repeated. "You better quit. Now."

Finally a couple of them broke off the fun long enough to turn and look at him. "Fuck off," one said. Then they saw the Magnum leveled in their direction. The verbal one grunted, and after a moment everybody else let go of the one poor bastard they'd been beating up. He collapsed in a heap.

"This don't concern you, dickhead," the apparent leader of the group said.

Well, technically that might have been true, but Robert didn't care. "Fuck this. You better just leave," he said. "Like right now. You don't know me, but I'm not into playing games. I'm really not."

They hesitated, then must have decided that he meant what he said. As one, they turned and disappeared into the darkness.

Robert stayed where he was, the gun still out, until even the echo of their running feet had faded. Then he reholstered the weapon and took a couple of steps forward. "You okay?" he said.

The boy on the ground didn't say anything. He was breathing, though, and trying to sit up, so whatever damage had been done probably wasn't too severe. Robert crouched down next to him. "You all right?"

"Yeah," the kid finally said in a shaky voice. He got to his knees with a grunt and glanced around the alley. A look of dismay crossed his face. "They took all my stuff."

"That's too bad. You're lucky they didn't do worse than that."

"But I didn't do a damned thing to them." The boy cleared his throat and spit bloody phlegm.

"Bastards like that, you don't have to do anything." Robert gave him a pat on the shoulder.

"You're going to be fine. Just take better care of yourself." He stood and started to walk away.

"Hey," the boy said.

Robert didn't stop and he didn't even really answer. He just sort of grunted.

"I don't have any money or a place to go," the boy said.

"Not my problem," Robert said.

"Please?"

Then, feeling a little guilty—why, he didn't know, because this still wasn't his business—he stopped, turned around, and looked back at the boy again. "You eat today?"

He seemed to consider the question seriously. "I don't think so."

Robert sighed. He took out his wallet and tossed a ten-spot down on the ground. "Eat something," he said shortly.

The boy picked up the bill, "Thank you," he said in a whisper. Then he looked up. "What if those guys come back? I can't fight them alone."

Robert gave up. One of these days he was going to get himself into trouble, being such a damned soft touch. "Well, come on," he said. "I missed supper, too. We'll get something."

The boy struggled to his feet without saying anything and followed Robert out of the alley. They jaywalked across Sunset to a twenty-four-hour coffee shop. It wasn't until they were inside under the glare of the fluorescent lights that Robert realized just how bloody the kid was. A passing waitress looked at them, paused, and made a face before moving on.

Robert spotted the men's-room sign in the back of the place. "This way," he said, and again the boy followed silently. Everybody in the place—losers most of them, of course, or why would they be here?—watched their journey curiously, but nobody said anything.

One man was in the john, standing by the sink. He was using a dripping-wet paper towel on a large mustard stain that decorated the front of his white shirt that badly needed laundering anyway. After a quick glance at the blood and then at Robert's face, he dropped the paper towel to the floor and scurried out without even taking the time to dry his hands.

Robert glumly surveyed the sight of the boy standing in front of him. "Jesus Christ, they did a real job on you."

"Yeah. The bastards."

"Well, you're starting to get mad. That means you'll be okay." Robert took a couple of paper towels, soaked them in cold water, and took an ineffectual swipe at the bloodied face.

His patient flinched away.

Robert sighed. "You have a name, do you?"

After a slight hesitation, the kid blinked. "Beau," he said.

"Okay, Beau, stand still, willya?" He tried again, remembering what the nurses had taught him about washing Andy. This time, Beau stood still and most of the blood was washed away. Robert took a step back. "That's better," he said. "But that shirt is a write-off."

Beau shrugged. "Yeah, well, it's all I've got. They took my stuff, remember."

"I remember."

After a moment, Robert sighed again and took off his jacket. When Beau saw the gun hanging there, his eyes widened and his face lost some color, but he didn't say anything. "Don't worry about it," was Robert's only comment. He removed the holster, then unbuttoned the pale-green sport shirt and took it off. Finally, he pulled the clean white T-shirt over his head. "Here. Take that off and wear this instead."

Beau made the change quickly, shoving the ruined shirt into the wastebasket. There wasn't anything that could be done about the jeans, but they didn't show the blood so much anyway. "Thanks," he said.

"Yeah, sure." Robert handed him his comb and watched as Beau used it.

Finally they were both ready to leave the bathroom. Nobody paid them much attention when they walked out and found a booth. Even a cop, newly arrived at the counter, only glanced at them before returning to his newspaper. The waitress, a weary-faced Chicana, finally came over. "You wanna see menus?"

"No," Robert replied. "Just bring us a couple cheeseburgers, double fries, and some Cokes." Then he looked at Beau. "That okay by you?" he asked belatedly.

Beau nodded.

The waitress dragged herself in the direction of the kitchen.

"Thank you," Beau said.

Robert shrugged.

"Not just for the food. For what you did in the alley."

"The odds sucked, that's all." He didn't want anybody thinking he made a habit of running around doing good deeds.

"I don't even know your name."

"Robert," he said.

Their Cokes were delivered.

Robert unwrapped a plastic straw and pushed it

into the glass. "What the hell were you doing out there in the middle of the night?"

Beau was stirring his drink. "What's anybody doing anywhere? I was just there. You were there, too. Why?"

"None of your damned business."

Beau gave a faint smile, then grimaced as his split lip objected. "Sorry." He took a packet of saltines from the plastic basket on the table and slowly turned the crackers into crumbs. "The thing is, I didn't have any place to go. I thought that maybe the alley would be a good place to sleep."

Robert looked at him in disbelief. "You haven't been on the street very long, I guess."

"Couple days."

"Well, you'll learn."

"I guess." He didn't sound very happy at the prospect.

The food arrived and Beau, after drenching his fries in a quart or so of ketchup, started to eat with enthusiasm. Robert chewed more slowly. A couple of hookers came in and took stools at the counter. He checked them out, just in case Marnie Dowd had decided to drop in for a bite between tricks. Both these women were much too young to be her. Marnie, judging by the mug shot, was on the downside of her good years. It must be getting harder every night to earn a buck. Why, after all, would anybody pay to fuck a wrinkled middle-aged broad when that was probably just what he had at home?

When you looked at it that way, maybe he should just kill Marnie; it would probably be a kindness. But he would avoid that if he could. No sense complicating things, right? If she didn't want to cooperate, he'd decide what to do then.

Beau picked up a kosher dill that had seen better

days and took a bite. "You a cop?" he asked between chews.

Robert shook his head.

"I only thought . . . because of the gun." He whispered the last word.

"No, I'm not a cop."

"Well, that's fine with me, you know? I don't think much of cops, actually. Back home, they're just nothing but a bunch of government assassins."

Robert finished his hamburger. "You must be from Chicago," he said with a smirk.

"No." Beau was frowning. "I don't like guns much either. They scare me, you know?"

"They're supposed to scare you. Everybody should be scared of them."

"Are you?"

Robert shrugged. "In the wrong hands, yeah." Meaning, of course, anybody's hands but his. He leaned across the table and spoke quietly. "Make me happy, buddy, and forget you ever saw the damned gun, okay?"

"Sure, Robert."

"You have enough to eat?" Robert asked as he checked the waitress's addition.

"Plenty. Thanks again."

"Sure, sure. No problem. I was hungry anyway." That made it seem less like a nice thing to do. Robert took an extra twenty from his wallet and put it on Beau's side of the table. "Here. I have to go."

Beau picked up the bill and rolled it in his palm.

"So long." Robert got up and walked to the cashier. As he stood waiting for his change, he looked back toward the booth. Beau was still sitting there. "Fuck it," Robert muttered.

"What?" the startled cashier said.

He ignored her and walked out. On the sidewalk, he paused and stared back into the diner. Beau was looking at him. Robert didn't know why he cared what happened to this boy, but he realized that if he just walked away now, he'd feel guilty later. It might be easier in the long run just to help the kid out a little. He stepped back inside and raised a hand to gesture toward the booth.

Beau jumped up immediately, starting to smile as he approached. "Yeah, Robert?"

"Come with me."

They left the coffee shop. The paper-reading cop was standing on the corner, talking to another patrolman. Robert barely glanced at them.

"Hey, where we going?" Beau asked, hurrying to keep up.

"Just for tonight, you can crash at my place. Just for tonight, understand?"

"Sure. Thanks."

Robert glanced sidewise at him, shaking his head. This boy was a real dope. Sleeping in alleys. Talking to strangers. Now going home with somebody he didn't know. Beau was just lucky that it was *him* he'd run into and not some pervert.

They reached the car and got in. Robert knew that he was going to regret this, probably by the time they got to the house. He wasn't Mother Fucking Teresa, after all, so why the hell should he get involved in the problems of some idiot street kid?

But he couldn't help remembering, with a sharp pang of hurt, that not so long ago, he and Andy had been a couple of homeless brats, bouncing around the system. More than once, it had been the two of them getting beaten up by the punks of the world. So maybe it was for Andy he was doing this. Instead of giving a freaking donation to the Cancer Society or something, he'd give this kid a little help.

It was no big deal. He'd let Beau crash for the night. No big deal.

9

1

The black woman led him through a long hall back to the kitchen. She was in the middle of baking the weekly supply of pastry which, she said, Mr. Epstein favored for his breakfast. The room smelled strongly of cinnamon and other good things.

The cook was a plump, cheerful-looking woman wrapped in a frilly pink apron. She insisted that Gar should call her Ruth. "Mr. Epstein, he just dotes on my tea cakes," she said, returning to a large bowl of dough, which she started to knead vigorously.

Gar was perched on a wooden stool, balancing the cup of coffee she had served him. "What about Beau?" he asked. "Does he like the tea cakes, too?"

She smiled. "You ever see a teenage boy who didn't inhale every bit of food put in front of him?" She patted the dough. "Beau eats everything."

The coffee was very good. Epstein certainly was well taken care of, both at work and at home. No wonder he'd lived so long. "What is Beau like?"

Ruth didn't take the question lightly. She poked and punched at the dough and thought about it for several moments. "Beau is a good boy," she said finally. "Real polite, in a sort of old-fashioned way. His poor folks did a nice job of bringing him up, even if they did live down there in the jungle."

"There seems to be a 'but' coming up here pretty soon," Gar said.

"Well." She paused, frowning. "Beau hasn't been happy here. I know he misses his momma and papa, but there's more to it than that. He's like a sad little duck out of water. This is a real different kind of life from what he was used to."

"And how about the relationship between Beau and his grandfather?"

Again she thought. "Mr. Epstein is happy to have the boy here," she said, "although he isn't one to show his emotions much. Which is too bad, because I think what Beau needs and what he wants is for somebody to grab him in a big hug and let him know he's cared about." She smiled a little. "Course, I guess you could say the same thing about everybody, right?"

He nodded. "But you don't think Beau is liable to get that from his grandfather?"

She sighed deeply. "Mr. Epstein loves the boy, I know that. But he's a proud man. Stubborn and set in his ways. I never met Jonathan, his son, but I do know that Mr. Epstein was very hurt by the way it went between them." She hesitated, loyalty to her employer seeming to war with her desire to help him find Beau. That desire to help won out. "The sad thing is, he can't see that maybe he was to blame some, too. Far as Mr. Epstein can see, he didn't do anything wrong with the way he raised up Jonathan."

"So he's doing the same thing with Beau?"

"Pretty much, I think, yessir." She began to roll the dough. "Mr. Epstein is a wonderful man in so many ways. He gives a whole lot of money to good causes. But he is also a man who has a lot of power. Men like that sometimes can't see that the power it takes to be rich and important outside doesn't work when they try to act the same way at home." She slapped the dough. "And Mr. Epstein, he was thinking that this boy would be like having his son back. You can't make one child take the place of another."

"No," Gar agreed. "You can't." Even if they'd had six kids, it wouldn't have made the pain any less when one vanished.

Ruth glanced at him. "One more thing about Beau."

"What's that?"

"He is a lot like some innocent little lamb. Smart like anything when it comes to school classes, but real ignorant about the world. He seems a whole lot younger than he is sometimes."

Gar digested this. "That's too bad," he said.

Ruth nodded. "If he's out there in this city," she murmured, "being an innocent child is no good."

He couldn't argue with that.

Derek Thorn must have spent hours each day polishing the brass buttons on his trim blue blazer. Each and every button gleamed like a miniature golden sun. And no doubt whatever time he had left from that chore was spent having his steel-gray hair styled. There was no denying that the headmaster of Paynor Academy was an impressive-looking man.

Gar felt a little guilty that his visit was serving to ruffle that magnificent facade, at least temporarily. It wasn't altogether clear whether Thorn was more concerned over the fact that one of his students was missing or over what that fact might mean to the reputation of his school. The only saving grace seemed to be that Beau Epstein had vanished after school was officially out for the summer. That might help keep Paynor blameless. Keeping Paynor's image clean—which really meant keeping Derek Thorn clean—was clearly the top priority here.

Gar's biggest concern at the moment was how to get comfortable in the damned plastic chair he'd been waved into. Even though it was made of plastic, that didn't mean the chair was a Kmart Blue Light Special or anything like that. The molded black poly-whatever was actually a very trendy item. As a work of art, it was probably okay. As a piece of furniture for actually sitting in, it was a disaster. After struggling in it for several moments, Gar gave up and just resigned himself to being uncomfortable. He rested the cane across his knees and hoped that he'd be able to get up when the time came.

Thorn was waiting for him to speak.

"I was surprised to find you here when I called," Gar said. "Don't you get the summer off?"

Thorn shook his head, an act which disturbed not a single hair on his head. "Many of our students benefit from additional educational opportunities during the vacation period," he said.

"Remedial classes, you mean?"

He admitted that with a reluctant nod. "Was Beau Epstein enrolled for the summer classes?"

"Yes. Although his grades were excellent for the short time he was here, his grandfather thought that he might best use the summer to improve his socialization skills."

"What can you tell me about Beau?" Gar shifted his butt a little, so that everything wouldn't go absolutely numb.

Thorn frowned. "We do our best with all the students at Paynor," he said. The words sounded as if they came from a canned speech. "Many of them live what might be termed stressful lives."

Gar wasn't sure that "stressful" was the word he would use. Most of them were spoiled brats. But he also knew that it could be very hard having everything in the world except a pair of loving, attentive parents. He realized, maybe better than most, that a lot of these kids were orphans in all but actual fact. Beau, of course, was the real thing. "How did he fit in with the other students? Given his pretty unique background, I mean."

"There were problems, naturally. He simply wasn't, how shall I say it, *accustomed* to the way of life here."

Gar could only imagine. "Did he make any friends at all?" That was the one piece of information conspicuously missing from the notes Epstein had given him. Usually the parents of even the most wayward youth could provide at least a few names to be pursued. But not this time.

Thorn was looking increasingly uncomfortable. "Well, as to that," he said, "unfortunately, I can help you very little." He made a pyramid of his fingers on top of the desk. "Young people have their own fairly rigid social structure. An adult authority figure like myself has a very difficult time penetrating its walls."

Gar thought it was pretty funny that Thorn seemed to think of himself seriously as having any real authority over the student body at Paynor. To the kids, he'd be willing to bet, this fool with his brass buttons was nothing more than a clown. A figure of ridicule, not authority. "Do I have your permission to speak to some of the students on campus?"

Thorn frowned again. "Well, ordinarily I wouldn't be terribly comfortable with that. But Mr. Epstein did ask us to give you our complete cooperation, and of course we want to accommodate him in every way possible."

Of course. Epstein was a man everybody wanted to accommodate. Except, maybe, his own grandson.

Gar used his cane as a sort of lever to get himself up out of the damned chair. He promised Thorn that he wouldn't disrupt any classes and left the impressive authority figure sitting glumly behind his desk.

Apparently, summer classes at Paynor were pretty low-key. A number of students were scattered around the lawn, soaking up the sun, eating frozen yogurt, and listening to music from a variety of radios. Some of them were even looking at books. It was clear that "remedial," at Paynor, did not have to mean dreary.

A young black man was selling the frozen yogurt from a small yellow truck parked in front of the school. Gar walked over and bought himself a cone of strawberry twirl. He licked it thoughtfully as he decided which students to approach. Three boys were sitting on the low stone wall that edged the lawn and none of them carried books. Gar went and sat on the wall near them.

One of the boys looked at him and Gar could see something like scorn reflected in the eyes. He could also see the effects of what was undoubtedly some recently smoked dope. "Hi, there," he said cheerfully. "Mind if I ask you a few questions?"

None of them said anything.

"Don't worry," Gar said. "I'm not a narc."

That earned him a snort. "No kidding," the kid with the stoned eyes said. "So you're not a narc. Gee, that's really interesting."

Gar smiled. "I do have a lot of close friends on the force, though. And some of them even work in narcotics."

"Big deal."

He shrugged. "Right. Big deal. Who the hell cares?"

"Not me," the boy said.

"Not me either." Gar finished his yogurt. "You can fry your brains with anything you like; it's none of my fucking business."

The boy grinned. "For an old crip, you have a pretty good attitude."

Gar shook his head. "You don't understand," he said. "The thing is, I don't have any attitude at all. I'm just here to do a job."

"What job is that?"

"First of all, do you have a name?"

"Scott."

"Okay, Scott. I'm trying to find a fellow student of yours."

Scott didn't look surprised. "Somebody hit the road, did they? Hell, that happens all the time. Who split?"

"Beau Epstein."

All three boys smirked.

"You know Beau, I guess."

"Nature boy? Sure, we know him."

"What do you think about him?"

Scott wrinkled his brow in a parody of thought; maybe that was all he was capable of. "Oh, Beau is pretty much of a complete dork," he said finally. "He walks around here like he's better than the rest of us. Like he's morally superior or something."

Gar wouldn't have thought that moral superiority was a subject that Scott would have been very concerned with. "Do you have any idea why he might have taken off?"

Scott shrugged. "Who knows?" Then he grinned unpleasantly, as if someone had just told a dirty joke. "Unless maybe it has something to do with Kimberly." His tone matched the grin in nastiness.

Gar wanted to sigh, but he was damned if he'd give these boys the satisfaction. Instead, he just took out his notebook. "Kimberly?" he said.

"Yeah. Kimberly Wyndham. She goes to school here."

"She and Beau friends, are they?"

Another snicker. "Well," Scott said, "that sort of depends on what you call a *friend.*"

Gar wanted to ask him exactly what he meant, but then he decided it would be better to hear the details from Kimberly herself. "You know where I can find her?"

Scott reached into his pocket and came out with a small electronic contraption. He quickly punched something into it, then turned its face toward Gar. "Kimberly's address," he said.

Gar read the digital readout and jotted it down. "There's nothing else you can tell me about Beau?"

Scott's momentary agreeability vanished. "You look in the jungle? Maybe he's back swinging through the trees."

"You're pretty funny, Scott. For an asshole."

Scott just grinned again and flipped him a finger.

Gar got up and walked away.

2

His daughter's name was Jessica.

One day when she was just past sixteen, Jessica

Lynn Sinclair had walked out of the house to go, they thought, to school. But she didn't go there and she never came home again, either.

No evidence of foul play was ever found.

Inside her denim schoolbag, she had tucked her diary, her teddy bear, and two hundred dollars in baby-sitting earnings. It seemed as if she had intended to vanish.

Gar stirred the high-octane chili that Harry served at his hole-in-the-wall diner on Alvarado Street. It wasn't the most convenient place to come for lunch, but some days nothing would do but a healthy dose of the spicy concoction. Or maybe it wasn't so much the chili as it was the memories. On Saturdays, years ago, he would bring Jessica here. A father-and-daughter sort of day. Maybe they would catch the Dodger game. Or a museum. But whatever they did, it always started with chili at Harry's.

It was as if the earth had opened up and swallowed his daughter.

Gar washed chili down with cold beer.

The doctors never said for sure, but he was convinced that the reason his wife succumbed so quickly to the cancer was that she just didn't want to go on without her daughter. Gar wondered sometimes if the fact that he *did* go on, was even happy most days, meant that he had loved Jessie less. He didn't think so. Maybe he still nourished some hope that sooner or later he would find her.

But probably not today.

Yeah, Jessie was gone, but he felt that Beau Epstein was still within his reach. Beau could still be saved.

Kimberly Wyndham lived in a large white house in the sacred heart of Beverly Hills. A Mexican housekeeper opened the door and told Gar that Miss Kimberly was around back by the pool. He followed the path she pointed out.

Kimberly was there, all right.

The girl was wearing a white string bikini on a body that was a perfect shade of brown; skin cancer undoubtedly waited several decades down the road, but Kimberly probably figured that there would be a cure by then, at least for somebody who could afford it. She might well have been right.

"Excuse me, Kimberly," Gar said. "Can we talk for a minute?"

She raised her head slowly and opened her eyes. "Who are you?"

He displayed his ID. "I wanted to talk to you about Beau Epstein."

She sat up and tied the bikini top, while Gar averted his gaze. It seemed as if he was spending a lot of time lately not looking at young girls' bodies. Next to her chaise was a small table that held a tall glass of what looked like tonic. Maybe there was something else in it, too, he decided, seeing the gulp she took before speaking again. "Beau?" was all she said.

"He's missing."

"Missing? What does that mean?"

How come this girl wasn't in one of those remedial classes at Paynor?

"I mean that his grandfather doesn't know where he is. I've been hired to find him."

"Like Magnum?" she said brightly.

"Something like that, yes."

She took another gulp; there was definitely something stronger than just tonic water in the glass. "How come you came here? I hardly know him at all."

Gar dragged a wooden deck chair closer and sat down. "I'm here because some of the kids at school told me that you might have an idea about why he took off."

She shook her head and reached for a bottle of coconut-scented tanning lotion. SPF 0.

Gar leaned forward. "Kimberly, maybe you don't know what it's like out there on the streets. It's very dangerous. A lot of very bad people. Beau might be in serious trouble."

She was slowly massaging lotion into her taut belly. "I don't think it's fair to blame *me*," she said, starting to pout. "It was only a joke."

Gar could feel a headache building behind his eyes. "What was only a joke?" he asked.

She was, to her credit, more than a little embarrassed by the story of what had happened between herself and Beau. It came out slowly, as she fortified herself with frequent swallows of the drink. When she was finished, she picked up a pair of dark glasses and put them on. Refuge from his gaze.

Gar closed his notebook and put it away without writing anything down.

"Do you really think that's why he ran away?" she asked finally.

"Maybe."

For almost ten seconds, it looked as if Kimberly Wyndham might actually be experiencing a crisis of conscience. Then she gave her head a toss. "Well, that's just dumb. Who would run away because of a little *sex?* Let me tell you, there are plenty of guys who would like to get lucky the way Beau did."

He didn't doubt it for a minute.

"So if he ran away because of that, he's just stupid. And I can't be blamed for that, can I?" She gave him a bright and perfect smile.

10

1

The boy was still sleeping.

Robert pulled on a pair of old cutoffs and walked quietly though the living room, where Beau was sprawled half-on and half-off the couch, dead to the world. Robert paused to look at him for a moment, then went on into the kitchen.

Coffee seemed like a very good idea. A heavy dose of caffeine and sugar might wipe out the lingering headache caused by drinking too much beer during his bar-hopping hunt for Marnie Dowd the night before.

All that damned beer probably also helped to explain why he was suddenly playing kindly uncle or whatever the hell he was doing.

He plugged in the electric coffeepot. If he was going to be a good host, he probably better feed the kid some breakfast. A quick check of the refrigerator gave him eggs, bacon, bread. Some orange juice.

Robert took everything out and set it on the counter.

Regular Betty Freaking Crocker, right?

It had been a long time since he'd made breakfast for anybody.

He was pouring his first cup of coffee when Beau appeared in the doorway. "Well, good morning, Sleeping Beauty," Robert said.

"Hi." Beau looked only half-awake and a little bewildered. "You're Robert, right?"

"Boy, you're sharp today. Yes, I'm Robert."

"I was confused. Real life was getting all mixed up with the crazy dreams I kept having." There was a bruise on one cheek and his left eye was swollen, but otherwise he seemed to have come through last night's beating relatively unscathed. He took a careful look around the kitchen. "This is your place, I guess?"

"Mine and the mortgage company's, yeah." Robert took a frying pan out of the cupboard. "If you want to take a shower or something, the can is that way."

"Okay." Beau turned around, then stopped and glanced back at Robert. "Thanks."

Robert shrugged. "You have any problem with scrambled eggs?" he said. "I don't feel like screwing around with them much."

"Scrambled is fine. The thanks was for what you did last night."

Robert frowned as he searched for a fork. "Yeah, all right."

Beau headed for the bathroom.

Robert lined up strips of bacon in the frying pan and turned on the gas flame. He leaned against the counter and drank coffee slowly as the fat began to sizzle in the pan. The plan was simple. Let the boy clean up a little, feed him, give him some more cash, and then send him on his way. Simple. He didn't have the time—or the desire—to fool around with the troubles of some hard-luck juvenile delinquint.

He started breaking eggs into a bowl.

God, the hot water felt wonderful.

Actually, it was sort of funny how quickly he'd gotten used to taking a hot shower every day at Saul's. A few days without one now and he started to feel really grotty. Everybody, Jonathan used to say, was corruptible.

His aching, battered bones and muscles began to relax under the stinging assault of the water. There was a bottle of green shampoo hanging on a hook. Beau dumped a big dollop of the stuff into his hair and rubbed vigorously. Suds and water swirled between his toes and disappeared down the drain. It felt like a lot of his problems were going along.

Robert was a really nice guy.

As he finished rinsing, Beau thought about something that he'd almost forgotten. The gun. If Robert wasn't a cop, why was he carrying a gun? It was a question he really would have liked to ask, but as he thought about it, there was something about the look in the man's green eyes that made him decide to keep the question to himself.

Beau had the feeling that he didn't want to get Robert pissed off.

The toast was made and the eggs hit perfection just as Beau walked back into the room, looking cleaner and a little damp. He also looked younger than Robert had thought. "Sit," Robert said.

Beau sat.

Robert filled two plates with eggs, bacon, and

toast, then joined him at the table. "You sleep okay on that couch?"

Beau set down the already-empty juice glass. "Fine. Thank you."

Well, he had good manners, at least. That was sort of rare these days. Robert approved. He poured some more juice into the empty glass. "So what's the story with you? Don't get along with your folks, I guess?"

"My parents are dead," Beau replied, keeping his gaze on the plate of food.

Robert chewed and swallowed some eggs. "I'm sorry," he said.

"Sure. Everybody is sorry."

He spooned grape jelly onto a slice of toast. "No, really, I can understand how you feel. My folks died when I was even younger than you. They were in a plane crash."

Beau looked up at him briefly, then returned his attention to the food. "So did you have to go live with some old fart of a grandfather?"

Robert shook his head. "No. There wasn't anybody else. Just my kid brother and me. We got dumped in a lot of foster homes. Some of the time, we couldn't even be together."

"It really sucks, doesn't it?" Beau said. "Other people just step right in and start making decisions for you."

"It sucks, all right," Robert agreed. "But when I hit sixteen, I took Andy out of the place he was living in and we came out here. Things were okay, then."

After a moment, Beau looked up and smiled. "You make great scrambled eggs, Robert."

"Yeah, right." Robert got up and went for more coffee. When he'd returned to the chair, he said, "I have to run out to Malibu on business today. You want to come along?"

"Sure. That'd be great."

Robert wasn't so sure about that and already he didn't know why the hell he'd issued the invitation. It wasn't part of the plan. But it was too late now.

Well, okay. So they'd go to Malibu, he'd see the man there and do what had to be done, and then tonight, when he returned to his search for Marnie Dowd, he could dump the kid right back in Hollywood where he'd found him.

2

Lonnie Jones owned a moderately priced fish restaurant down on the beach. Because the location was fine and the food acceptable, though unextraordinary, he probably would have made a decent living even if the joint had been strictly legit.

But the only thing legit about Lonnie Jones were the diamond rings that adorned four of his fingers. And even those were probably hot.

Robert parked in the empty lot behind the restaurant. "You go down to the beach," he ordered Beau. "I have to see a guy inside."

"Okay," Beau said cheerfully. He headed for the water.

The restaurant wasn't open for lunch, only dinner, and so even the staff hadn't arrived yet. Only Jones himself was there, sitting at the bar, going over some purchase orders and bills. When the door opened and Robert came in, he looked up with a frown. "Not open," he said. Jones looked a little like a young Belafonte.

Robert didn't say anything as he walked over and took a seat at the bar.

"You deaf, pal, or what? I said, we're not open."

"That's okay. I'm not here to eat."

Jones set his gold Cross pen down on the bar carefully. "Then why are you here?"

"Mr. Campion sent me."

That was not what Jones wanted to hear. But he tried to pretend that the news didn't make him very nervous. "Yeah? What the fuck for?" The Better Business Bureau member was gone suddenly; Jones had started in the gutter and that background wasn't far beneath the surface.

Robert reached out and toyed with the pen, spinning it in a slow circle. "He wants the book back, of course."

"What book?"

Robert smiled and shook his head. "Oh, Lonnie, Lonnie," he murmured. "We don't have to dance around this, do we? You know damned well what book. I know what book. Everybody knows what fucking book."

Jones didn't say anything.

Robert got up and walked over to the sliding glass door that led to the patio. He slid the door open and stepped out. Beau had rolled his jeans way up and was wading in the Pacific.

"How do I even know you're really from Campion?" Jones said from the doorway.

Robert shrugged. "Call him, if you want. My name is Turchek. Ask him if I'm here on his behalf."

"Maybe I will," Jones said. He rubbed one of the diamond rings as if it were a magic lamp and he was wishing for a genie to pop out. "Turchek?" he said after a moment.

"Right." Robert knew that Jones wasn't going to

call Campion. "Why don't you just get me the book?" He was still watching Beau.

"How about we deal?" Jones offered.

"Sure. Okay. Here's the deal. You get me the book and I won't blow your fucking brains out. Does that sound like a pretty good deal to you?"

"Hey, come on—"

"Fuck it, Jones. That's the deal. The only deal."

Beau looked up suddenly, saw him watching, and gave an enthusiastic peace sign. God, when was the last time he'd seen anybody do that? Robert returned the gesture. Then he turned and looked at Jones again. "Well, Lonnie? It's your call."

After a moment, Jones went back inside the restaurant. Robert followed him and slid the door closed. "I'll get the book," the black man said.

"That's smart, Lonnie. And don't even think about trying anything that isn't so smart."

"It's in the safe. You wait here."

"Oh, I'll wait."

Jones disappeared.

Alone, Robert took out a handkerchief and used it to wipe the doorknob. He went back to the bar and picked up the pen, wiping it as well. He hadn't touched anything else in the place. Then he took the handgun from his pocket.

Jones reappeared, a small black spiral notebook in one hand. He dropped it onto the bar. "Tell Campion this isn't over yet," he said.

"I'll tell him," Robert said.

He raised the gun and shot Jones in the head. After using the handkerchief once more on the gun, he dropped it next to the body. Ditch the weapon and you were a lot safer. It was very easy to get another cheap gun.

Then he left the restaurant.

* * *

Beau was sitting on the sand now, watching the water. "Business all done?"

"All done." Robert dropped down next to him and lit a cigarette. "I'll take you back to Hollywood tonight," he said. "Then you'll be on your own again."

Beau frowned, then looked away quickly. "Okay."

"I'll give you some money."

"You already gave me thirty."

"Oh, hell, that's not enough."

Beau was drawing ragged lines in the sand. "You don't owe me anything, you know."

"It's got nothing to do with owing you. I just want to do it." Robert stared at the scratches. "What's that mean? That picture."

"Nothing." Beau rubbed it out. "It doesn't mean anything."

Robert sighed and pushed himself up. "Let's go," he said.

Beau followed him back to the car.

3

"Does that hurt?"

Robert looked up from the menu he was reading. "Does what hurt?"

Beau fingered his earlobe. "Having those holes in your ear."

"No, it doesn't hurt at all. You decide?"

"I don't care. Steak, I guess."

"Good choice." The waitress came back and they both ordered the sirloin dinner. Robert settled back to drink his beer. It was time to get tough on this kid. To tell him the facts of life before he went back onto the street. "What I want for you to do, Beau, is smarten up a little, okay? Hide your money. Stay out of dark alleys. And for Christ's sake, don't get so chummy with strangers. You don't know who might be a psycho or a pervert. You hear what I'm saying?"

Beau nodded.

Robert still wasn't sure that any of what he was saying was actually getting through. "Maybe what you really ought to do is just go on back to your grandfather's. Hell, I'll even drive you there, if you want."

Beau's chin lifted a little. "No," he said. "I won't do that."

They paused as the waitress delivered salad and rolls. When she was gone again, Robert picked up one of the warm rolls. He tore it apart and smeared butter on both halves. "Does the old man beat on you or something?"

"No." Beau dumped salt and pepper on his salad. "Nobody pays me that much attention."

"So your feelings got hurt, is that it?"

A quick flash of anger passed through the usually placid blue eyes. "Look, Robert, you don't understand the situation. He never cared about my father and he doesn't care about me, either. And so why the hell should I care about him? I'm not going back there."

Robert shrugged. "Hey, it's your life. None of my fucking business what you do."

They glared at one another and concentrated on eating, not talking.

Both steaks were nearly gone before Beau spoke again. He set his fork down. "I'm sorry," he said. "I don't have any right getting mad at you."

"It doesn't bother me," Robert said. "Sometimes getting mad is the only way to survive."

Beau shook his head. "But you've been real great. Saving my ass last night and all."

Robert didn't want to get all tied up in this boy's emotions; there wasn't any time for that. "Hey, Beau, it was no big deal."

Beau just looked at him for a moment, then picked up his fork and started eating again.

As they were finishing the apple pie à la mode, Robert pushed an envelope across the table. "Take this," he said. "It should keep you going for a while."

Beau opened the envelope and quickly counted the money inside. "There's two hundred dollars in here," he said.

"I can afford it. Just remember to hide the bread in different pockets, like I showed you. And in your shoes."

"I will. Don't worry about me," Beau said, going for toughness. "I can take care of myself."

"Sure. Just like you were doing last night, right?" Robert checked his watch. "Well, it's getting late and I've got things to do. You ready to take off?"

Beau swallowed hard. "I'm ready, yeah."

Robert paid the check and they walked out of the restaurant, stopping on the sidewalk. Robert held out a hand. "You hang tough, Beau."

They shook. "I will. You too. Thanks."

Robert walked away quickly. Beau was a nice kid. It was only too bad that the street would probably devour him whole before very long. The world could be a shitty place for somebody that dumb. Dumb wasn't really the right word. Naive, that was it. Now that he thought about it, there was something about Beau that reminded him of Andy as a kid. A sort of goofy sweetness.

But there wasn't anything more he could do for

him. His business right now was finding Marnie Dowd and then Danny Boyd. And he'd already gone to a lot of trouble for somebody who wasn't his responsibility at all.

He turned around for one more quick look, but Beau was no longer standing in front of the restaurant.

Beau stayed in the shadows until he was pretty sure that Robert wasn't going to turn around again. Then he stepped back out onto the sidewalk and walked after him.

What he hoped to accomplish by following Robert wasn't real clear. But since Robert was the first person in a long time to seem interested in what happened to him, Beau wasn't going to give up the link just like that. Even Jonathan, a determined pacifist, had always admitted that there might be some things in life worth fighting for. Beau decided that this qualified.

Ahead of him, Robert walked for several blocks and then went into a bar. Beau crouched across the street in the doorway of a closed record store. Maybe if Robert got a little drunk, like last night, he'd be in a more receptive mood. They could be friends, Beau thought, if only Robert would give it a chance.

He hadn't been lonely with Robert and he hadn't been scared. The black hole in his stomach was gone. Yeah, that was worth fighting for.

Even if it was Robert himself he had to fight with.

4

It was nearly two hours and several bars later before Robert finally spotted Marnie Dowd.

She wasn't aging very well. Of course, junkie hookers rarely did. Her long hair was dyed a harsh orange-red color, sort of what Lucy Ricardo's hair might have looked like if the old shows hadn't been done in black and white. She was wearing a purple miniskirt and a tight yellow blouse. A heavy mask of makeup didn't hide the wrinkles on her face. For an instant, Robert almost felt sorry for Danny Boyd, coming out of prison after all that time and finding this worn-out broad waiting for him.

He stood in a corner of the bar, nursing one beer, until Marnie, apparently deciding that her income prospects weren't very good in the Diablo Bar, walked out. He went after her, following the woman for almost a block, until she stopped to light a cigarette. Then he walked up to her. "Hi," he said.

"Hi, yourself, sweetie," she said, the Virginia Slim hanging from one corner of her mouth. "You looking for a date?"

"Maybe." This close, the evidence of drug use was even clearer on her ravaged face. How desperate would a man have to be to get laid to let her touch him? "How much?" he asked.

"How much for what?" Marnie probably thought that she was being real cagey, making sure that he wasn't a vice cop.

He leaned closer, almost gagging on her perfume. "Blow-job," he whispered. "How much for a blow-job?"

"Twenty."

"You any good?"

Impatient and bored, she flicked ashes away. "I'm experienced," she said. "It doesn't take a lot of brains to suck a cock and do it right."

What a charmer. "Okay," he said.

"You don't have any diseases, do you?"

"None to speak of. Let's go to my car."

She followed him this time, around the corner and into an alley. After taking several steps into the darkness, she tossed the cigarette away. It made a shower of orange sparks as it fell. "Where the hell are you parked, lover boy?"

"In here a little further. I don't especially want an audience, you know."

She sighed and followed him again. Thank God for a druggie who needed a fix badly enough to be stupid. Abruptly, he stopped and turned around to face her. "This is far enough, Marnie."

"I thought—" She broke off and peered at him in the dim light. "You know my name? Who are you?"

"I'm just a man with a few questions."

"I don't like this," Marnie Dowd said. "You can get somebody else to suck you off, buddy, 'cause I'm outta here."

She started away, but he grabbed her by one arm and pushed her up against the side of the building. "Not yet, sweetheart. I said there were some questions."

She glared at him.

"I'm looking for Danny Boyd. Where is he?"

She blinked. "Who?"

"Danny Boyd," he repeated tightly. "And don't bother with the dumb act. I know you used to shack up with him."

"That was a long time ago. Before he got sent up."

"Well, he's out now and I'll bet you've seen him lately. Maybe you're even playing house again."

She glanced around, as if looking for help, but there was none to be found. "What if we are? Why is that your fucking business anyway?"

"It's my business, okay? Did your boyfriend ever

mention somebody named Andy Turchek? From when he was inside?"

She shook her head. "No, he never mentioned nobody."

But Robert knew that she was lying. "He tell you that he killed Turchek?"

She didn't say anything.

"Where's Boyd now?"

"Go away," she said, her voice beginning to rise with hysteria. "Just leave me alone."

"Not until you tell me where he is."

Suddenly, she got very calm. There was a certain pathetic dignity in her face. "Boyd ain't yours. I waited a long time for him to get out. You ain't gonna spoil it all now."

"Oh yes," Robert said with a smile, "I'm going to spoil it. I'm going to find that bastard and kill him."

She tried to get away again and he shoved her back. She stared at his face, long and hard, as if trying to catalogue what was there. "I know you now," she said smugly. "Anything happens to my Danny, I'll go straight to the cops. What you have to say about that?"

Robert shook his head. "I say you're a stupid bitch, Marnie. Real stupid. I'm sorry, but you don't leave me any choice, do you?"

He knew that she would never tell him where Boyd was. Even on the threat of death. It wasn't loyalty or even love that would keep her quiet. It was desperation; Boyd was her last hope. And if he took that away, she would do just what she threatened: go straight to the cops.

Now it was he who was pushed to the wall.

There wasn't any choice.

He took the gun out of his pocket, pressed it to her head, and pulled the trigger.

The noise seemed loud, but he knew that it wouldn't be heard above the traffic sounds just beyond the alley. And even if it was, who the hell would pay attention in this neighborhood?

He wiped the gun clean and dropped it next to the body. Then he turned around to go back to his car.

Beau Epstein was standing there.

They just stared at one another for maybe a year or so. It was Beau who finally broke the terrible silence. "You killed her," he whispered hoarsely. "How come you did that?"

Robert got over the immediate shock of seeing the boy standing there. "What the hell are you doing?" His voice was also a whisper. "Why are you here?"

Beau, who was now shaking violently, didn't say anything.

Robert could hear the sound of a siren in the distance. Probably it didn't have anything at all to do with this, but he couldn't take that chance. Almost without his thinking about it, one hand moved toward the Magnum under his arm.

Beau flinched away. "Robert?" he said.

"Damn." He grabbed Beau by one arm and moved, dragging the unresisting boy after him.

They went all the way back to the car like that. Once there, he unlocked the passenger door and shoved Beau into the seat. "Don't move," he said. He ran around the car and got in behind the wheel, just as a squad car, lights and siren on, raced by and kept going. He waited until the car was out of sight and his breathing had slowed. "Beau, what the fuck are you up to?" he said then.

Beau was huddled against the door, as if he were

trying to get warm. "I was following you," he said in a low voice.

"Why?"

"Just because. I wanted to, that's all."

Robert pounded the steering wheel in frustration. "You *wanted* to? Great. Well, you're in deep shit now. I hope you fucking know that."

"Are you going to kill me, too?"

"I ought to. God, what an idiot you are."

"I'm sorry," Beau said.

Robert started the car. What the hell was he going to do now? The kid could burn him; the kid could burn him real good.

Lacking any other bright idea at the moment, he drove home.

He pulled the car into the garage and turned off the engine. It seemed very quiet. He finally got out of the car and walked around to the passenger door. Beau didn't say anything as Robert reached in and yanked him out by the arm. Neither did he object to being dragged down the hall to the bathroom, the only room in the house without a window. Robert shoved him into the room so hard that Beau stumbled and almost fell into the bathtub.

Beau sat on the floor and looked at him.

After a moment, Robert shut the door. He went into the kitchen and took some rope from the junk drawer. Hopefully, Beau wasn't taking advantage of this opportunity to escape.

But he didn't. The bathroom door was still closed when he got back. He double-knotted the rope around the doorknob, stretched it across the narrow hall and did the same to the other end, using the closed door of Andy's room.

When that was done, he stood still for a moment. A drink. God, he needed a drink. He went back to the kitchen and found a bottle of Scotch in the cupboard. He also needed some fresh air.

He left the house, slamming the door, and headed for the beach a couple of blocks away.

Robert Turchek didn't know what the hell he was going to do next. He didn't like feeling that way. It scared him a little, and he didn't like that, either.

Beau heard the door slam and then it was still.

He got up and went to the bathroom door, testing it almost nonchalantly. Robert would surely not let him leave that easily, he knew, and so the knowledge that he couldn't open the door didn't surprise him.

He sat down again, resting his back against the tub. Maybe Robert would come back and kill him, but Beau didn't think so. He was pretty sure that Robert liked him. And there had to be some reason why the man who seemed so kind had suddenly erupted into deadly violence. Robert could probably explain it all to him.

Beau realized that he was still shaking. He closed his body into a tight ball and tried to do some meditation.

Robert sat on the beach for nearly two hours. When the bottle of Scotch was empty, and he was drunk—although not so drunk that he didn't know he was—he threw the bottle into the Pacific and headed home.

Inside the house, he stopped by the bathroom door and pressed his ear against it. There wasn't a sound from inside.

He went to bed.

11

Sex was a great way to relax after an unproductive, frustrating day.

At least, Mickey seemed to think so. Or maybe her day hadn't been as unproductive or frustrating as his. Whatever. Anyway, she relaxed so much that within moments she had rolled over in the massive waterbed and was sound asleep. Gar, unfortunately, wasn't that lucky.

Which didn't mean that the lovemaking hadn't been great, as it always was with Mickey, or that it didn't leave him lazily satisfied.

He just couldn't sleep.

After almost thirty minutes of staring at the orange numbers on the face of the digital clock, he gave up the fight and got out of bed—always a lot of fun, given his bad leg, his weight, and the wave action of the mattress.

He dressed again, without turning on the light, although he knew from experience that it would have taken a lot more than that to wake Mickey once she was out.

The dog looked up hopefully as Gar passed through the living room, but when his master picked up the car keys and his cane, Spock just settled more deeply into his spot on the couch and sighed.

This was not the first time that Gar, all keyed up over a case, had left the house when most decent people were tucked away in their beds. As a cop, he'd done the same thing. Like a vampire, he often worked at night by choice. Of course, the streets of Hollywood were the perfect place for Count Dracula to ply his trade. So that was where he headed this night.

Gar sometimes wondered why he continued to do the job he did. Looking for lost kids was a really shitty way to earn a living, mostly because happy endings were so rare. Most often, the missing child had run away by choice, because life was so bad at home. Maybe the reasons for the leaving were valid and maybe they weren't; either way, the runaway wasn't especially thrilled to be brought back.

An increasing number of cases he handled were the result of custody battles between parents, with the child caught in the middle. In those instances, too, somebody always ended up miserable. Usually the kid.

Only once in a very great while he discovered the truth that every parent feared the most—that their son or daughter had been snatched away by a terrible stranger. A killer or a sex creep.

If people only knew going into parenthood all the ways that having a baby could make them miserable over the years, nobody would ever have the guts to do it.

He sure as hell wouldn't have.

Gar parked not far from a run-down taco stand that was a favorite gathering place for the kids. The dump attracted both those who actually lived on the streets and those Gar liked to call wannabees. They dressed just like the others, affected the same society-be-damned attitudes, and sometimes did drugs with the best of them. The only difference was that, at the end of most nights, anyway, the pretenders went home, which usually meant the suburbs.

There wasn't even a name on the place. Just the single word TACOS on a hand-painted sign. Day or night, there were usually a dozen or so kids hanging out on the tiny patio, eating cheap, greasy tacos that they washed down with gallons of watery soda pop.

Gar's was such a familiar face by now that several almost-friendly greetings were tossed his way as he stood at the counter to order a couple of chili dogs and a root beer. He carried the midnight snack to a table under a shabby red-and-white-striped umbrella. The sidewalk just beyond where he was sitting was as alive with people as if it were midday, instead of so late at night. Gar always entertained himself, sitting here, by imagining that one night, as he chowed down on the heartburn specials Carlos served up, whatever kid he was looking for at the moment would just walk by. So far, it hadn't ever happened, and Beau Epstein didn't set a precedent by showing up just then.

But sometimes he could pick up a good tip here, frequently from the girl dressed all in black who was approaching his table slowly. She was accompanied by a boy with a half-shaved head and a swastika hanging from one ear. They sat down across from him. "Hi, April," he said. That was the month they'd met in, not her real name.

She lifted a weary hand in greeting. "How's it hanging, Sinclair?" April looked like hell and Gar wondered how many more times she would show up. Eyes once bright with intelligence were now dulled.

"It's hanging okay," Gar said. "Who's your friend?"

"Call me Joe," the boy replied, giving a furtive glance over one shoulder.

"Pleased to meet you, Joe." Gar continued to eat his chili dog.

"Who are you looking for this time?" April asked him after a moment.

She was undoubtedly broke again. Gar tried not to have any illusions that these kids spoke to him out of much genuine fondness. He was simply known as a man who always paid a fair price for the good information he received. He sometimes wondered when being a snitch had become fashionable. It was one more thing he tended to blame on Ronald Reagan.

He wiped his chili-covered fingers on a napkin and took out Beau's picture. "Him."

April looked at the photo carefully, then shook her head regretfully. "Don't know him. Sorry." And no doubt she really was; no info meant no cash.

Gar finished the last hot dog in one bite. "How about you, Joe?" he said after chewing and swallowing.

The ear ornament rattled as Joe shook his head. "Nope." Then he frowned. "Unless . . ."

Gar felt a glimmer of hope. This was how it happened, slow step by slow step. "Unless what?"

Joe thought it over. "Last night," he finally said. "I was having a sandwich down the street and these two guys came in. One of them was old, maybe thirty or forty, and the other one looked sort of like this. 'Cept that he was all bloody," he added as an afterthought.

"Bloody?"

"Yeah." Joe made a face. The swastika notwithstanding, he was apparently a boy of delicate sensibilities. "Like, the front of his shirt and all. They hit the can, he cleaned up, and then they ate. They were still there when I left."

"And you think this was the kid?"

"Maybe." Joe looked at the picture once more, then nodded firmly. "I really think so, yeah."

"Anything else? What did the older guy look like?"

He shrugged. "Just a guy. Nothing special. Baseball cap. Just a guy."

Gar kept looking at him.

"Hey, that's all I can say, man. But ain't it worth something?"

He nodded and gave Joe a couple of bucks. The two kids got up and drifted away as he sat still, finishing the root beer.

Mickey and Spock were in the kitchen when he got back home. She was eating frozen yogurt and the dog was watching. Gar dropped into the chair opposite hers. "You woke up," he said.

"Yeah." She took a big bite of the frozen yogurt, swallowed, and smiled. "I got hot again and you weren't there."

"Sorry about that."

"You should be." She pushed the empty bowl aside, got up, and came over to him. Her mouth bent to his; she tasted cold and minty.

His hands slipped under the T-shirt she was wearing and gently massaged her breasts. "I'm here now," he said into her neck.

"Umm-humm," she murmured.

Nobody said anything for several moments.

"I don't think your mind is on what your hands are doing," she said, her voice muffled against his neck.

"You're right," he said. "I was thinking about those kids out there. The way I use them." Gar sighed. "Sometimes I wonder what makes me any better than the creeps who buy their bodies," he said. "I use them for my own purposes, just like the johns. I get what I can, pay them off, and walk away."

She pulled back and looked at him. "You're not like them. You try to help the kids."

He shrugged.

Mickey frowned. "Damn it, Gar, you're a kind man. Why do you think I love you?"

He studied her face, touched her lips gently. "Sometimes I wonder." This was getting dangerously close to things he knew were better left unexplored. She loved him and that should be enough.

"You don't really wonder, do you?" she asked.

He nodded.

"Lord, what an idiot." She smiled. "Because you're a good man." She planted a kiss on his cheek. "You're a good man and there aren't so many of those out there." The smile grew even brighter. "Plus the fact that you're sexy as hell."

He snorted. "Sure. *Cosmo* wants me for a centerfold."

"Well, they can't have you. You're all mine."

Gar felt a sense of peace wash over him. He wasn't as good us Mickey thought he was, but as long as she believed in him, he would keep trying.

Christ, that sounded like something out of a bad old movie. Could it be that life was really just a "B" melodrama? It wouldn't surprise him a bit.

They kissed again and this time when their mouths separated, they were both panting a little. "Bed," Mickey said.

"Bed," Gar agreed.

Spock watched them leave the kitchen.

12

1

He woke up with a real bastard of a headache.

It took all of thirty seconds for him to remember in excruciating detail all that had happened the night before. When the whole miserable experience came back to him, he groaned aloud and pulled the sheet up over his head.

What a complete fuck-up. When the history of fuck-ups was written, this little incident would be right at the top of the list. Never in his entire professional life had everything gone so wrong.

And it wasn't over yet, because now he had that damned boy locked in his bathroom. Could that be considered kidnapping? Probably so, and that was just fucking great, wasn't it?

Finally realizing that just lying in bed all day wasn't going to help things at all, Robert came out from under the sheet and then got up from the bed. He pulled on some jeans and walked down the hall to the bathroom. Carefully, he untied the rope from around the knob and pushed the door open slowly. He was half-expecting to be jumped or something. Maybe the kid had armed himself with a Bic razor. But nothing happened and so he took a cautious step into the room.

Beau was asleep in the bathtub, using a rolled-up towel as a pillow. He was breathing softly and steadily. Robert looked at him for a moment, then turned and left the room, not closing the door this time.

He plugged in the coffeepot and went to fetch the *Times* from the front porch as it brewed. Although it was much too soon for there to be anything in the paper about Marnie Dowd's killing, he looked anyway. Nothing.

Two cups of the strong black coffee settled his stomach enough for him to take a chance on a bowl of heavily sugared Shredded Wheat. Caffeine and sugar were two of his favorite hangover cures.

"Hi."

He looked up quickly from the sports page. Beau was standing in the doorway, looking hesitant. "Come on in," Robert said flatly. "Sit down."

Beau paused, gnawing on his lower lip, then moved slowly to join him at the table. He still didn't relax, but sat perched tentatively on the edge of the chair.

Robert shoved another bowl and the box of cereal toward him. "You might as well eat."

Beau dumped some Shredded Wheat into the bowl, covered it with sugar and splashed milk on top, all without saying anything or even looking at Robert. He took one bite, chewed, and swallowed slowly, then set the spoon down. "Are you still mad at me?" he asked in a near whisper.

"Hey, don't you think I have a damned good reason to be pissed?"

Beau nodded. "Yeah. And I'm really sorry."

"That's great. Except that being sorry doesn't help at all."

"No. I guess it probably doesn't. But I didn't know . . ."

"And now you do." Robert got up and poured himself another cup of coffee. "Does knowing make you happy?"

Beau shook his head. After a moment, he sighed and started eating again. Between bites, he asked, almost casually, "Are you going to kill me, too?"

"I damned well should," Robert said glumly. "It would serve you right."

Beau just kept eating.

Robert pinched the bridge of his nose. The headache was better, but still there. "The only problem with that is, I just don't want to."

"Thanks." The blue gaze flickered his way. "How come you wanted to kill the woman last night?"

"You don't know a damned thing about what was going on last night. About why I did what I did."

Beau finished the cereal and pushed the bowl away. He rested both arms on the table and leaned forward, staring at Robert. "You could explain it all to me," he said. "Then maybe I could understand."

Robert played with the gold ring in his ear. How much to tell him was difficult to decide. "You remember me telling you about my brother?"

Beau nodded.

"A few years ago, he got into some trouble and he pulled a jail term. While he was inside, a man named Danny Boyd hit him. Andy went into a coma. Stayed that way for over three years. He just died."

"I'm sorry," Beau said.

Robert looked at him. "Thank you. Anyway, Boyd is out of prison now and I'm going to kill him." He said it flatly.

Beau was quiet.

"That broad last night—she was just a junkie whore, by the way, no loss to anybody—she was Boyd's girlfriend. She threatened to turn me in. So I was only protecting myself when I whacked her. I was just doing what had to be done." He met Beau's gaze and tried to read the expression there. He couldn't tell what the boy was thinking.

Finally Beau lowered his head and rested it on his folded arms. "I do know how you feel," he said in a muffled voice. "If I could get the bastards who killed my parents, I'd do exactly the same thing. So I really understand, Robert."

"I'm glad," Robert replied, meaning the words without knowing why he cared a damned bit about what this boy thought of him. There was more, of course, that he should tell Beau, but that would lead him into very dangerous waters. No sense doing that until and unless it became necessary. "But there's still a problem, you know," he said.

Beau raised his head and looked at him. "What to do about me, you mean."

"What to do about you, right."

Beau smiled faintly. "Well, you're not the first person to have that problem. I'm trouble for everybody."

Robert stood and carried the cereal bowls to the sink. He rinsed them extra carefully, using the time to think. "I can't just let you go. I'm sorry, Beau." He turned around in time to see the expression on Beau's face. "I'm not going to kill you," he said quickly. "But I can't just let you go, either." The implications of what that meant he wasn't prepared to deal with at the moment.

Beau closed the milk carton and carried it to the refrigerator. He shrugged. "I don't have any place to go anyway." He leaned against the fridge, looking at Robert. "So you're going to find that guy Boyd and kill him, is that it?"

"That's it."

"Okay. I won't get in your way. Promise."

Robert shook his head. "This is pretty crazy."

"Yeah, I guess so. But things have been that way lately." Beau pushed himself away from the refrigerator. "I'm going to take a shower." He paused. "I don't want to bitch or anything, but my clothes are starting to feel pretty crummy."

"All right. We'll take care of it." Robert dumped the coffee grounds down the garbage disposal.

Beau nodded and left the kitchen.

Robert was still wondering what the hell he was getting into when the phone rang. He reached for it. "Turchek," he muttered.

"Mr. Turchek? This is Mr. Brown."

Right.

"That package we talked about last week?"

"Yeah?"

"Please take care of it for me. As soon as possible."

"All right." He hung up. Damn, this was a job he couldn't afford to turn down, but it was going to get in the way of his search for Boyd.

And it was going to make the problem of Beau even more of a problem. He sighed and wiped the counter with a wet paper towel.

Robert exchanged empty smiles with the shiny-clean teenaged sales clerk at the Gap. Beau was in the dressing room trying on a pair of jeans. Already some khaki pants and several shirts—with color-coordinated socks, of course—were piled on the counter.

Life was not going as planned.

But since he couldn't see any other way to play it at the moment, Robert was just trying to stay calm. He even managed another smile as Beau emerged from the cubicle, the 501 button-fly jeans in his hand. "Those okay?"

"Fine," Beau said, adding them to the pile. "Thanks for this. I'll pay you back."

"Sure you will. Out of your inheritance, right?"

"Right." Beau seemed serious.

Robert took out his wallet and handed the credit card to the clerk.

When they first walked into the mall, he was more than a little nervous about what the kid might do. Maybe he'd run yelling to the first security guard who appeared. But a uniformed hire-a-cop walked by almost immediately and Beau did nothing. Still, Robert couldn't let himself really relax. He kept a close eye on him.

When the clothes were all paid for, Beau picked up the bulky plastic bags and followed him out of the store. Their next stop was the Taco Bell in the food court.

Beau ate quietly for a few minutes, then paused and wiped hot sauce from his chin. "Can I ask you something?" he said in a confidential voice.

"You can ask," Robert said, unwrapping his burrito.

"Do you have your gun with you right now?"

Robert frowned and glanced around quickly. No one was sitting close enough to hear or seemed to be paying them any attention at all. "I always have it with me," he said shortly. "Why? You planning on making a run for it? Go ahead. I'm not very likely to pull my piece and blow you away in front of several hundred witnesses, am I?"

Beau picked up another taco. "I'm not going to make a run for it. Like I said, there's no place for me to go. And I'm not afraid you'll shoot me." He ate half the taco. "I only asked because . . . well, maybe somebody is looking for *you*. Like you're looking for that guy Boyd."

Beau was staring at him. It took Robert a minute to understand what the kid was saying. "Don't worry about that," he said. "I can take care of myself. And I can take care of anybody else, too."

Beau looked relieved.

"Finish up," Robert said brusquely. "There's things to do. By the way, we're going to drive to Vegas tonight."

"Las Vegas? Why?"

"Business" was all Robert said. "We need to buy you a toothbrush, right?"

"Right."

Robert sighed. "Me and fucking Mary Poppins," he muttered to himself.

2

Robert figured that, if necessary, he could make the drive north on I-15 to Las Vegas blindfolded. Over the years, for one reason or another, he had been required to make the trip more times than he wanted to remember. Always for business reasons; Vegas was not a place he would ever go to for fun.

Whenever possible, he liked to make the trip at night. It was just after midnight now and the miles were slipping away almost painlessly.

Beau had been asleep in the passenger seat for most of the trip, but suddenly he was awake again. "What kind of business are we going to Las Vegas for?" he asked.

Robert accelerated around a truck. "Have to find a man named Tony Drago," he said. "A gambler. Very low-level kind of guy."

For a moment, he thought that Beau was going to ask him something else about Drago and Robert didn't know what the hell he would say. But instead, Beau said, "I'm hungry."

"Again?" Christ, there wasn't any satisfying his appetite.

They went another two miles or so and then spotted a diner. Robert pulled into the lot, parking between a truck and an old Pontiac. Right inside the door, two state cops were having coffee and doughnuts at the counter. At the sight, Beau stiffened and looked at Robert. He ignored them and chose a table by the window. "Sit down," he ordered.

Beau dropped into a chair, still looking at the cops.

"Knock it off," Robert said.

"They don't scare you?"

"No, they don't. Not a fucking bit." He yanked a menu from the plastic holder. "I'll tell you what does scare me," he said.

"What?"

"You. You scare the shit out of me, Beau."

Beau blinked, bewildered. "Me? How come?"

Robert didn't answer.

After a moment, Beau reached for the other menu.

* * *

He really did hate Las Vegas.

The insistent neon, noisy casino-hotels, the glitzy broads all decked out in sequins. And everywhere you looked, the clusters of tourists in their polyester clothes, propped like Robotrons in front of the slots. It all came together in such a cacophony of sound and light that he wanted to run the other way as quickly as possible.

Instead of doing that, however, he drove directly to a motel on Tropicana Avenue; it was a place where he could always get a room, even with no reservation. They knew him and they knew the people who were his clients. They called him Mr. Turchek and always gave him the best room in the place.

It was nearly 4 A.M. by the time they hit the room. Beau went into the can and came out a few minutes later, wearing his undershorts and T-shirt. He sat on one of the beds.

Robert sat on the other bed and looked at him. "Beau, there's something I have to tell you."

"Sounds like bad news," Beau said, smiling faintly; his eyes, however, were darkly solemn.

"It's not good or bad," Robert said. "It's just a fact. Something you need to know now, because I can't take a chance on having you freak out later."

"I don't freak out much."

"Yeah, well." Robert lit a cigarette. "I told you before that I'm here to see a man named Drago, remember?"

"Yeah," Beau said tentatively.

"Well, when I find him, I'm going to kill him."

Beau bit his lip and didn't say anything for a time. "Did he have something to do with Andy getting killed? Like the hooker?"

Robert shook his head. "I'm not going to lie about it. This killing is different. This is just business."

"What kind of business?" Beau said in a low voice.

"*My* kind. That's what I do, Beau, I kill people. For money."

"Why?"

"Who the hell knows? Mostly because I'm good at it, I guess. And it pays well, if you're good at it."

Beau shook his head. "But I like you. You don't seem like a killer."

"The truth is the truth. Sorry if this shatters any illusions." Robert stood and went into the bathroom. He leaned over the sink and splashed cold water into his face. Maybe he was just giving the kid a chance to take off if he wanted to. Robert knew that if Beau did leave, he wouldn't go after him. It might be stupid and dangerous, but life itself was a crapshoot. Somehow, he had the feeling that even if Beau did run away, he wouldn't squeal to the cops. Robert thought he was a pretty good judge of character.

He stripped down to his Jockeys and went back into the other room.

Beau was in bed, with the blanket pulled up to his chin. He didn't say anything, but his eyes watched Robert cross the room.

Robert got into his bed and switched out the lamp.

"Robert?" Beau said into the darkness.

"What?"

"I don't understand. How come you do this?"

"Life just turns out that way sometimes." Robert sighed. "Look, Beau, I was only a kid when I hit L.A. with Andy. We needed money to live on, just like everybody else, and it seemed like the only people willing to pay me enough wanted me to do things that weren't quite legal."

"What things?"

"Hot-wiring cars. Heisting merchandise. Running numbers. Bill collecting. Little things that got bigger and bigger. Then one day I killed a guy, mostly by accident." His voice was low; nobody had ever heard this story before and Robert didn't quite know why he was telling it now to Beau. "Somebody heard about what I'd done and wanted me to do it again." Even though Beau couldn't see him, Robert shrugged. "That's just the way it happened."

"It makes me feel funny," Beau said. "Sort of nauseated."

Robert didn't say anything.

"Who do you kill?" Beau asked then.

"Mostly whoever they pay me to. We're not talking your regular kind of folks here," he said. "It's basically the scumbags of the world. Bad guys. They ask for it, most of them."

"Like Drago? Did he ask for it?"

Robert snorted. "Yeah, you could say that. I mean, how stupid do you have to be to run off with the wife of one of the biggest gangsters in the whole fucking state?"

Beau was quiet for so long that Robert thought he had fallen asleep. Then, suddenly, he spoke again. "You wouldn't just go out and kill somebody good, would you? Like my parents?"

What to say? Robert sighed. "No, kid. I wouldn't just go out and kill people like your parents."

"Okay."

That was all Beau said.

It took Robert a long time to fall asleep.

* * *

Beau woke up first.

It took him several beats to remember where he was. And why.

He rolled out of bed and went into the bathroom. As he peed, he wondered just how he ought to be feeling about all of this. And how he really *did* feel.

Probably he should be scared. But he wasn't, really. Not of Robert anyway. Maybe the *situation* scared him a little. But if he wanted to be completely honest with himself—and Jonathan had always said that telling the truth to yourself was the most important thing—well, then, he had to admit that it was all sort of exciting.

Most of it, anyway.

Seeing that woman get shot hadn't been a whole lot of fun. It brought back some very bad memories. But he could accept Robert's reasons for why she had to die.

The rest of it was harder to understand.

Robert was a paid killer. It sure didn't make any sense. But Beau decided that he just had to accept Robert's explanation for why the people almost deserved to die. They seemed to be asking for it most of the time. Like this Drago. Dumb, very dumb.

Of course, Beau admitted to himself, what choice did he have *but* to accept what Robert said and did? Unless he wanted to find himself out on the street again, or back with Saul. Or maybe even dead himself. None of those things sounded good to him. So, if Robert said somebody had to die, deserved to die, then that was pretty much how he would see it, too.

After all, good people (like his parents, for example) got shot down every day for absolutely no reason at all. Why waste tears on jerks and creeps like this Drago?

Still, it was a scary thing. Robert wasn't like the people who had killed his folks, was he?

Then Beau shook his head firmly. No. This was a much different thing. It was. What seemed real strange to him was that Robert—who was about as different from Jonathan as anybody could be and still belong to the same species—treated him much as his father always had. Like a person. Like somebody who mattered.

Beau went back into the bedroom. Robert's eyes were still closed. The holstered Magnum was resting on the nightstand next to his bed. Beau walked over and bent down for a better look at the weapon. He touched it carefully.

"Don't do that," Robert said unexpectedly.

He pulled his hand back quickly.

Robert sat up. After a moment, he got out of bed and walked over to the window. Parting the draperies a little, he peered out at the sun-bleached scene. "God," he said, "I hate this city. I want to find Drago today and get the hell out of here." Then he walked into the bathroom and closed the door.

Beau didn't touch the gun again. Instead, he turned on the television and watched "Scrabble" as he dressed in some of his new clothes.

"Now I know why you don't like this city," Beau said with a sigh. They had spent a very long day going in and out of bars and casinos looking for Tony Drago.

Robert just grunted. He was used to this kind of thing. There were easier ways to find people, but those ways were also more dangerous, because they called more attention to what was going on than was healthy. He crushed out the latest in a long chain of cigarettes. "Well, come on, Tonto," he said. "We're not done yet."

He was trying to get a reading on just how Beau was feeling about what he'd found himself in the middle of, but it was hard to do. On the surface, at least, none of it seemed to matter to the boy. He was acting just as he had before finding out that the freaking Lone Ranger was a hired gun. But every once in a while, Robert would look up suddenly and see two very blue, very speculative eyes on him. It was unsettling.

Less than an hour later, he finally spotted Drago, who looked pretty much the way he had in his most recent mug shot. The man was fat and balding, with the few strands of hair he had left combed up and over his naked scalp. It didn't help. Neither did the sport jacket he wore, which looked as if it would be more at home covering the back of a Kentucky Derby loser. Gold chains, of course, and a broad with more boobs than brains hanging on his arm. That was not a woman Robert would give up his life for. But Tony Drago was going to.

They watched the happy couple at the craps table for a while, then went back outside to the car. Beau was looking a little nervous now. "What next, Robert?" he asked, tapping on the dashboard.

"We wait," Robert said, reaching for still another cigarette. "And hope like hell that Drago leaves alone."

Their hopes paid off, because Drago and the woman parted company, with obvious anguish, in the parking lot. After all, he was a family man. Drago got into a shiny black Porsche and took off. Robert followed at a discreet distance.

Beau was tapping again.

Before very long, they had left the lights and glitz

of the city behind and were driving through a quiet residential neighborhood. A nice place to raise a family, probably. It was at one of the largest houses on the block that the Porsche turned in.

Robert parked on the street, leaving the engine running. "You wait here," he said quietly. "Don't move, understand?"

Beau just nodded.

He got out and walked quickly up the driveway. Drago was still standing by his car, locking the door when Robert reached him. "Drago," he said pleasantly.

Drago whipped around. "Jesus," he said with a nervous laugh. "What you trying to do, asshole, give a guy a heart attack or something?"

Robert just smiled.

"Who the hell are you, anyway?"

"My name is Robert Turchek. Maybe you've heard of me?"

After a moment, Drago nodded. "I know who you are. But I don't know what the hell you're doing here."

"Ah, man, think about it for a minute. Did you really and truly think that you could dip your wick into a bitch belonging to somebody like Nicky Whalen and just walk away clean? Are you that dumb?"

Finally it sank into Drago what was happening here. "Hey," he said, "I got family in the house."

"Maybe you should've thought about them before you started fucking Nicky's girl."

"What're you gonna do to me?"

"You said you've heard of me. What the hell do you think I'm going to do?"

Robert brought the gun up from the shadows and fired.

A light went on inside the house. He wiped the gun quickly and dropped it on top of Drago's body, then he turned and ran back up the driveway to the car. Beau was slumped down in the seat, hands covering his ears. They drove away at a moderate speed.

On the way back to the hotel, Robert stopped to buy a bucket of fried chicken and then a six-pack. At the last minute, he remembered Beau, waiting in the car again, and added some Coke to his purchases.

Back in the room, they sat on his bed and ate the meal while watching an old episode of "Barney Miller," which was brand-new, of course, to Beau.

During one of the commercial breaks, Beau stopped chewing long enough to ask, "Can we go home now?"

Robert used a wadded-up paper napkin to wipe chicken grease from his chin. "First thing in the morning," he said.

"Good." Beau turned back to the television.

3

Robert stepped out of the shower and wrapped a towel around himself. He shaved quickly and opened the door to let Beau know the bathroom was his.

Beau was sitting huddled on his bed.

There were four men in the room. Robert knew only one of them by name but he was the only one who mattered very much, even though it was the other three who had guns, two trained on him and one on Beau.

Robert swallowed a couple of times and then forced a smile to his face. "Well, hello, Mr. Marcello. This is a little early for a visit, isn't it?"

"Maybe it's a little late," the old man corrected him gently. "When people come into my town and start eliminating my employees and I don't know anything about it until after the fact, then maybe it's a little late."

Robert shrugged.

Marcello turned his cold gaze on Beau. "You take on a partner, Mr. Turchek?"

"No."

"Get rid of him."

"Tonto," Robert said, "why don't you go out and soak up some sun by the pool."

After a moment, Beau got up from the bed. He pulled on his jeans and walked, barefooted, to the door. There, he stopped and turned around. "Robert?" he said.

"Go on, do like I said."

He went out, closing the door very quietly.

Robert leaned against the desk and lit a cigarette. "You're here about Drago," he said.

"Of course. The tragedy that occurred in his driveway last night."

"Yeah, a real heartbreaker, right? Maybe you ought to send flowers," Robert said dismissively. "Actually, I was going to touch base with you this morning. I thought it would be a good thing to do."

"You have always been a wise and cautious man," Marcello said. "However, I am forced to point out that this is coming after the fact."

Robert acknowledged that silently.

"It is a lucky thing, therefore, that the individual in question was of very little consequence."

Now Robert smiled faintly. "I knew that ahead of time, sir."

For just a moment, Marcello smiled, too. Then he got serious again. "Why?"

"It was a personal matter, sir, nothing to do with

business. The man who contracted for the job had a grudge against Drago. He was fucking the man's woman. Brought her to Vegas, in fact. Drago was really stupid, sir."

Marcello nodded. "This was an isolated thing, then?"

"Yes, sir. I'm leaving town today."

"Very good. And it would probably be better if you stayed away for a while."

"I will."

The old man glanced toward the door. "That boy," he said. "He have a part in this?"

"No," Robert said flatly. He straightened. "Life just gets complicated, you know?"

"Well, as long as I do not have to become involved in your private complications," Marcello said.

"You won't."

That seemed to end the conversation. One of the goons opened the door and all four of them left.

Robert pulled on his jeans and walked out to the pool. Beau was sitting in a plastic chaise, watching an empty beer can float across the pool. Robert sat on the end of the chaise. "That old man," Beau said, "was he like the godfather or something?"

"Something like that, yeah."

"He didn't look like so much to me."

"Right." Robert glanced at him. "That man would have you killed in a minute if you aggravated him."

"We didn't do that, did we?"

"Nope." Robert grinned at him. "I've been at this a long time, Tonto. Trust me."

"I guess I have to, don't I?" Beau said.

Robert looked at him for a moment and then nodded. "I guess so." He patted Beau's leg. "Come on, let's get the hell out of this town."

13

1

Gar was beginning to run out of ideas.

He'd been working hard, checking all of the usual places—the arcades, the beach, the shelters for runaways, even the freeway overpasses under which a lot of kids lived—and talking to the street sources that were usually the most reliable. So far none of what he'd done had moved him one step closer to finding Beau Epstein. The only lead he'd managed to discover so far, and it was pretty damned vague, was the tale of the bloodied kid coming into the coffee shop. Maybe it had been Beau and maybe it hadn't, but whichever was the case, so what? The unknown man and boy, whoever they were, seemed to have dropped from sight.

Gar was having one last beer before calling this a (worthless) night's work when a familiar face appeared in the midst of the crowd in the Touchdown Bar. After the woman had picked up her drink, Gar got her attention and waved her over to the table. With obvious reluctance, she joined him. "Evening, Kiki," Gar said.

She took a ladylike sip of her pink gin drink. "Hi, Sergeant Sinclair." The honorary title was a holdover from his days on the force. Back then, he had busted Kiki regularly. She never seemed to hold that fact against him, however, and sometimes she even came through with some pretty solid information.

"How's business these days?"

"'S okay," she said with a shrug. But she looked tired. No surprise; how easy could it be, after all, for a hooker pushing forty to keep pulling in the bucks?

"You ought to retire, honey," Gar said. "Find a nice guy and settle down in the suburbs."

"Sure. They're lining up to marry me." Her tone was characteristically self-mocking, but now that he looked more closely, Gar could see that it was more than simple weariness that showed in her face. It almost looked like fear.

She seemed to have forgotten that he was even there; her manicure was getting an intense examination. More from pure habit than out of real expectation that she would be able to help him, Gar took Beau's picture from his pocket and dropped it on the table. "I've got a tough one here, Kiki. Maybe you can help me out. Have you seen this kid around?"

She glanced down automatically, blinked, then looked at the picture again. Even with the thick mask of make-up she was wearing, he could see the color drain from her face. The fear that had been subtle before was now obvious. Her lips trembled and she took a healthy gulp of gin.

"What's wrong, Kiki?"

"Nothing. I ain't seen the kid."

"Are you sure?"

"Sure I'm sure. What you think, I got nothing better to do than look out for some stupid kid?" Abruptly, she stood, "I gotta split. Bye."

"Kiki, wait—" But she was gone.

Gar left his beer on the table and went after her. By the time he reached the sidewalk, she was already disappearing around the corner. He picked up his speed, which still didn't mean he was going to break any records, but he did manage to catch her by one arm. Old whores didn't move much faster than old cops. "Kiki, what the hell is wrong?"

She tried to pull away, then gave up with a sigh and leaned against the side of the building. "I don't know anything about it," she said in a nervous whisper. "Please, just let me go."

Gar loosened his grip on her a little, but did not let go. "You don't know anything about *what*?" he asked in exasperation.

"I didn't even know that Marnie was dead until the next day."

Gar felt as if the situation had slipped completely out of his control. "Kiki, I don't know what the devil you're talking about."

Kiki didn't seem to believe his protestations of ignorance, but she allowed herself to be talked back into the bar anyway. Gar ordered up two fresh drinks and they sat again. "Okay, honey, you want to tell me what the hell you're talking about? Who's Marnie?"

Kiki still didn't want to talk, but she sighed and did. "Marnie was a friend of mine. Marnie Dowd. She got killed the other night." Her eyes darted fearfully around the crowded room. "If you tell the cops I said anything, I'll tell them you're lying."

"So you haven't spoken to them about this?"

Her face turned scornful. "Who's fucking stupid enough to talk to them about anything that matters?"

"I'm not a cop anymore, Kiki. And I'll keep your name out of it if I possibly can. But tell me what you know."

She was holding on to the glass of gin with both hands. "I had a customer, see, and he only wanted a quick blow-job. Not worth going back to the room for, right? So we found this doorway and transacted our business arrangement. Okay?"

Gar nodded.

"We get all done and he takes off. I was, like, having a quick smoke break there in the doorway. Just enjoying the dark and the quiet, you know? Until I heard the shot."

"One shot?"

She nodded.

"What'd you do?"

She gave him a look that questioned his sanity. "What do you think I did? Stayed hiding right where I was. That's when I saw them coming out of the alley."

"Them?"

"Yeah. A man and a kid. They came out together and walked away. Marnie was dead back there and they just walked away. He was, like, dragging the kid by one arm."

"And you think it was the boy in the picture?"

"It was him, yeah." She sounded very sure of herself.

Now it was Gar who took a restorative gulp of alcohol. After swallowing a mouthful, he said, "You say he was dragging the boy. So the kid was trying to get away, is that it?"

After a moment of consideration, she shook her head. "I don't think so. More like, he was just trying to keep up with the man."

After getting what he could about the man—which wasn't much, beyond the fact that he was just "regular," whatever the hell that meant—Gar slipped Kiki a twenty and watched her leave the bar. His mood was not improved by what she had told him. He didn't like this more than he hadn't liked anything in a very long time.

But since it was late and there didn't seem to be much he could do at the moment, Gar decided to go home to bed.

Just to wrap up a crummy evening perfectly, Mickey was out someplace and so he had nobody to sleep with except Spock.

2

It was still a sort of homecoming every time he walked into the cop shop. There were always a lot of new faces, of course, men and women who didn't know Gar Sinclair from any perp in the place. But even so, there were still enough of the old guys around to shake his hand, slap his back, and talk bullshit about getting together for a beer one day real soon.

The next morning Gar made his way through all the buddy-buddy crap as quickly as possible and headed for Walter Dixon's office.

The black man still had the build of the linebacker he'd once been, but now that tanklike shape was clothed in a three-piece suit and an air of cool authority. Instead of "Monster," which had been his nickname in the NFL, he was now called Lieutenant. Except by his former partner.

"This is what you do all day now, Wally?"

Dixon's feet, which had been propped on the desk, hit the floor. A sheepish look crossed his face until he saw who it was standing in the doorway.

"Shit, they're letting anybody into this place nowadays, aren't they?"

"Yeah, even gimpy pensioners." He sat down, noticing the half-eaten jelly doughnut in Dixon's massive hand. "Don't let me interrupt your breakfast."

"I certainly won't." Dixon took a big bite. He was the only man Gar knew who could eat a doughnut that was oozing grape jelly and not get even a drop on his expensive gray suit.

Gar let him chew and swallow before asking, "You know anything about the murder of a hooker the other night?"

Dixon drank coffee from a mug emblazoned with a drawing of a jolly-looking pig in a blue police uniform. "You talking about Marnie Dowd?"

"That's the one." It was immediately interesting that the name of a woman who should have been just another dead whore came so quickly to Dixon's mind. It wasn't as if anybody really *cared* about a case like that.

Dixon finished the doughnut in one last bite. "An unknown perp shot Ms. Dowd in an alley."

"That's all you have?"

"Yep."

Gar looked at him. "I'd like to know why a big-shot lieutenant even knows about one more dead hooker in an alley."

Dixon grinned. "Funny. I was just about to ask you why a hotshot locator-of-lost-kids cares anything about that same dead hooker."

Gar quickly debated with himself how much to reveal to Walter Dixon, who was probably the best friend he had in the world, but who was also still part of the bureaucracy. And while he knew that Wally didn't always move in lockstep with the establishment, he also knew that Dixon was still enough of a company man to be a black in the position he was in.

Gar finally smiled. "I don't have any interest in Dowd herself at all. What I do have is a suspicion that a kid I'm looking for might have been a witness to the killing."

Dixon's brows elevated. "Really?" He seemed interested in that.

Gar finally noticed that one of the two files on Dixon's desk was, in fact, labeled DOWD, MARNIE. "You really do seem especially interested in this whore's killing," he said, nodding toward the file.

"Hey, it's my job."

"I told you my motives," Gar said.

Dixon tapped the file. "Well, there is one pretty interesting thing about this case," he admitted.

"Yeah?" Gar moved his leg and it hit the cane, knocking it to the floor with a crash. "Shit," he said mildly. He left the cane where it had fallen. "What's interesting?"

"The gun was found at the scene."

Gar tried not to show his impatience. Wally always went about things in his own way. Trying to rush him would only have the opposite effect. "Prints?" was all he said.

"Oh, no, not one." Dixon smiled again, showing that he knew exactly how aggravated Gar was becoming. "Okay." He turned businesslike. "Over the last few years, there's been a triggerman in town. Good at his job. Quick, clean, a real pro, who's done some very big hits. And he always leaves a gun, wiped clean, at the scene. Bastard must buy his cheap firepower by the carton."

Gar had to admit that this was fairly interesting, even if he couldn't see that it had much bearing on his search for Beau Epstein. "And?" he said.

Dixon shrugged. "And I'm just a little curious why a man like that wasted his time and considerable talents on a two-dollar whore. It seems out of character." Dixon had studied psychology in college and never forgot it. "Maybe now you ought to tell me just what it is *you* know about the Dowd killing," he suggested.

"According to what I heard on the street, a man was seen leaving the alley right after a shot was fired."

"Oh, yeah? We didn't turn up any witnesses."

"I got lucky."

"Yeah?" Dixon said sourly. "What did this lucky witness tell you about the man?"

"Not much. A regular sort of guy."

"Regular?" Dixon sighed. "What the fuck does that mean?"

"Who knows? He was wearing a baseball cap," Gar added helpfully.

"Great. A regular guy in a baseball cap. That certainly narrows down the field."

"Sorry, but that's all I got."

Dixon glared at him. "Would you like to tell me just where you learned all of this helpful stuff?"

"From one of Marnie's sisters in the business."

"Does she have a name?"

Gar raised his hands helplessly. "Sorry."

"Sorry you don't know, or sorry you won't tell me?" Dixon asked.

"Whatever."

The big black man wasn't pleased. "When you start screwing around in open murder investigations, Mr. Private Eye, you begin to walk a very dangerous line."

"I know that."

Dixon was still glaring. "Who's the kid you're looking for?"

"That's not cop business," Gar said. "The family wants it kept quiet."

Wally's face was grim. "It's not police business yet, you mean," he said.

Gar bent to pick up his cane. Straightening, he looked at Dixon. "Not yet," he agreed.

As he left Dixon's office, there was a knot beginning to form in the pit of his stomach. And his leg was throbbing. He stopped at the drinking fountain in the hallway and swallowed one of the little pink pain pills.

By the time he got home that night, after a day that gave him nothing more to go on, the knot was bigger and tighter. Mickey was already there, with dinner ready, and they ate a meal of cold salmon and salad out on the deck. She could see that he wasn't in the mood for conversation, so it was a quiet meal. That was one of the things he loved most about Mickey. Nobody had ever really read his moods as well.

Afterward, they both took the dog down to the beach and let him chase birds for a while. When he asked her about her day, Mickey began a steady flow of conversation. Glad now for the sound of her voice, Gar just listened, nodding at all the right moments, and watched Spock terrorize the gulls.

Mickey stopped her commentary suddenly. "You're really worried about the Epstein boy, aren't you?"

"I guess. Hell, I don't know why it's getting to me." Spock tired of playing tag with the birds and brought a stick to his master. Gar threw it as far as he could and the dog went after it cheerfully. "I just have a very bad feeling about this case. I think it could go wrong at the end. I don't think I want to be around for that."

"But you're already involved."

He shrugged. "I could quit."

She looked surprised. "You've never done that before. Given up on a kid."

"There's always a first time." Besides, maybe it wasn't the first time. Hadn't he sort of given up on his own daughter?

Mickey leaned against him. "How about you stop thinking about it for tonight? We could go back to the house and lose ourselves in some sweaty sex."

He bent forward and inhaled the clean scent of her hair. "That sounds pretty damned good to me," he said.

Spock tried to delay things by playing games, so finally Mickey picked him up and carried him all the way home.

14

1

He was on his third cup of coffee the next morning when the newspaper story caught his eye. Why he even bothered to read the details surrounding the killing of some second-rate hood who'd gotten himself iced, Gar didn't know. Murder was the kind of thing that happened every day to guys like that. Who cared?

But once he'd read the short item and seen the details—which said that the victim had been shot once in the head with a gun that was found, wiped clean of prints, next to the body—Gar's interest level increased dramatically. It seemed like sort of a funny coincidence, given what Wally had told him. At the same time, he was honest enough to admit that his flutter of excitement over something so totally insignificant only proved the depths of his desperation.

Shrugging that aside, he reached for the telephone.

Wally Dixon wasn't really interested in a killing that had happened so far out of his jurisdiction. Nevada, for Chrissake, he said testily, was a whole different *state*.

Gar pointed out that there were some strong similarities between this killing and that of Marnie Dowd.

Wally conceded that, but did not find it sufficiently interesting to spend either his time or departmental funds in checking further. And if that was all, he *did* have work to do. Thanks for calling.

Gar hung up. He decided that while the time and money of the police department were limited, he had plenty of the former and Saul Epstein a whole lot of the latter. It probably wouldn't do a damned bit of good to ask some questions in Vegas, of course. But it couldn't hurt either.

He left a note for Mickey, who was still in bed, and headed for the airport.

The commuter flight put him into McCarran just before lunch. He caught a cab and went directly to police headquarters. Unfortunately, he didn't have any friends in the department there. That meant he was shuffled around for some time before he was finally pointed toward the desk of Sergeant Luis Alverado, who was in charge of the Drago case.

Alverado looked more like a high school history teacher than a homicide cop. He was thin, with graying hair, a suit that had to have come from Sears, and horn-rimmed glasses that had been repaired with a piece of masking tape. He straightened the glasses on his nose and gave Gar's ID careful study. "Well, a big-city private eye. This is a real honor," he said. The slightly mocking words were said in such a gentle tone that it wasn't possible to take real offense. "I was about to get some lunch," Alverado continued. "Do you mind?"

Lunch, it turned out, meant sandwiches and drinks from a row of vending machines. They sat at a Formica table in an otherwise empty room, the walls of which were tastefully decorated with "Wanted" posters, and Alverado unwrapped his egg salad on rye. "So what brings you to us, Mr. Sinclair?"

"The Drago hit," Gar replied, peering with some suspicion at his own American cheese on white. "I'm interested in what you might be able to tell me about that."

"Ah, yes. Tony the Toad. Well, somebody shot him down in his own driveway."

"Actually, I know that much already. It was in the *Times*. One shot in the head. The weapon was a cheap handgun found by the body."

Alverado smiled. "So now you know as much as I do." He opened a small carton of milk. "How come you want to know about Tony?"

"Tony I don't give a flying fuck about. But the MO of his death is just like that of a recent homicide back home."

"And?"

"And I'm hoping that something you can tell me about this might help me find a runaway kid I'm looking for."

Alverado finished his sandwich and started work on a small package of Oreo cookies. "That sounds pretty thin to me."

Gar nodded glumly. "I know it's thin. Very thin. Fucking anorexic. But when that's all you got, run with it, right?"

"I guess so. I hate to be the one to bring you down, but I would bet City Hall that this was a paid hit. Nothing to do with any runaway kid."

Gar carefully wrapped the second half of his sandwich in its cellophane and pushed it away. "Could I get a copy of the report on this?"

"I guess so. Hell, it's as thin as your theory." Alverado glanced at him. "If anything comes of it, you'll let me know, of course?"

"Of course. And there is one more thing."

Alverado was finally finished with his meal. "There's always one more thing." He popped a Tums into his mouth. "What is it?"

"Who in town could I talk to about the Drago hit?"

"Besides me, you mean?"

Gar smiled. "Uh, yeah. Somebody from the other side is what I had in mind."

Alverado chewed the Tums thoughtfully. "Frank Marcello," he said finally. "He's the one to talk to. If you really want to do that kind of stupid thing."

"*Want?* Oh, want has nothing to do with it. If it did, I'd be home with a cold beer right now. But that wouldn't help me find the missing boy."

"And talking to Marcello will?"

Gar shrugged. "Probably not. But it's worth a try."

Alverado took a business card from his pocket and scribbled something on the back. "You might try here," he said. "Give Frankie this card. He knows me."

Gar took the card. "Thanks."

The cop grimaced. "I haven't done you any favor, pal. Be careful with Marcello. You might be getting in over your head."

That was entirely possible, but Gar decided not to think about it at the moment.

The country club crowd was lunching on the veranda. There wasn't a cellophane-wrapped sandwich anywhere in sight. A tennis tournament was in progress below and the diners divided their attention between the match in progress, their radicchio, and muted but lively conversation.

The hostess, a blond snow queen dressed in virginal white, didn't bother to hide her disdain for Gar's wrinkled linen jacket, lack of tie, and, he felt, his cane. After he told her who it was he wanted to see, she frowned prettily and consulted a complicated seating chart. "This way, please."

He trailed her through the maze of tables to one that had a very good view of the tennis court. One old man sat there, along with a couple of much younger women, and some efficient-looking yuppie gentlemen who were probably lawyers. They all seemed to be having a very good time. At the very next table were three sturdy representatives of the lower middle class. This trio was visibly not thrilled by either the cuisine or the tennis. Their suits didn't fit right. They watched Gar's approach with stone-cold eyes as their hands moved ever so slowly toward their jackets.

Gar just shook his head gently at them and spoke to the old man. "Mr. Marcello? Could I have a few words with you, please?"

Marcello looked up from his trout and frowned. "I'm having lunch," he said. "And anyway, I don't know you."

Gar held out the card that Alverado had given him.

Marcello took it, saw the name, and sighed. He waved off his thugs and stood. "This way." The old man led him into the adjacent bar, which was nearly empty. He ordered a shot of bourbon, but didn't offer Gar anything. "So?" he said. "What's so important that I have to interrupt my lunch?"

"Alverado said I should talk to you about Tony Drago."

"I don't know the man."

Gar leaned his weight against the sturdy oak bar, giving his leg a rest. "Whether you do or not doesn't interest me at all. Whether you know anything about his recent demise doesn't interest me either."

Marcello seemed to be paying more attention to his bourbon than to what Gar was saying. "So? What does interest you then?"

Gar took out the Epstein photograph. "This boy. Forget Drago. Forget about who killed him. All I want to know is, have you ever seen this boy?"

Marcello looked carefully at the picture. "One of life's complications," he murmured after a moment.

"I beg your pardon?" Gar said.

"Complications," Marcello repeated. "I'm too old for the complications that belong to others."

Gar put the photo away. "I'm not trying to complicate things for you. I only want to find that boy before he gets hurt." He eyed the old man. "His grandfather wants him back. I'm sure that you can understand that. Maybe you have grandchildren of your own?"

Marcello hesitated, again studying the amber liquid in his glass. "I may have seen that boy," he said carefully. "But I cannot say where or with whom."

"Cannot or will not?"

The face was bland, but the voice was icy. "However you prefer. I will not discuss this matter any further and it would be better for you not to ask me to. Understand?"

Gar understood. Marcello was perfectly willing for him to walk away now, knowing what he knew, and to leave Vegas in an undamaged condition. To press him any more would only lead to severe complications for everybody. Including himself. "Thank you," was all he said.

Marcello took his drink with him as he turned around and walked back out to the veranda. Instead of sitting back down to his lunch, though, he stopped by the table with the three goons. He bent down and said something into the definitely unshell-like ear of the biggest, meanest-looking ape. The man nodded and jumped up like the trained gorilla he was. He hurried away.

Interesting.

Gar glanced at his watch. He had twenty minutes to make the next flight back to Los Angeles. He could make it, assuming that he didn't run into any traffic cops en route. And also assuming that King Kong, who'd just left the veranda, wasn't waiting in the parking lot to beat the shit out of him.

2

He was sitting in the dark living room when Mickey came home. She didn't bother to turn on the lights, but just came and sat next to him. "Problems?" she said, toying with the hair that straggled over his collar.

"Deep shit," he replied. He took a long gulp of beer.

"Is it still Beau Epstein?"

"Oh, yeah. It's still Beau. Somehow that stupid boy has gotten himself mixed up with a couple of killings. And I don't mean your basic street crime. I'm talking highly paid mob killing. A pro."

"That's scary."

"It sure as hell is. I don't have any idea what's going on."

She patted his cheek. "You'll figure it out. I have faith."

"I'm sitting here thinking that maybe I really should just step out of this. Turn it over to the cops."

"Are they looking for Beau, too?"

"Not yet. But they could be."

Mickey leaned back and stared at him in the pale moonlight that was filtering into the room. "You're serious about quitting?"

He didn't say anything, because he didn't know how serious he was.

The phone rang.

"I don't feel like talking to anybody," he said. "Get that, will you?"

She stood and went to answer his phone. About three minutes later, she came back into the room. "That was Mr. McClure," she said in a very soft voice.

Gar moaned. "If Tammi has gone missing again, he'll have to hire somebody else to track her down this time. I'm too busy."

Mickey shook her head. "It's not that." She stood there for a moment not saying anything.

Gar felt a spasm of something—fear, maybe?—go through him. "What, then?"

"She killed herself, Gar. Last night. An overdose of her mother's sleeping pills."

Gar bent forward a little, as if someone had gut-kicked him. "Fuck," he said. "Fuckfuckfuck."

Mickey came over and sat next to him again. She took his hand and held it tightly between both of hers. "You okay?"

After a moment, he nodded. "I'm fine." But he

wasn't fine at all, and she knew it. "I have to go see Saul Epstein," he said suddenly.

"To quit the case?"

Gar shook his head. "No. No, not to quit. I'm going to find Beau, damn it. And it's time we got some publicity, no matter what the old man thinks." He stood.

"Are you going now? It's pretty late."

"So Saul Epstein gets out of bed. This is his grandson, for Chrissake. This boy is all he has left. He can get out of bed."

She nodded. "I'll wait up for you."

He bent to kiss the top of her head. "Thank you."

A black man in a neatly tied robe opened the door after Gar had knocked for several minutes. He didn't want to wake his boss at first, but when Gar made it clear that he wasn't budging until the old man appeared, the butler went to get him.

It took nearly fifteen minutes for Saul Epstein to appear. He wore a velvet smoking jacket and leather slippers, and his hair was neatly combed. "Have you found my grandson?" he asked immediately.

"No."

Epstein nodded and they walked into the library. The black man had already produced a pot of coffee and two cups. He served them and then slipped out of the room. "What is the news, then?" Epstein asked. "It must be important for you to come here at this hour."

"It's important. Mr. Epstein, I want you to bring the cops in on this. And the press. I want some publicity."

Epstein frowned. "I thought it was made clear that I wanted to keep this a family matter." He drank a little coffee. "And no matter what you might be thinking, Mr. Sinclair, this is as much for Beau's sake as for mine. The position I occupy, the publicity couldn't hurt me. But Beau is just a boy. I don't want to do anything that might mess up his life."

"But what you don't know is that this whole thing has gone way beyond just a simple runaway kid." The coffee burned the tip of his tongue and he paused. "I think that Beau is in big trouble."

"What kind of trouble?"

He sucked on his sore tongue briefly. "He's been seen at the sites of two murders. Possibly in the company of the killer. Willingly or unwillingly, I don't know. But we have to move quickly, before it's too late to save him."

Epstein looked much older than he had moments ago. "Beau? With a killer? You don't think he . . . ?"

Gar shrugged. "As far as I know, he's not killing anybody. I think the boy is probably a hostage." He wasn't sure about that, but there wasn't any sense in laying too much on the old man right now.

"There haven't been any ransom demands."

"Well, that doesn't mean much. Look, whatever is going on, we need some publicity."

After a moment, Epstein nodded. "I'll take care of it."

"Fine." Gar finished the coffee and stood. "I'll be in touch," he said.

"We have to find Beau," Epstein said. "I don't care what it costs or what has to be done. I want my grandson safe."

"I know," Gar said. The face of Tammi McClure flashed through his mind. And then the face of his own daughter. All the lost ones. "I'll find him," he said.

It was the first time he'd ever promised.

15

1

It was surprising and maybe even a little scary just how quickly the strange could become routine. Robert was thinking about that as he automatically set the breakfast table for two and waited for Beau to come out of the shower. After living alone for so long, he couldn't quite understand why the situation felt this comfortable so fast. Given the circumstances, the two of them seemed to be getting along fine. Robert even admitted to himself that he sort of liked having the kid around.

Not that he would ever say so out loud. But it was almost as if the clock had been turned back and Andy were here again. Then he felt a little disloyal for even thinking something like that. Beau wasn't Andy. Beau was just a kid he was stuck with temporarily. Still, it was nice.

He poured a cup of coffee and sat down with the newspaper.

A few minutes later, Beau came into the room, moving as usual with a certain manic speed. He sat down and reached for the Wheaties. "I just thought of something," he said.

"What's that?" Robert said absently.

"Today's my birthday."

He lowered the paper. "No shit?"

"No shit. I'm sixteen."

"Terrific." Sixteen. God, he was still such a baby. Robert felt a stab of what almost felt like guilt over what he was doing to someone who was still, basically, a child. It would probably be called corrupting the morals of a minor or something. Wonderful. He set the newspaper aside and started eating. Maybe because of that stab of guilt, he said, "Since it's such a big day, we should do something special."

Beau stopped with a spoon halfway to his mouth. "Like what?"

"Hell, I don't know. Something." He chewed cereal and thought about it. Then he got an idea, God knew from where. "Have you ever been to Disneyland?"

Beau shook his head.

"Well, neither have I." Once, a long time ago, he and Andy were supposed to go, but for some reason he'd now forgotten, they never made it. He hadn't ever even thought about going since then. "How about we hit the freaking Magic Kingdom today?"

"For real?"

"Sure."

Beau smiled. "Wild."

Wild. Yeah, you could say that. Disneyland and birthdays and who knew what next. There were people in this town who would find the idea of Robert Turcheck playing whatever the hell game he was playing here pretty damned funny.

He had planned on talking to one of those people this very day, in fact. But Camden Hunt would have to wait twenty-four hours. It was almost like a reprieve for the old buddy of Danny Boyd. Robert hoped that Hunt appreciated that.

Traffic on both the Santa Monica and Santa Ana freeways was moving with unusual speed, so the trip to Anaheim was easier than he'd expected it to be. Robert was beginning to feel a little stupid about this. What the hell was he thinking? The last thing in the world he wanted to do was spend the whole damned day at Mickey-fucking-Mouseville. He had important things to do. As his doubts grew, he almost changed his mind and headed for the nearest off-ramp. A glance at Beau's face kept him heading toward Anaheim. So, give the kid a little fun. What could it hurt?

Nothing. Except maybe his wallet.

Getting a parking place in the vast lot was a couple of bucks. Then he had to cough up twenty apiece just for them to get through the gate. They better have a lot of damned fun, he thought, after laying out over forty dollars in the first five minutes.

They paused as Beau bent over the detailed map of the park, deciding where they should begin this adventure. His choice was Pirates of the Caribbean and several choruses of "Yo-ho, Yo-ho, a Pirate's Life for Me." Robert felt very much out of place crowded in with what felt like every damned happy family in the country, but Beau didn't seem to mind. "Pretty neat, huh?" he said at one point.

Robert nodded.

Maybe Beau was playing a game, too. The game that they were a happy family.

Everything in the park was painfully clean, kept

that way by what seemed to be an army of white-suited young people with brooms and dustpans. "Maybe I could get a job here," Beau said thoughtfully, watching them work.

Robert looked at a bright-faced, obviously Republican kid sweeping up a stray candy wrapper. Then he looked at Beau. "You'd have to cut your hair," he said dryly.

"Yeah, I guess so. And they probably wouldn't let me wear an earring like yours, either."

"You don't have an earring," Robert pointed out.

Beau only grinned and shrugged.

They stopped for some lemonade and freshly baked cookies and Robert had a cigarette. Beau, he thought, was looking more as if he'd just turned ten instead of sixteen. And, although it irritated him to admit it, Robert realized that he was having fun, too. It had been a very long time since he'd relaxed this completely, maybe not since those long-ago summer afternoons watching Andy pitch. For this one day, at least, there was no pressure. The job was forgotten, the search for Danny Boyd was set aside, and even the memory of a mounting pile of messages from Maureen didn't annoy him.

They decided to get really brave and ride the big Space Mountain coaster. Neither of them had ever been on a roller coaster before, so as they settled side by side into the rocket-shaped car, enthusiasm was tempered slightly by nervousness. The thirty-two-mile-per-hour journey, most of which took place in pitch-darkness with stars whizzing by on all sides, left Beau red-faced and breathless. Robert was glad that, this once, he'd left his gun at home.

A moment later, however, he was wishing like hell that he hadn't been stupid enough to leave his gun in the closet.

He recognized Pete Franco immediately, although it was hard to imagine what a two-bit triggerman like him was doing hanging out in the Magic Kingdom. Unless, of course, he was there because Robert was.

Robert swore softly.

"What's wrong?" Beau asked instantly.

"Nothing. Just . . . nothing." He shoved Beau in the direction of a refreshment stand. At the counter, he stepped in front of a woman about to order, silenced her complaint with a glance, and ordered a Coke. He handed the paper cup to Beau. "Stay here. Drink this. I'll be right back."

"Where are you—?"

He didn't wait to hear the rest of the question. Instead, he moved into the crowd and headed in the same direction Franco had gone. Surely, surely, nobody would have been dumb enough to send an asshole like Franco after him. *Franco*, for Chrissake? If it wasn't so funny, he might be insulted.

Except that Robert didn't really feel like laughing either, because having Franco here spoiled the day. One lousy day, when Robert Turchek was just trying to be like everybody else. One day, and a creep like Franco had to show up.

It wasn't fair.

In another moment, he saw Franco just ahead, sitting on a bench and looking at a map of Disneyland. Acting as if he were just another tourist. Robert reached into his pocket and took out the knife, holding it against his side as he walked to the bench quickly and sat. "Why are you tailing me, asshole?" he whispered, pressing the point of the knife into Franco's side.

Franco froze and then turned his head very slowly. "What?" He blinked. "Turchek? What the fuck are you doing?"

"What I'm doing is none of your goddamned business. What you're doing is the problem."

Franco was being very careful not to move. "What the hell do you think I'm doing? I brung my kid to Disneyland. Anything wrong with that?"

"You just happen to be here on the same day I am?" Robert said.

"Looks like." Franco dared a small snicker. "Didn't know you went in for this kind of shit."

"You're not tailing me?"

"Hell, no."

Robert relaxed a little, but didn't put the knife away.

Franco squinted and stared at him. "I heard that you've been playing some stupid games, Turchek. Maybe you need a long vacation somewhere. Out of town."

"Fuck you," Robert muttered.

They both saw the woman and little boy approach at the same moment. "Don't you do nothing to scare my kid," Franco said.

"Yeah, yeah," Robert said. He got up and walked away quickly.

Screw Franco.

Beau was still waiting by the refreshment stand. He watched Robert approach, frowning. "What's wrong?" he said.

"Nothing. There was just a guy I know. I had to talk to him."

"That's all?"

Robert nodded shortly. "Come on," he said. "Let's have some more fucking fun."

They tried, but something had gone out of the day. The loss made Robert angry. Beau just seemed bewildered. Finally, desperate, Robert glanced around and spotted the Davy Crockett Pioneer Mercantile.

"Come on," he said brusquely. "Let's buy you a present. It's your fucking birthday, right?"

"You don't have to."

Robert pushed him toward the store. "Maybe not, but I want to, so shut the hell up."

After considerable looking and debate, they chose a fringed leather vest. It was too damned expensive, but Robert had decided not even to think about money for the rest of the day. They left the store.

Beau shoved both hands into his pockets and walked backward, facing Robert. "This is the best birthday I've ever had," he said as they moved through Frontierland.

"I'm glad," Robert said. He wasn't sure that one day of fun made up for everything else, but it was all he could offer. It would have to do.

Beau stopped suddenly, still looking at Robert. "What's going to happen? To you and me?"

The noisy crowd surged around them as Robert searched for an answer that he didn't really have. Finally, he just shrugged. "I don't know," he said.

"Are you scared? Not of me like you said before, that's just dumb, but of . . . " He gestured helplessly. "Of everything."

A fat woman in pink polyester bumped into Robert and he gave her a dirty look. She started to say something, then, after looking into his face for a moment, kept quiet and moved on. "Bitch," Robert muttered. Beau stood where he was, waiting for an answer. "For whatever it means, sometimes I'm scared, yeah," Robert finally said.

"Me, too."

"That's life, I guess."

They finally had a fancy dinner in the Blue Bayou Restaurant in New Orleans Square. Beau devoured the last bite of cake and leaned back with a deep sigh.

Robert quit studying the check. "What's wrong?"

"Nothing. I'm just feeling lucky we met when we did. Otherwise, I'd probably still be out on the street."

Robert wanted to tell him that, in the long run, he'd probably be better off out there. At least on the street the dangers were visible and familiar. But he didn't say that. Instead, he just tossed his platinum card down onto the table for the waiter. "Hey, Tonto, you like champagne, do you?"

Beau shrugged. "Never had it."

"We'll stop on the way home and get a bottle. Just to wrap up this damned celebration."

"Terrific."

They ended up with two bottles of the ridiculously expensive Bollinger Tradition R.D. It cost more than he'd ever paid for booze before, but by this time he figured what the hell. Instead of staying home to drink it, he just parked the car and they walked down to the beach. There was no one else in sight as they stretched out on the sand and drank champagne straight from the bottles.

Beau watched the waves for a time. "You know," he said then, "I can hardly remember what my parents looked like. If I close my eyes and concentrate real hard, I can get sort of a fuzzy picture, but that's all."

"I know what you mean," Robert agreed. "Andy's hardly been dead any time at all and I can hardly get a picture in my mind. Funny thing is, I can remember what he looked like when he was sixteen like you, but not when he was older."

"That is funny." Beau gulped the Bollinger as if it were water. "My folks, we had a party every August sixteenth. The anniversary of Woodstock, you know? It was neat. Music and stuff. They were at the real Woodstock."

"It sounds like they were okay people," Robert

said, although, to be honest, he thought Rachel and Jonathan must have been a little strange. A couple of overage hippies. Which explained a lot about why Beau was the way he was. Sort of spacey and innocent-like. He was like the youngest survivor of the freaking Age of Aquarius.

"Yeah, they were fine. Only, they were so close to each other that sometimes I felt like an intruder. Does that sound dumb?"

"If that's how you felt, then it's not dumb."

"Oh, well, I guess it doesn't matter so much now anyway, does it?"

"I guess not. But, Beau, what about living with your grandfather? Was it really so bad?"

"I didn't like it." Beau's words were slurred. "He wasn't seeing me, anyway. Just Jonathan. It was like this was another chance for him, you see?" Beau lay back and gazed up at the stars, real ones this time, not the Walt Disney make-believe kind.

"I see." Robert had an uncomfortable feeling that maybe he was sort of doing the same damned thing. Looking at Beau and seeing Andy. But that was a shot of self-knowledge that Robert wasn't ready to accept. So he pushed it aside.

"You're not gonna make me go back there, are you?"

"No," Robert said. "That's not my fucking job."

Beau giggled, then got quiet and tilted the bottle again. It was empty. "I fucked a girl once," he said.

Robert knew that he was far from sober himself. "Oh, yeah?" he said. "Well, good for you."

"It wasn't so great."

Robert shrugged. "Yeah, well, that happens."

Beau rolled over and looked at him. "She did it as a joke, see? So she could get into some damned club at school. She had to make it with the Paynor Academy freak. How's that?"

"Well, it sucks," Robert said. "She sounds like a real cunt to me."

"Yeah," Beau agreed. "A real cunt."

Robert leaned close and whispered, "Want me to kill her?"

They both laughed.

When they were quiet again, Beau said, "Do you think I'm a freak, Robbie?"

Nobody had called him that for a very long time. Robert blinked back a sudden hot dampness in his eyes. Christ, he thought, I'm drunker than I thought. "No," he said. "I think you're fine."

"How come nobody likes me, then?"

"I like you."

"Really?"

"Sure."

Beau smiled with little-boy sweetness. "Thanks. I like you, too."

"Good."

"And you can trust me, Robbie. I won't ever tell anybody about . . . about anything."

"I know you won't." Robert reached out a hand and lightly ruffled Beau's hair. "I mean, I'm trusting you with my life. Would I do that if I didn't like you a lot?"

"I guess not."

Robert left his hand where it was for a moment, lost in thought. Then, realizing again just how drunk he was and that drunk people sometimes did or said crazy, stupid things, he yanked his hand away. "We better go home," he said.

"You think so?"

"I know so."

They struggled to their feet.

"Shit," Beau said with another giggle. "I feel sort of funny."

"You won't feel funny in the morning," Robert warned him. "And neither will I."

"Race you home," Beau said suddenly.

"You're kidding, right?"

Beau's only response was to take off, laughing, across the sand. Robert left the empty champagne bottles where they were and set off after him. It was pretty much of a tie as they hit the front porch and banged into the house. As one, they collapsed onto the couch, both panting.

By the time Robert was able to speak, he realized that Beau had fallen asleep. Or passed out, which was more likely. Robert pushed himself up and managed to turn the dead weight of Beau's form lengthwise on the couch. He removed his shoes and socks, stuck a pillow under his head, and tossed a blanket down.

Then he went to bed.

2

Beau woke with a start and realized that he'd been sleeping in his clothes. His feet were bare, but otherwise he was completely dressed. The second thing he realized was that his head hurt. This, he decided, was his first real hangover.

He sat up slowly and then had his third realization of the day: he was going to throw up.

Immediately. He made a quick dash for the bathroom and got there just in time.

Amazingly, he felt better almost instantly after puking. He brushed his teeth, then stripped off the rumpled, sandy clothes, and got into the shower. By the time he'd finished and wrapped a blue towel around himself, he felt quite normal. Whistling cheerfully, he went into the kitchen.

Robert was sitting at the table, holding on to a cup of black coffee with both hands. "If you don't stop that fucking noise," he said mildly, "I'm going to cut your lips off."

Beau stopped. "Morning," he said, studying Robert critically. "You look a little sick."

"Yeah? Well, I feel worse than that. How're you?"

He shrugged. "Fine. I threw up and that made me feel better."

Robert made a face. "Must be nice to be young."

Beau poured himself a glass of juice and gulped it down a little desperately, which made Robert smirk slightly. "Thanks for yesterday," he said.

"Yeah, sure." Robert looked at him with blood-shot eyes. "You better put some clothes on. We have a lot to do today."

Beau knew what that meant and the thought made him feel a little sick again. He wished that Robert didn't have to keep killing people. Sure, he was trying to understand *why*, and all that, but it was scary. What if one of them had a gun, too, and shot Robert first? Beau didn't know what he would do if that happened.

He dressed quickly, putting the new fringed vest on over his T-shirt. Everything that had happened yesterday was already fading into memory. All he had left were the vest and a sort of good feeling inside. He could only hope that it wouldn't fade away, too.

Back in the kitchen, he made himself some toast. Robert refused his offer to make him some, too, and just stuck with the coffee. Beau sat at the table to eat the toast and jam. Halfway through the second slice, he looked up. "Robbie, is it business we have to do today?"

As Robert met his gaze, something Beau couldn't quite read flickered through the man's eyes. "No," he said after a moment. "This is personal."

Beau sighed. "Looking for Danny Boyd, you mean."

Robert set his cup down carefully. "Looking for Boyd, yes," he said. "I'm going to keep looking until I find him."

Beau didn't say anything.

"You don't have to hang around here, if that bothers you," Robert said. "I trust you. Take off anytime you want."

Beau couldn't decide if that was a suggestion or an order. He licked at the strawberry jam above his lip. "Do I have to?"

"What?"

"Do you want me to leave?"

Robert closed his eyes and carefully massaged his forehead. "I don't give a damn, Beau. Do what you want."

"Okay," Beau said. He picked up the rest of the toast.

The day was actually pretty boring.

After spending some time on the phone, speaking in a low voice that Beau, watching TV, couldn't quite hear, they left the house and drove over to Melrose Avenue. Robert parked across the street from a place called Hunt's Fine Antiques and they just sat and watched the customers come and go.

A couple of times during the afternoon, Beau left the car and ran up the block to a small croissant place for sandwiches and cold drinks. Robert smoked a lot of cigarettes and Beau read the newspaper.

Finally, when Beau was just about to decide that boredom could be fatal, businesses started closing along Melrose, including the antique store.

"You're whistling that fucking song again," Robert said.

Beau glanced at him sheepishly. "Sorry."

"Never mind. I'm just feeling a little edgy. Maybe I'll find out where Boyd is from this guy. This means a lot to me."

"Yeah, I know." Beau folded the newspaper and tossed it into the back seat. "Who is this man anyway?" he asked after a minute.

"Camden Hunt? Oh, he's a terrific guy. He likes to pretend to be a legit antique dealer. But what he really is is a fence. A heavy-duty, high-class fence, but still just a fence. Boyd is an old friend of his. If Danny Boy is trying to hustle up some bucks, this would be the guy he'd come to see."

Beau rubbed newsprint ink from his fingers onto his jeans. "You're just going to talk to him, right?"

"That's my plan, Tonto, that's my plan."

It was already getting dark when Camden Hunt came out of the store. He was tall and thin, with long blond hair. He locked the door of his shop and got into a new green Jag.

Beau looked at Robert, but didn't say anything, because Robert was already intent on his prey. They followed the car for several blocks before it turned into a dark parking lot. They watched Hunt pause a moment to comb his hair before going into the building. Robert drove in a moment later, going past the other car to the far corner of the lot.

"Gay bar," Robert said, mostly to himself. "So what I heard about him is true."

Beau didn't say anything.

Robert tapped the steering wheel, thinking out loud. "If he comes out with somebody, I can't make a move. And I can't afford to wait much longer. This whole thing is dragging on too long. It's dangerous for me. And Boyd is liable to split town or fuck up and end up back inside before I can get to him." After another moment, he turned and looked at Beau thoughtfully. "You want to help me out, Tonto?"

"Me? How?"

"Go in there and see if you can't get him to come out here with you."

Beau swallowed hard. He didn't want to do that. He wasn't even sure exactly what it was that Robert expected him to do. "I don't think I can."

"Sure, you can," Robert said, studying him with eyes that were suddenly cold. "You sure as hell don't look legal, I know, but this joint doesn't look all that particular. And maybe Hunt likes them young."

"Robbie, please, I don't want to."

"I'm asking you to do me a favor, that's all."

Beau couldn't stand the look of betrayal he thought was on Robert's face. "Okay," he said in a whisper. "What do I have to do?"

"Simple. Just go inside and try to get friendly with Hunt. Get him to leave with you, so I can talk to him."

Beau's mouth was dry. "He won't try anything, will he? You know what I mean?" He swallowed hard.

Robert shook his head. "Hell, would I let you walk into something like that? You know I wouldn't, Tonto. Just get him out here. I'll be waiting." He punched Beau lightly on the arm. "Go to it."

Beau got out of the car and walked slowly across the lot. At the door he stopped, glanced back toward the car, and straightened his shoulders. He walked into the bar.

The music was loud and the air thick with cigarette smoke. Beau coughed once and then started looking for Hunt. A couple of men around the bar spoke to him, but he ignored them. Finally he saw Hunt sitting alone at a table. Beau walked over that way, but he still didn't have any idea what to say, so he just stood there, staring at Hunt until the man looked up.

"Yes?"

"Can I sit here?" Beau asked.

"Sure. But aren't you a little young to be in this place?"

"My birthday was yesterday," Beau said truthfully as he pulled out a chair and sat.

"Many happy returns," Hunt said. "You can sit, but all you're getting to drink is a Coke."

"Okay." Beau leaned back in the chair and crossed his arms. Maybe it wouldn't take too long. The thing was not to think about what he was doing, but just to do it.

Robert smoked his way through half a dozen cigarettes as he waited in the car. He was feeling a little guilty again; hell, he was feeling a *lot* guilty over using Beau this way. It was damned unprofessional, for one thing. There were other ways to get at Hunt. He shouldn't have sent Beau into this place. He felt almost like a pimp and it wasn't a feeling he liked. What the hell was he trying to prove? Or make Beau prove?

Just thinking about it made him uncomfortable.

But sitting there he didn't have anything else to do but think about it. The question that was nagging at him was just how far would he go in using Beau? What came after sending him into a fag bar to pick up somebody like Hunt?

Robert didn't like to think that maybe he could be the kind of bastard who could hurt a kid. But who knew, until push came to shove?

When the door of the bar opened again, he watched without much hope. But this time, Beau appeared, followed closely by Hunt. Hunt had one hand on Beau's shoulder as they walked across the lot.

Robert reached under the seat and pulled out the gun he'd stashed there, just in case. He got out and headed after them quickly. They were standing by Hunt's car when he reached them. "Go back to the car, Tonto," he said quietly.

"What's going on?" Hunt asked.

Beau hadn't moved yet.

"Back to the car, I said," Robert ordered more sharply.

Beau glanced at Hunt quickly and then ran off.

Robert shoved Hunt more deeply into the darkness.

"I wasn't doing anything with the boy," Hunt said. "He simply wanted a ride. Good Lord, he's just a child."

"I know."

Hunt was looking increasingly desperate. "He only wanted a ride."

"I'll give him one."

"No problem," Hunt said.

Robert just looked at him. "I'm looking for Danny Boyd," he said. "You being an old buddy of his, I thought maybe you could help me out. Wouldn't you like to do that?" He smiled.

Hunt shook his head. "I haven't seen Danny in a long time," he said. "We don't run in the same circles anymore."

"How come I don't believe you?" Robert said. He took the gun from his pocket and quickly stuck it under Hunt's chin. "Maybe you want to try again and this time try harder to convince me."

Hunt didn't say anything. But he didn't have to. The sound of the switchblade clicking open said it all. Where the hell had the knife come from? Robert was irritated with himself for not having anticipated something like this.

"Bastard," Hunt said tightly.

His arm and Robert's finger moved at the same time. Robert fired and moved back quickly; the knife blade just grazed his chest as Hunt pitched forward.

Robert wiped the gun on the front of his shirt and dropped it before running for the car. There, he just had time to slip into the driver's seat before the door of the bar opened and several men came out. They looked around, saw nothing, then seemed to shrug collectively, and went back inside.

Only then did Robert start the car and drive away slowly.

Beau was slumped in the passenger seat, his eyes squeezed closed. Both hands were over his ears.

Neither of them said anything.

When they got back to the house, Beau went directly to the bathroom. Robert, standing in the hall, could hear him throwing up. He didn't think it was the champagne this time. After a moment, he went into the living room and sat on the couch.

Beau finally emerged, pale and trembling.

"You okay?" Robert asked.

"No, I'm not okay," he replied. "I feel like shit. I feel like it was me who killed that guy."

"Well, it wasn't. I did it."

"You told me it was only to talk to him. That's what you said."

"Hey, the punk pulled a knife on me."

"Yeah? Well, he seemed nice to me. He was going to give me a ride."

"Right," Robert muttered. "He wanted to do more than that, you know."

Beau glared at him. "Maybe so, but he wasn't going to kill me."

Robert was tired. "He might have killed me, though. Would that have made you happy?"

"No," Beau whispered. "But couldn't you have just hit him or something?"

"That's not the way I play," Robert said. "You want to see what his fucking knife did to me?"

Beau shook his head. "The thing is, Robbie, you make it seem so easy. Probably you could kill me just as easy. Maybe you will before this is over."

"Don't be stupid," Robert said angrily.

"I'm not stupid. I just don't like being made to feel like some kind of accessory to murder."

And *he* didn't like the way Beau was looking at him. "Why don't you just go to hell, then," he said in a tight voice. "Leave me the fuck alone." He went into his bedroom and slammed the door.

It was only a moment later that he heard the front door slam, too.

3

Beau hitched a ride with a solitary tourist, a priest from Wisconsin. It turned out that back home, he ran a shelter for runaways. As they rode along, he tried to persuade Beau to leave the streets. To go home.

When they reached Hollywood, Beau thanked him and got out, promising to think about what the man had said. Which was a lie, of course, because there was no way he'd go crawling back to Saul.

He just walked up and down Sunset until it was very late and the crowd had dwindled down to the hard-core street regulars. Beau found a doorway that was empty and he crouched down there wearily. He didn't know what the hell he was going to do.

Finally, exhaustion took over.

He didn't know how long he'd slept when he was jerked from a restless dream by the feel of rough hands on him. "What?" he said, startled. He found himself peering up into a strange face, a face that was pale and sweaty and crazy-looking.

"Shut up," the man said in a wheezy voice. "I want your bread. I want all your fucking bread. And your shoes. Gimme your bread and your fucking shoes, or I'll fucking kill you."

Beau didn't move.

The man slapped him hard and his head bounced back against the door. "Give it to me."

Beau was trembling so hard that he could hardly untie his Nikes. "Here," he said, shoving them toward the man. Then he fished a few crumpled bills from his pocket and tossed them down.

The man clutched the shoes with one hand and grabbed for the bills with the other. "That all? That all?" he said, slapping Beau twice more.

Beau nodded. "Yes," he whispered.

Instantly, the man was gone.

Alone again, Beau started to cry. He hated himself for being such a baby—Robert would never be this scared—but he couldn't stop the scalding tears that rolled silently down his face.

Robert was sitting on the couch, where he'd been all night. On the table in front of him were several empty beer cans and an ashtray overflowing with butts. He hadn't slept at all.

It was just after dawn when he heard the soft tapping on the door. He got up quickly and went to open it. Beau stood there, barefooted and dirty. His face was dirt-streaked and pale, except for a small bruise on his cheek. "I'm sorry," he whispered.

Robert stared at him for a moment, then tugged him inside and into a hug. "It's my fault," he said, pulling back. "I shouldn't have asked you to do that."

Beau shook his head. "I owed you."

"No, you don't owe me a goddamned thing. Everything I've done was because I wanted to. You don't owe me."

They finally went and sat down.

"I'm glad you came back," Robert said.

"Yeah, well, I didn't have any place else to go." He wriggled his bare feet. "And I don't seem to do so well by myself."

Robert lit a cigarette and looked at him through a cloud of smoke. "In other words, you're here because this is all there is."

Beau shook his head. "Not only that. I came back mostly because I wanted to. Except . . ."

"Except what?"

He took a deep breath. "Please don't make me do anything like that again."

"I won't." Robert lifted a hand, only half-mockingly. "Scout's honor," he said.

"So I can stay?" Beau asked.

"If you want to."

"Okay. Thanks."

After a moment, Robert got up. "Come with me," he said.

Looking curious, Beau followed him to the hallway. Robert unlocked and opened a door that hadn't been opened before. Beau looked in. The room was a shambles—broken furniture, books thrown everywhere, drawers yanked out and emptied.

He glanced at Robert.

"Soon as we get the time," he said, "we'll clean this up. It'll be your room." He turned and walked away. "You want some fucking breakfast or not?" he added, not looking back at Beau.

16

1

Gar ordered a stack of pancakes, two eggs over easy, sausage patties, hash browns, and coffee. It was an old habit of his; the worse he expected a day to be, the bigger the breakfast he would eat. It was as if he needed to be fully stoked to face whatever was ahead.

He didn't know why he thought that today was going to require the Lumberjack Special, but then again, the way this case was going, it seemed like a pretty safe bet.

He was still waiting for his food when the massive shape of Wally Dixon slid into the booth. "Bad habits never change, do they, Gar? You're not a cop anymore. So how come you're sitting in a grease factory like this at the crack of dawn?"

"I'm having breakfast," Gar replied.

"Uh-huh. It's pretty early."

"Eternal vigilance," he said. "That's why I get big bucks from my clients."

The waitress brought Dixon a cup of coffee. When she was gone again, he said, "You still on the same case?"

"Yes." Gar decided not to wait any longer for his client to talk to the police. "I'm looking for a kid named Beau Epstein. Saul Epstein's grandson."

Dixon gave a low whistle. "You're really playing in the big time now, aren't you? I didn't even know that old bastard had any family."

"Well, I'm not quite sure that 'family' is the right word. He has a grandson who was living with him. But the kid took off."

Dixon considered his coffee briefly. "I'm surprised the word hasn't reached me. A high-profile case like that."

Gar shrugged. "The old man wanted to keep things under wraps, but I finally persuaded him to go public with it. He should be filing a missing-person report any minute, or maybe he already has."

Dixon nodded. "And the Epstein kid is the one who witnessed the hooker getting killed, is that it?"

"That's it."

Dixon was looking at him knowingly. They had been partners a long time. "What else?"

Gar waited as his breakfast was finally delivered. He poured warm maple syrup over the whole plate. "What else?" he repeated. Well, when there was nothing else to do, you went to the cops. "Just for starters, I think that maybe Beau was in Vegas when the Tony Drago hit went down."

"That's interesting," Dixon admitted. "How old is this kid anyway?"

"Fifteen. No, sixteen," he corrected himself, remembering the date Epstein had given him. "He just had a birthday."

"Sounds a little young to be going around killing people." Dixon snitched a slice of toast and piled apricot preserves onto it.

Gar frowned. "Beau isn't killing anybody. The way I see it, he's with whoever is offing these people. Your paid triggerman."

"You think so? Is he going along willingly or unwillingly?"

Since Gar didn't know the answer to that and he didn't even want to think about it much, he didn't say anything. He just concentrated on finishing the food on his plate. He was nearly done when Dixon's beeper went off. The black man headed for the pay phone in the back of the diner. While he was gone, Gar had another cup of coffee.

Dixon returned to the table looking grim.

"Trouble?" Gar asked.

"Do I ever get beeped for good news?"

Gar wiped his mouth, "What?"

"Somebody just found a stiff a couple blocks from here. Guy found shot to death behind the Domino Lounge."

"Gay bar, right?"

"Right." Dixon picked up his coffee cup and took one last swallow. "You might be interested to hear that the deceased was shot once in the head."

"Yeah? And was there a gun at the scene?"

"I didn't ask that."

But Gar had a bad feeling. "Would you have any objection if I followed you to the scene? Just out of idle curiosity."

"You'll do anything for a cheap thrill, won't you, Gareth? But come on."

He paid the check and followed Dixon from the diner.

The body was lying behind the trash bin at the edge of the parking lot. A middle-aged man with blond hair, nice clothes, and a face that, in the one quick glance he got, looked vaguely familiar to Gar. After that fast look, he stayed politely out of the way as Dixon did the things a lieutenant of homicide was supposed to do at a time like this. It all made Gar feel just a little nostalgic.

Dixon finally came over to where Gar was leaning against his car. Wordlessly, he held up a plastic evidence bag. Inside was a handgun. "Looks clean," he said.

"The victim?"

"One Camden Hunt. Owner of an antique store down on Melrose. And a regular here apparently. He was in the bar last night."

"Hunt?" Gar thought for a moment. "The guy was a fence, right?"

Dixon grinned. "Nice to see that your mind is as sharp as ever, partner."

Gar returned the smile. Then, because he could read Dixon as well as Dixon could read him, he sobered, knowing that there was more. "What else?" he said wearily.

Dixon wasn't smiling anymore either. "Hunt left the bar with a boy last night. Nobody knew him, and it looked like he was underage, but since the kid wasn't drinking anything but Coke, nobody made a fuss. This is all according to the bouncer."

"Can I show him the photo?"

"Be my guest." Dixon turned to talk to a woman from forensics.

Gar made his way through the small army that had descended on the parking lot. A massive young man with a long ponytail was standing in the doorway of the bar, smoking nervously.

"Helluva thing," he said to Gar.

"Sure is," Gar agreed. "You told the detective that the victim left the bar with a young boy, right?"

"Yeah. I never saw him before and I know most of the hustlers who work this area."

Gar didn't really want to do it, but he held the picture out. "Is this him?"

The bouncer stared at the photograph, then nodded decisively. "That's the kid. You don't think this boy killed Mr. Hunt, do you?"

Gar just shrugged. "Anything else you can tell me?"

"Afraid not."

"Well, thanks for the help."

"Sure. Helluva thing," he said again.

Dixon was still standing by the car. This time, he held up a bag with a switchblade inside. "Hunt tried to get the drop on his killer," he said.

Gar didn't say anything.

"So?" Wally said, with a nod toward the bar.

"He just ID'd Beau Epstein."

Dixon shook his head. "This is getting pretty involved. For what started out as just another runaway kid."

"This," Gar said, "is a totally fucked-up mess." They watched in silence as the loaded body bag was carried by. "Damn it," Gar said to no one.

Dixon looked at him. "Your boy seems to have become a sort of Judas goat," he said.

Gar just sighed.

Mostly because he couldn't think of anything else to do at the moment, he followed Dixon again, this time to Hunt's apartment. There was already a squad car in front of the building. The young uniformed officer got out and walked over to them. "We talked to the boyfriend," he said with a mild smirk. "Seemed pretty broken up about it."

Dixon just looked at him. "Thank you," he said flatly.

Camden Hunt had liked to think of himself as a respected antiques dealer, and he lived the life to fit that image, including a fancy address. But that he hadn't managed to cast off his roots completely became obvious when the door of his apartment opened.

The young man standing there looked about two weeks off the street. He was maybe twenty, wearing tight black jeans, a sleeveless black T-shirt, and a hostile expression. Whatever grief he'd felt at first hearing the news seemed to have diminished.

Without saying anything, he led them into the living room, They all sat on a vast curved velvet sofa. "What's your name?" Wally asked.

"Jimmy Lee Hoskins," he mumbled, lighting a cigarette. "That other cop already told me that Cam is dead. What else is there to say?"

"How long have you known Mr. Hunt?"

"Three months." He glanced around the fancy living room and sighed. "Three fucking months of the good life. I guess it's over now."

Dixon smiled slightly. "Unless he put you in the will, Jimmy Lee."

Hoskins snorted.

Gar hadn't said anything yet.

"Do you know why anyone would want to kill your benefactor?" Wally asked.

"My what?"

"Your meal ticket."

Hoskins shook his head.

"You *do* know about his business? Not the antiques, the other stuff."

After a moment, Hoskins nodded. "But Cam was a good guy," he said with sudden heat. "Nice, no matter what he did."

"Just a nice neighborhood fence who took in strays, right?"

Hoskins shot Dixon a dirty look. "What the fuck do you know about it?"

Gar stepped in finally. He held out the picture. "Do you know this kid?"

A quick glance. "No. Should I?"

"Hunt left the bar with him last night."

"Yeah? Well, I don't know the kid. And I don't think Cam was up to what you think he was. Cam was getting everything he needed here."

"Did he seem worried lately? Scared?"

"No." Hoskins stared at the smoke trailing up from his cigarette. "There was one thing," he added. "Some guy Cam used to know was bugging him. Cam told me the guy was just out of jail and he was trying to work some kind of a deal. Cam wasn't very interested."

"You know this old pal's name?"

"No."

Dixon asked a few more questions, none of which gave them much more than what they already had. Then Hoskins walked them to the door. "Shit," he said. "When do you think I'll have to clear out of here?"

Wally shrugged. "Talk to a lawyer."

Hoskins didn't seem too thrilled with that answer.

Riding down in the elevator, Gar took another look at the photograph. He was suddenly struck by how damned sad the face in the picture was. It seemed to him that a child this sad could get into a lot of trouble just trying to find a little happiness. Realizing that didn't make him feel very good about how this case was liable to come out.

2

Beau had decided to start smoking.

Cigarettes, that was. "I used to do grass back home," he said. "But my folks, they were really down on tobacco."

Robert greeted the news with a shrug and pushed his lighter and cigarettes across the table. "It's your funeral" was all he said.

Beau shook one cigarette out of the pack and lit it, then looked around the café to see if any of the other late breakfasters had noticed. No one had. "Actually," he admitted, "they weren't all that thrilled with me doing grass either, but they figured it was just a phase I was going through."

Robert looked at him for a moment, then shook his head slowly and returned his attention to the newspaper. "I catch you smoking anything but tobacco," he said mildly, "your ass is back on the street. Understand?"

"Yeah."

He turned the page of the paper and instantly felt his heart fall to somewhere down around his ankles. "Jesus H. Christ," he said.

Beau took the cigarette out of his mouth. "Is something wrong?"

"Yes," Robert said grimly. "I'd say something is wrong." He shoved the newspaper toward Beau. "They've got your fucking picture in here."

"For real?" Beau smoothed the page. "Shit."

"You didn't tell me that your grandfather was Saul Epstein."

"I didn't think it mattered."

"Oh no? Christ, he's probably got the whole goddamned FBI out looking for you. He and J. Edgar were good buddies, I heard." Abruptly, Robert shut up and looked around the small café. Nobody was paying them any attention at the moment. He took off his baseball cap and sunglasses. "Put these on," he ordered.

Beau did.

"Now let's get the hell out of here." He paid the check quickly and they went straight to the car. Safely there, he opened the paper again for another look at the picture. "Jesus, Beau," he said, "I don't believe this."

"I'm sorry," Beau said in a low voice. "I didn't know the old man would do anything like this."

"Saul Epstein. Richer than God and just as powerful around here."

Beau took off the sunglasses and looked at him with worried eyes. "What are we going to do, Robbie?"

Robert thought for a moment, then started the car. "Can't do a damned thing about what's already happened. But we can make sure nothing else does."

He drove several blocks to a drugstore, told Beau to wait in the car, ignored Beau's question about what he was going to do, and went into the store.

After a brief tour of the aisles, he picked up some brown hair color, battery-operated clippers, and another pair of sunglasses. At the last minute, he added a cheap baseball cap with a Batman logo on the front to his purchases. He also picked up a couple packs of cigarettes, figuring that if somebody else was going to keep bumming them, he'd run out pretty fast.

Beau looked very relieved when he got back into

the car; what did the idiot think, that he'd been planning to duck out the back door? Not that it didn't sound like a pretty good idea, in fact. "What'd you buy?"

"We're going to transform you."

"What's that mean?" Beau asked warily.

"You gotta lose the hair, Tonto. And we're changing the color." He opened the sack and took out the sunglasses and hat. "And from now on, you don't go out without wearing these."

"Okay." Beau pointed at the paper. "It says in there that some private detective is looking for me."

"Yeah, well, some stupid rent-a-dick is the least of our problems." But Robert wondered, hearing this, if maybe the sense of being observed that had come to him at odd moments over the last couple of days had to do with the fact of that detective. It made him nervous.

Beau leaned back, chewing on his lower lip.

At home, Beau stripped off his shirt and stuck his head over the kitchen sink while Robert poured the thick coloring gel onto his hair and rubbed it in. They didn't talk much for ten minutes, waiting for the color to take, then Beau rinsed it out as Robert had a beer.

He emerged from the sink with dark-brown hair. A few reddish streaks. Already he looked like a different person. Maybe this was going to work. They went outside to the patio. A high row of shrubs gave them lots of privacy. Beau perched on a redwood chair and Robert applied the clippers to his nearly shoulder-length hair.

He had the haircut looking like something straight out of the 1950s by the time he finished. It was just at that moment that the silence was broken by the sound of a completely unexpected voice. "Hi, Bobby," Maureen said.

He almost dropped the damned clippers, then recovered and turned to look at her. "Maureen," he said in a neutral voice.

Beau just sat very still.

"You haven't answered any of my messages or called, so I decided to just come by and see if you were okay." She paused. "I guess you are."

"I'm fine, yeah."

"So I see." She peered around him at Beau. "So, you working as a barber now in your spare time?"

"No." Robert glanced over his shoulder. Beau, from somewhere, had produced the new sunglasses and slipped them on. With the short brown hair and glasses hiding his blue eyes, he didn't look like himself at all—Robert hoped. "Go inside, Tonto," he said.

Without a word, Beau disappeared into the house. His parents, weirdo hippies or not, must have brought him up right; most of the time, he obeyed orders.

"Who's that?" Maureen asked.

Robert started to sweep up the hair. "Just a friend of mine."

"Oh. I thought maybe he was another long-lost brother or something."

Robert looked at her sharply. "I only had one brother. This is just a friend."

She nodded and swept her hair back. "So you have a friend visiting. Is that why you haven't gotten in touch with me?"

He shrugged. "I've been busy is all."

She seemed to digest that. "Okay." Her eyes moved over him slowly, thoughtfully, and finally she nodded. "I probably shouldn't have bothered to come. Obviously, we're a thing of the past. Right?"

Robert nodded. "This happens," he said.

When she spoke again, there was bitterness in her voice. "Thanks for letting me down so easily."

He didn't say anything to that.

She gave a sniff and tossed her head. "You're a real bastard, Bobby."

"I'm sorry." He realized that maybe he should have felt something—pity, at the very least—but he didn't.

"No, I don't think you are." She smiled a little. "I'm sort of surprised that I never noticed that before."

"What?"

"How cold your eyes are. You really do have very cold eyes."

He only shrugged.

Maureen turned around and walked away.

Robert threw the shorn hair into the trash can before going into the house. He stopped in the kitchen long enough to take a can of beer from the refrigerator and then walked on into the living room.

Beau was stretched out on the couch, watching CNN and smoking. It was a mild shock to see him looking so different. The short brown hair made him seem older and somehow harder. He glanced at Robert. "That your girlfriend?" he asked.

"Used to be. Not anymore."

"How come?"

Robert took a gulp of beer and then held the can out. "Want some?"

Beau took a quick swallow, but he hadn't forgotten the question. "So how come she's not your girlfriend anymore?"

"I'm tired of her is all. Besides, we're too busy right now to bother with broads anyway, right?"

"Right," Beau said cheerfully.

Robert started to take another swallow of beer, then lowered the can, staring at the television. "Fucking grandfather," he said.

Beau looked at the screen again and saw his own face staring back at him. He pushed himself back into the sofa.

They listened to the short piece—grandson of movie mogul missing, feared kidnapped, et cetera—and when the smiling anchorperson went on to the next story, Robert used the mute button on the remote control. "This is getting too hot too fast," he muttered. "I have got to make the hit on Boyd and then get out of town for a while."

Beau looked at him, but didn't say anything.

"I'm going out tonight," Robert said. "Talk to some people."

"About Boyd?"

"Right. You can come if you want to or stay here. Whatever."

"I'll come," Beau said promptly.

"You sure?"

"Yeah." Beau sucked in smoke, held it, and then exhaled noisily. "I need to be there. Just in case."

Robert sat on the back of the couch and looked down at him. "Just in case what?"

It was a long moment before Beau spoke again, and when he did, his voice was so soft that it was hard to hear what he said. "In case something goes wrong, of course."

Robert crushed the empty beer can. "What the hell are you talking about?"

Beau was staring at the silent TV screen. "Well, I

can't just hang around here, wondering what's going on. That would be worse."

After thinking about it, Robert nodded.

He stood. "I need to pick up some cash, too," he said. "Things are moving too damned fast and I don't want to get caught short."

Beau looked at him. "Where are we going to get money?"

Robert grinned. "Hey, I've got bread stashed in banks all over this damned town. A man has to be ready for anything."

Beau just nodded.

17

1

He told Spock to answer the phone.

But the dog only looked at him, seemingly heart-broken because he couldn't do what his master asked him to do. Gar told him that was okay and got up to take the call himself. "Sinclair," he said.

"Is this the detective in the newspaper? The one looking for the missing kid?"

"Yes," he said.

The woman didn't say anything.

"Can you tell me something about Beau Epstein?" Gar asked quietly.

"He . . . he . . ." There was a sharp intake of breath. "No," she said then. "I better not. I think he might even kill me." She hung up.

Gar listened to the dial tone for several moments, then replaced the receiver. He walked into the bedroom.

Mickey, wearing a T-shirt and some shorts, was

exercising in the middle of the room. Gar sat on the bed and watched her count sit-ups. There was a faint sheen of sweat on her face as she smiled fleetingly at him.

"Some woman just called. She knows something about Beau, but she's too scared to tell me."

"Scared?" Mickey said breathlessly. "Of what?"

"Someone who might kill her if she speaks up," Gar said glumly.

"Maybe she'll call back." Mickey stopped moving and looked at him.

"Maybe. Sweat is very sexy, do you know?"

She laughed. "Is that a proposition?"

He thought about jumping into bed with Mickey and putting all this other crap aside, at least for a few minutes. One fast roll in the hay; what could it hurt? But then, unfortunately, he thought of Beau Epstein and the mounting pile of bodies. He sighed. "Later?" he said hopefully.

Mickey nodded. "I have to run anyway. There's a rumor that Tom Cruise might show up at this benefit tonight."

Gar stood, held out a hand, and pulled Mickey to her feet. He leaned close and tasted the sweat on her face. "Maybe we need a vacation," he said.

"Sure. Have your girl call my girl and we'll coordinate schedules."

He grinned, but it wasn't all that funny.

Gar deliberately avoided going anywhere near Wally Dixon's office on his late-evening visit to headquarters. Instead, he headed directly for the records department. Luck was with him for a change, because Della Horn was on duty. Della was a tall, attractive woman, a long-time acquaintance with whom he had managed to stay friendly despite the fact that her hopes for a much closer relationship had been destroyed when he moved in with Mickey.

She greeted him with her usual smile and a slightly wary attitude. The wariness was justified, because every time he came around these days, it was for her help. Both of them knew damned well that some of the information she slipped him was not, strictly speaking, supposed to be his.

On some days, Gar felt a little guilty about the way he used her. But not this time. Tonight, he had no qualms about exploiting her or anybody else, because he was desperate. Time, he felt, was running out for Beau.

"I'd like to see a couple of files," he said. "One a fence named Camden Hunt and another a hooker named Marnie Dowd. Both recently deceased."

"This have something to do with a missing kid?" Della asked. Childless, divorced, she took a deep interest in the children he looked for. Maybe that was why she helped him, for the kids, and not because she secretly had the hots for him. Gar felt a little disappointed when that thought came to him. "Yes," he said. "And this is a special case. The boy is in real trouble. It could be the fatal kind of trouble, unless I can find him damned fast."

"And if you see the files on Hunt and Dowd, it will help?"

"Couldn't hurt," he said with shrug.

He hadn't taken more than two sips of coffee when she returned with the files. "That was fast."

"Well, Lieutenant Dixon had them out and I hadn't put them away yet."

If there was anything to be found, it was a safe bet that Wally would already have found it. But Gar decided to look anyway, for two reasons. First, there was no guarantee that Wally would be willing to share what he knew with a private snooper, especially since the name of Saul Epstein was now hovering over the police case. When the big money came into it, the cops could get pretty close-mouthed, even with a best friend.

Second, since his main motivation was different from Wally's—the cops were mainly interested in finding a mob hitman and he wanted the boy—it was possible that a fact that meant nothing to Wally might be just the one he needed to bring the picture into focus.

So he sat down and started to read through the files.

It was so insignificant that he almost missed it. And maybe it didn't mean a damned thing. But Gar decided to believe that it did.

"Find something?" Della asked.

"Maybe. At one point in his illustrious career, Hunt was caught buying hot jewelry from a second-rate thief named Danny Boyd."

"So?"

"So, Marnie Dowd lived with that same second-rate thief."

"And what does that mean?"

"I don't know," Gar said truthfully. "But it's a link between the two of them. It might be what got them both killed." He handed the files back to Della. "Maybe I should drop in on my old buddy Wally."

"He'll be thrilled," Della said.

Gar smiled and thanked her. She accepted his gratitude stoically.

Wally's office was lit only by a small lamp on the desk. He was leaning back in the chair, his eyes closed. Gar came in quietly and dropped into the visitor's chair. "No, thanks," Wally said without opening his eyes. "I don't want to buy any."

"Any what?"

"Whatever it is you're selling."

"Maybe I'm here to give you something."

"Right." Wally opened his eyes and straightened in the chair. "You'll forgive me if I'm skeptical."

"You're a cop," Gar said with a shrug. "That's a job requirement."

Wally nodded. "You haven't found the Epstein kid yet, I guess."

"No. Have you come up with anything?"

"Nada."

They sat in silence briefly.

"What can you tell me about a guy named Danny Boyd? Jewel thief, at one point in his life anyway."

"Off the top of my head, I can't tell you a damned thing, because I never heard of him. Although the name sounds vaguely familiar," he admitted after a moment.

"He used to live with Marnie Dowd."

"Oh, yeah." Wally rubbed his eyes. "I haven't been home for fifteen hours," he said.

"Why?"

He shrugged. "I don't really know. There's nothing so extraordinary going on. Maybe it's just easier to stay here."

Gar decided not to pursue that at the moment. "Can you find out about Boyd for me?"

"Why don't you just get Della to pull it for you? Doesn't she do all your research for you?"

Gar grimaced. "Well, she's already done her quota for one night. Besides, she wants my body and I'm afraid to get too indebted to her."

"Uh-huh." Wally reached for his phone.

While waiting for the information to come back,

they talked about baseball and the weather—carefully avoiding the topics of Beau Epstein or why Wally didn't want to go home.

When the phone buzzed, Wally picked it up and listened for several minutes, then grunted thanks to whomever was on the other end, and hung up. "Boyd just got out of San Quentin on parole," he said. He scribbled a name on a slip of paper. "This is his PO."

Gar took the paper.

"What's the connection between Boyd and your missing kid?" Wally asked.

"I'm not sure. Probably there isn't one, but . . ." He shrugged.

"Keep in touch," Wally said.

Gar left the office. He turned around and looked back through the glass. Wally was leaning back again, his eyes closed. There was trouble going on in his friend's life and Gar wanted to help.

But it was late, he was tired, and his leg was throbbing. There wasn't anything he could do for Wally right now—or with the name of Danny Boyd's parole officer—so he went home.

To find that his woman was still out chasing around after Tom Cruise.

2

Robert drove the car around to the back of the deserted warehouse and parked. He glanced at his watch and then at Beau, who had been uncharacteristically quiet all evening. "You better stay here," he said. "Even the way you look now, there's no sense taking chances, right?"

"Okay," Beau said.

Robert squeezed his shoulder. "Hey, don't worry. I'm not going to whack this guy."

"Whatever you say," Beau mumbled.

"Look at me."

After a moment, Beau glanced up at him. "Yeah?"

"I'm telling you the truth, Tonto. This isn't like it was with Hunt. Or the hooker. The guy I'm seeing here is too smart to pull a knife on me and too well-connected for me to off him without a very good reason. We're meeting here by mutual agreement. Mostly because he owes me and wants to clear up the debt. You understand all that?"

"Sure, Robbie," Beau said more cheerfully.

Robert nodded. "Good. You lock the door after me and sit tight. This shouldn't take long."

He got out of the car, waited to hear the lock click into place, and then headed for the side door of the warehouse. Rocco—that was actually his name—was supposed to be waiting right inside.

And he was.

Shiny gray suit, greasy hair and all. "Hey, Bob, it's been a long time."

"I've been busy." He didn't like Rocco, who seemed to try his damnedest to come off like a character from a road-show production of *The Godfather*. Or maybe *Guys and Dolls*. But even an idiot like him could have his uses. Rocco remembered the time Robert had whacked the guy who had been hired to whack *him*. It was all tied up in mob politics, which Robert always did his best to avoid.

Now, finally, was the time to collect on the debt.

"So? I understand you can tell me where Danny Boyd is."

Rocco was smoking a fat black cigar. "Well, not right now."

—201—

Robert frowned. "What the fuck am I doing here then?"

Rocco waved off the words. "Hey, chill out, buddy. All I meant was I don't know where Boyd is right this minute. But I know where he'll be tomorrow night about now."

"Where?"

"Right here. There's a high-stakes poker game going on. Boyd is trying to raise a bankroll."

Robert nodded. "Okay."

"Anything you do to Boyd is okay with me—and with Mr. Carson. Just don't get anybody else at the game mixed up in it."

"I won't. Thanks, Rocco."

"This clears it between us?"

"It's clear."

Rocco nodded. "Okay. Then this next thing is a freebie."

Robert, who already had the door open, paused. "What next thing?"

"Watch your ass. There are some people who aren't real happy with you. I hear talk that maybe they're out to have you taken care of."

Robert stared at him for several seconds. Then he nodded. "Thanks, Rocco."

All the way back to the car, he felt a faint prickling at the back of his neck, as if somebody were watching each and every step he took. When he got to the car, he tapped impatiently on the window and as soon as the lock clicked open, Robert slid in behind the wheel.

"How'd it go?" Beau asked.

"Fine," he replied shortly. "Boyd will be here tomorrow night. I can kill him then."

Beau looked at him, but didn't say anything.

* * *

Robert was too tense to stay inside, so they went back to the beach, to the same spot as the other night. The empty champagne bottles were gone, and this time they were drinking root beer. Robert wanted to keep his mind fully operating.

He was still thinking about what Rocco had told him. Who the hell would put a contract out on *him?* It didn't make sense; it had to be a mistake, that was all, and as soon as this business with Boyd was over, he'd clear it up. He could handle it.

Now he had to concentrate on Boyd.

Beau was sitting cross-legged next to him, working intently on a sand sculpture. Robert gazed at him, still not used to the way he looked now. Beau patted the damp sand thoughtfully. "We could go to Santa María," he said.

Robert leaned back against a boulder. "What would we do there?"

"Live in my house. It *is* my house now, you know. I used to make belts and wallets to sell at market. I could do that again."

"And what about me?"

Beau shrugged, concentrating on the sculpture. "You could do whatever you wanted."

Robert shook his head. "I don't think so," he said. "I think I'd rather stay in this country."

"Okay," Beau said. "We'll stay here." He pulled back from his handiwork. "How's that?"

"Looks terrific to me. Maybe you should be an architect or something."

"Maybe. I don't know." The thought of the future seemed to depress him.

And it made Robert suddenly very tired. "Let's go home, Tonto," he said.

Beau nodded and stood.

Robert looked up at him. "Tomorrow night this business with Boyd will all be over," he said. "That will make things easier."

"Yeah, I guess it will." Beau, in a sudden frenzy of movement, kicked the pile of sand down. When that was done, he grabbed Robert's arm and pulled him up. "Home," he said.

Robert looked at the pile of wet sand, then sighed and followed Beau.

18

1

Robert suddenly realized that it had been over
three weeks since his last visit to the gym. Under
normal circumstances, he tried to make it there
twice a week. Of course, his life lately had been far
from normal. God, yes. Which fact, he recognized,
was absolutely no excuse for letting his body fall
into disrepair. It even occurred to him that what was
happening to his body might be seen as a reflection
of what was happening to his whole damned life.

And wasn't *that* a cheerful thought.

In the daylight, he was less concerned about
what Rocco had told him last night. The sunshine
seemed to eradicate the shadows of lurking gun-
men. He pushed aside the second jelly doughnut
that he'd been about to eat for breakfast. "I'm going
to run," he said suddenly.

Beau was eating his third doughnut and reading
an old *Mad* magazine he'd found in a drawer. "Run?
From who?" he said, not looking up.

Robert frowned at him. "Not *from* anybody, stupid. I'm just going to *run*. For my health. I'm getting too damned soft."

Beau looked skeptical at that, but then he nodded agreeably. "Okay. I'll run, too."

That wasn't exactly what Robert had in mind, but he didn't say so. Besides, maybe it was a good idea to keep the kid close to him. Just in case somebody was looking for him, it wouldn't be a good idea to have him stumble across Beau alone.

The idea of a solitary and simple run immediately got complicated, of course. Beau needed to borrow shorts and a T-shirt. He came out of the john in the somewhat oversized clothes looking like a recent refugee from some Third World nation. Only the brand-new Nikes, bought to replace the ones stolen the other night, fit properly.

They went out to the patio and Robert showed him some warming-up and stretching exercises. When Robert pulled his sweatband on, Beau immediately decided that he needed one, too, so that meant some more time spent searching through drawers until another one was found.

Finally they set off. Robert kept the pace slow enough so that neither one of them would get winded. After a few minutes, he started getting into the rhythm of the run and it felt good. Maybe, if he worked on getting back into shape really fast, the rest of his life would fall back into place at the same time. It was worth a try, anyway.

Keeping pace at his side, Beau had been quiet for about as long as he could. "So tonight is it, huh?"

"Yeah. Tonight is it."

"What happens then?"

They ran in place at a corner, waiting for the traffic to pass. "Nothing happens. I'm done chasing around after Boyd, that's all. Life can get back to normal." They started across the street.

"Can it? What about me? The detective and all?"

"I don't know what about you, Tonto." He remembered his conversation with Marcello in Vegas. "You're a complication."

"I'm sorry."

They parted to get around a woman pushing a baby in a stroller. "Don't sweat it," Robert said when they were side by side again. "I can handle it."

Well, that sounded tough and competent.

And why the fuck not? He *was* tough and he *was* competent. To hell with Rocco and his warnings. To hell with old man Epstein and his hired dick. This wasn't some two-bit hood they were dealing with. Robert Turchek had a rep and it was a rep he'd earned honestly.

Beau came to a stop suddenly and pointed. "Ice cream," he said. "All this running makes me hungry. How about it?"

"We've only been running fifteen fucking minutes," he said.

"I could *really* use some ice cream," Beau wheedled.

Robert wanted to argue some more; they were out here to run, for Chrissake, not to pig out on Haagen-Dazs. But then he gave up and followed Beau into the crowded little shop.

Shit. You'd think he had adopted the damned kid or something. Here he was again, taking care, just as during all those years with Andy. Taking care, and because of that, he couldn't get on with things the way he wanted to. Not that he had ever begrudged Andy the time and trouble; not at all. And, he admitted only to himself, he didn't really mind all the trouble Beau was causing him. But it did sometimes seem that things were moving in sort of a vicious circle.

He ordered extra hot fudge on his ice cream, just to help even up the score with fate a little.

2

George McBain, Boyd's parole officer, was home sick with the flu, but when Gar called, he agreed to a visit. The house Gar parked in front of was a tidy bungalow on a quiet side street in Glendale.

A plump white-haired woman opened the door to his knock. She didn't seem to approve of this intrusion into her husband's convalescence, but her greeting was polite as she led him into the tiny living room.

McBain himself was as plump and white-haired as his wife. He was watching a nature documentary on TV, but he muted the sound as Gar came into the room. "Mr. Sinclair," he said, half-rising to shake hands.

"Sorry to bother you when you're sick," Gar apologized, sinking into a worn overstuffed chair.

"Hell, I'm okay," McBain said. His wife had left the room and he leaned forward. "If it was left up to me, I'd be back at work, but you know how it is with wives."

Gar nodded. "Well, this is a real crisis or I wouldn't have come."

McBain picked up a pipe and began to fill it. "You're the detective looking for the Epstein boy, right? I saw your name in the paper."

"That's right. And I'm hoping you can help me find him before it's too late."

"If I can help, sure."

"The name of one of your parolees has come up in my investigation. Danny Boyd."

McBain nodded. "Boyd is one of mine, yes. But I don't see him involved in a kidnapping, if that's what you're leading up to."

Gar shook his head. "No. In fact, I don't think that he's necessarily involved directly with Beau at all. I'm really just hoping that he can point me in the right direction. But first I have to talk to him."

"And that's where I come in."

"That's it."

McBain finally got the pipe going and he puffed thoughtfully for a moment. "Okay, I'll give you Boyd's address. If you find out that he knows anything about this, you'll let me know, of course?"

"Of course."

McBain got up and excused himself.

Alone, Gar stared at the voiceless picture on the television screen. A flock, if that was the right word, of penguins was waddling across an ice floe.

Gar was trying his damnedest to work himself into a party mood. This was the anniversary of the date on which he and Mickey had moved in together, so they were celebrating with dinner at Il Giardino's in Beverly Hills. Pasta and then *battuta*, all washed down with a good red wine. It was an evening that they'd planned for weeks.

He wasn't feeling really festive because of the hours he'd spent—wasted—sitting in front of a cheap motel near downtown, waiting for Danny Boyd to show up. Which Boyd never did.

Mickey, of course, looked beautiful and extremely desirable in a very short white dress that sparkled under the lights. Every man in the place had watched her walk across the room to their table. Gar knew that they were all wondering what a woman like that was doing with him.

Well, let them wonder.

The dinner was delicious, and listening to Mickey tell him about her encounter with Mr. Cruise the night before almost took Gar's mind off business. Almost. But he still found himself glancing at his watch frequently, although he tried not to.

During dessert, Mickey finally gave up. "What's the matter, Gar?"

He gave a guilty shrug. "I'm sorry, Mick. It's just this damned case. I can't get it out of my head. I know that something is going to happen tonight, I just *know* it, and I'm scared for Beau." He wasn't quite sure where the hell the word "scared" had come from, but, thinking about it, he didn't change it.

She slowly licked frosting off the spoon, which probably made more than one male in the dining room groan inwardly. "In that case, Sam Spade, maybe you should be out there doing something about it, instead of sitting here."

But he shook his head. "No. We've been looking forward to this. I want to be here."

Mickey fed him some cake from her spoon. That should make the horny males watching them grit their teeth. "I've been looking forward to spending an evening with you, yes. *All* of you. And, frankly, darling, your body is here, but your mind is somewhere else."

"I'm sorry," he said again. He took a sip of coffee to wash the sweet taste of the frosting from his mouth. "Damn it, I don't want to be obsessed by this case."

She laughed softly. "Gee, can you choose your

obsessions? I can't." She patted his hand. "I think you should go. I'll sit here and finish my dessert, maybe have some more coffee, and then catch a cab home."

"I can't do that," he protested, although it was exactly what he wanted to do.

"Of course you can." She leaned closer and whispered, "We'll finish the celebration whenever you get there. No matter how late it is."

"Promise?"

She smiled and he felt a lurching in his gut. "Absolutely."

He felt only a little guilty as he left her sitting there.

There was a light on in Danny Boyd's motel room.

Gar thought about it for a moment, then decided that he'd had enough of this sitting-around-and-waiting shit. It was time for some direct action.

He gave a solid rap on the flimsy motel door, a cop's knock, which an ex-con like Boyd would recognize immediately. It was nearly a minute before the door slowly opened. Danny Boyd was tall, blond, handsome in a rough-hewn way. Clean him up a little and any mother would be glad for her daughter to bring him home to dinner.

"What?" Boyd asked.

"We need to talk, Boyd," Gar said.

"Show me a badge."

"Did I say I was a cop?"

Boyd frowned. "Then who the fuck are you?"

"I'm a private investigator. Trying to find a missing kid named Beau Epstein."

"Never heard of him."

"You have heard of Marnie Dowd, though, right? And Camden Hunt?"

Boyd had started to close the door, but now he paused. "Marnie Dowd is dead," he said.

"And so is Camden Hunt."

A flicker of surprise crossed his face. "Shit, I didn't know that. Guess that explains why he never returned my calls."

"I guess. He was killed in the same way as Marnie. Probably by the same person."

Boyd frowned. "You ain't trying to pin the rap on me, are you? I had no reason to off either of them."

"No, that's not why I'm here. I'm just trying to follow a trail that goes from Dowd and Hunt to you and then maybe to the killer."

"I don't get you."

Gar sighed. "Who do you think might have killed Marnie?"

"Marnie was a hooker," Boyd said. "It could have been a john."

"It was a hit, Boyd."

Boyd shook his head. "Man, I just can't get into this. I don't know nothing about Marnie getting killed or Hunt. I never heard of that Epstein kid." He glanced at his watch. "And I've got things to do. Places to go."

"You might be next on the killer's list, you know," Gar said as the door started closing again.

Boyd paused. "Anybody comes after me, he'll be fucking sorry." The door closed firmly.

Great. Tough prison talk. Boyd was an idiot.

And, Gar knew, the hitman they were dealing with wasn't that stupid.

He went back to his car, swallowed a pain pill, and settled back to wait for Boyd to come out.

Boyd led him to a darkened warehouse down by the docks. Gar drove past the building for half a block or so, then made a U-turn and went back. He parked at the far side of the building. Boyd had already disappeared inside.

Something was going on in the warehouse. There were several other cars—all of them newer and fancier than Boyd's—parked nearby. Gar couldn't really convince himself that whatever Boyd was into here had a damned thing to do with Beau Epstein. But at the same time, he also still had the feeling that something was going to happen tonight, and since Boyd was all he had, this was where he'd stay.

He got out of the car and walked around to the rear of the building. After a quick tour of the premises, he stood in the shadows and lit a cigarette. He stood there and thought about the many pleasures he was missing out on by being here rather than at home with Mickey. He wondered, when all was said and done, whether Beau Epstein would appreciate the sacrifice.

Probably not.

It was about thirty minutes before another car appeared, cruising slowly through the lot, its lights off. Gar didn't like that much. The car didn't stop where the others had, but moved on into the shadows. Inside the car, he could see two dark forms in baseball caps. He dropped the cigarette and crushed it out. A surge of adrenaline coursed through him. Just as he'd known it would, something was going to happen. And he was going to be in on it.

A moment later, the door opened and the driver got out, fleetingly illuminated by the inside light. He headed for the building. The passenger stayed put, sliding down into the seat until all Gar could see was the top of the baseball cap.

Now Gar wished that he had a gun. But who went

armed to an anniversary dinner? Or maybe he
should try to find a phone and get some backup. But
it could take him a long time to find a working
phone in this neighborhood. It was pretty stupid of
him to be out here alone, with only his cane.
Unfortunately, it was a little late to be worrying
about that.

Keeping to the darkest edge of the lot, he started
moving toward the newly arrived car. One part of
him wondered if maybe he should do something to
warn Boyd, but hadn't he already tried to do that?
Boyd thought he could take care of himself, fine.
Gar's only job was to find Beau Epstein.

He was willing to bet that the slouched-down
figure in the passenger seat was the missing boy.

Finally, he reached the car from the rear and
peered in. Beau—if it was actually him—was staring
straight ahead, both hands over his ears. Assuming
that the door was unlocked, Gar figured that he
could reach in, grab the boy, and be gone before—

His silent planning got no further, because all of a
sudden there was the unmistakable feeling of cold,
hard metal being pressed against the back of his head.

"Move, motherfucker, and you're dead." The
voice was quiet, almost gentle, and for that reason
all the more threatening.

"Okay," Gar said. "I'm not armed. All I want is the
kid. That's Beau Epstein in there, right?"

"Shut up," the voice said.

Gar realized that the boy in the car had turned
around and was watching them. He couldn't get a
good look at the face, but he was even more sure
now that it was Beau.

The boy shook his head, not at him, but at whomever it was with the gun.

Gar thought he heard the man sigh, then, abruptly,

his cane was kicked out from underneath him. He lost his balance and almost fell flat, catching himself at the last minute on the car. It was a hell of a time to be embarrassed, but he could feel heat flooding his face.

"Without looking back," the quiet voice said, "I want you to walk away. One glance back and you're dead. Is that clear?"

"Very clear."

"I'm glad. Now move."

He did as ordered, leaving the cane where it was, and moving slowly. Just as he finally reached the end of the lot, he heard the other car drive away quickly. Stumbling as he went, Gar finally made it to his own car, and managed to be after them in only a moment. It wasn't clear what he planned to do if he caught them, but having come this close, he just couldn't let them get away without doing something.

The Saab ahead of him turned off onto a side street. Gar, remembering a shortcut, headed through an alley in pursuit, punching the accelerator.

The plan worked perfectly. Sort of. His car collided with the Saab at the end of the alley.

His car did a slow bounce off the other and then died. The Saab, meanwhile, faltered, did a sort of half-spin as if the driver had lost control momentarily, and then took off.

All he could do was sit and watch it go.

And wish to hell he'd noticed the license number.

Saul Epstein took a gulp of his brandy. "You actually saw my grandson. Is that what you're telling me?"

"Yes. I'm sure the boy I saw was Beau."

"But you didn't get him."

"Not yet."

Epstein was quiet for a minute. "And you believe that he is actually in the company of this killer willingly?"

Gar shrugged. "It's hard to say. All I know for sure is, he was sitting in the car alone. He made no attempt to escape. Of course, for all I know, he might have been tied up. Or drugged. Whatever."

Epstein nodded and sipped more brandy. "Perhaps I should start to make some arrangements for Beau's return."

"Arrangements?" What was he going to do? Throw the kid a "Welcome Home" party?

Epstein set his snifter down decisively. "I want to have a doctor on hand. A psychiatrist. To offer help. And also to prepare the groundwork for a legal defense, if that should prove necessary."

Gar was reminded suddenly that he was dealing not only with a distraught grandfather, but also with a very powerful man. A man who knew how to pull all of the strings to get what he wanted. Under normal circumstances, it was the kind of abuse of privilege that would annoy him. But in this case, he wanted whatever it took for Beau to come out of this safe and whole. "Maybe you should do that," he said.

He downed the rest of his brandy and then finally went home. As promised, Mickey was waiting and they finished the anniversary celebration.

He kept one ear attuned to the phone, just in case.

19

1

Beau couldn't seem to stop shaking. And he was afraid that any minute he was going to throw up all over the car. Robert, meanwhile, just kept driving, swearing, and muttering under his breath. Already an enormous bruise was visible where his forehead had hit the steering wheel in the collision. He hadn't really blacked out, but he drove like a man half-drunk or something.

Beau swallowed hard, tasting bile and fear.

The car stopped at a red light.

"Can we go home now, Robbie?" Beau asked softly.

Robert glared at him. "What're you? Dumb or something? No, we can't go home now. That guy saw the car, which means he maybe got the license number. Right this minute, the cops are probably camping on my front porch. I figure that asshole with the cane was the detective your fucking grandfather hired. You beginning to get the picture here, dummy? No, Beau, we can't go home now." He made a sharp left turn, causing several other motorists to blow their horns angrily, which he ignored or maybe even didn't hear. "In fact, I can probably never go home again."

"I'm sorry," Beau said. "This is all my fault, isn't it?"

"Damned right it is."

Beau shut up then, figuring that Robert was only going to get mad at anything he said, so it was better to say nothing. If he was lucky, Robert wouldn't push him out of the car here in the middle of Sunset Boulevard.

They rode around for nearly another hour in silence, before Robert finally pulled into the parking lot of a run-down motel in a neighborhood Beau didn't know at all. Robert drove way around to the back so that the car couldn't be seen from the street and turned the engine off. Then he leaned back against the seat with a sigh. "Christ, my head is killing me." He poked at his right side carefully. "And I think I must have bruised a rib or something."

Beau didn't say anything.

Robert glanced at him. "You all right?"

"Yeah. My seat belt was fastened."

"That's terrific." Robert pushed and shoved at the smashed-in door until, with a grinding noise, it opened slowly. "Well, you just sit here all safe and sound and seat-belted, while I go get us a room."

"Okay, Robbie."

He could see into the motel office as Robert, moving slowly and carefully, went inside and talked briefly to the old man behind the counter. The man handed Robert a key and pointed. Then Robert stepped back outside and waved at Beau. Unsnapping the seat belt, Beau got out of the car and followed Robert up a flight of stairs.

Outside room 203, Robert handed him the key. "Open the damned door, will you?" he said in a hoarse voice.

Beau hurried to do so and they stepped inside. Robert leaned against the wall immediately, his eyes closed. Beau switched on the light and stared at his pale, sweaty face. "Robbie? You don't look so good."

"I don't feel so good either, Tonto," Robert said. With that, he pitched forward and landed on the floor, out cold.

Beau, stunned, just stared at him for several seconds. Then he finally went into action. He managed to haul Robert's dead weight up onto the bed. Once that was accomplished, he removed the unconscious man's shoes and socks. It took more of an effort to slip him out of his jacket and, carefully, the holster and gun. He unbuttoned Robert's shirt and opened it to look at the bruised stomach. Guilt flashed through him; it *was* all his fault, and he couldn't blame Robert for being mad. He couldn't even blame Robert if he kicked him out as soon as he woke up. He watched to be sure that Robert's chest was moving up and down steadily, which he figured was a very good sign. Not like when his parents were shot. He could still remember crawling out from under the wagon where he and his friends had been hiding during the attack, crawling out, and running to Rachel and Jonathan's bodies. It was the terrible *stillness* he would never forget. Death was so still.

When he was absolutely sure that Robert was breathing okay, Beau went into the bathroom. He ran some cold water over a skimpy washcloth, squeezed it out, sort of, and took it back to the bed. Robert didn't move as he plastered the cloth to his forehead. That seemed to be the best he could do at the moment.

He perched gingerly on the edge of the bed, staring hard at Robert's face.

Next door, a man and a woman were having a very loud argument in Spanish. Beau half-listened to the fight, which seemed to be about the equal division of some coke, at least when it started, but then got sidetracked onto their sexual preferences.

Pretty soon, they started screwing, which was just as noisy as the fighting had been.

It seemed to be a very long time before Robert finally stirred and then slowly opened his eyes, which looked blankly at Beau. He leaned down close. "Robbie? You okay?"

Robert blinked a couple of times and recognition came into his gaze. "Yeah. I guess. Shit." He struggled to sit up. The washcloth fell to the bed.

Beau picked it up and twisted it nervously. "Maybe we better call a doctor or something, huh?"

Robert gave him another one of those Jesus-how-can-you-be-so-stupid? looks. "I *don't* think so," he said. Then he flinched. "Christ, my head is still hurting."

"You probably got like a concussion or something."

"I'll be okay."

Beau sat down again carefully. "I'm really sorry. If it wasn't for me, this wouldn't have happened. You must be really mad at me."

Robert rested back against the shaky headboard. "No, Tonto, I'm not mad," he said wearily. "Actually, it should be the other way around. I think you're probably in the deep shit right along with me now. I should have let that damned detective take you."

Beau folded and unfolded the damp cloth. "I'm glad you didn't kill him, Robbie."

"Yeah, well, I'll probably live to regret that. Shit, I regret it already. But the paper said the guy was an ex-cop. I already got enough people pissed at me. But I should have let him take you."

Beau didn't say anything.

Robert sighed. "But since I didn't do that, and you're still here, you might as well be useful. Go out and find me some fucking aspirin or something. And coffee, black coffee. There should be some-place across the street."

"Okay."

"You have money?"

"Yeah."

Robert looked at him for a moment. "Be careful."

Beau wondered if maybe Robert thought he wouldn't come back. "I'll be careful," he said. "And I won't be long."

"Right."

Beau got to the door and then paused. "You stay right there in that damned bed," he ordered.

"Sure thing, tough guy." Robert tried to smile, but it came out as more of a grimace.

Beau made sure to lock the door as he left.

He walked nearly two blocks before finding an all-night drugstore, where he picked up some extra-strength painkillers and an ice bag. Then, on the way back to the motel, he hit a McDonald's and ordered the coffee, along with fries and two Big Macs. And two hot apple pies.

While he was waiting for the food, he watched two cops who were in a booth having supper. Amazingly, he wasn't scared of them anymore. He didn't know whether that was because he was really getting braver, like Robert was, or whether it was simply that a person could only get so afraid before it just sort of leveled off. Maybe he was merely too tired to be scared.

Whatever.

Beau wondered idly what would happen if he just walked over to those cops, told them who he was, and that he'd been kidnapped. He'd probably be a freaking hero or something.

Not that he would ever do such a thing, of course. How could he just abandon Robert, who was counting on him? It was sort of an interesting sensation, feeling needed. Beau had never felt that way before. His folks loved him, sure, but they hadn't *needed* him. And Saul, who owned the whole damned world, it seemed like, certainly didn't need him. Didn't want him, either. All Saul wanted was to have Jonathan back again.

But Robbie needed him.

He grabbed the bag of food, averted his face from the cops as he passed them, and left the restaurant.

2

Robert heard the key turn in the lock, but he couldn't quite summon up the strength to sit up or even open his eyes immediately.

So the kid had come back. He didn't know whether to be relieved or dismayed.

"Robbie?" Beau whispered.

"I'm awake," he said.

"I got you some pills. And the coffee you wanted."

"Okay." Robert gritted his teeth and managed to sit up. Beau was standing by the bed, holding several capsules in one hand and a cardboard cup filled with coffee in the other. Robert took them from him, swallowing all four capsules at once.

Beau sat at the small table and opened a bag. "I got some food, too, if you're hungry."

Robert wasn't, but he thought that maybe getting

something into his stomach would help. He waved off Beau's offer of assistance and got himself over to the table. Beau was already eating enthusiastically. Robert nibbled on a couple of fries and took a small bite of the burger. As he chewed carefully, he was aware of Beau watching him with a frown. "We'll be okay," Robert said.

"Sure we will." Beau smiled and ate quietly for a moment. "Robbie," he said then, "did you get him? Boyd, I mean?"

"No, damn it. I would have. It was a fucking perfect setup. He comes out of the game, I off him. Nobody else in the game cares. Perfect. But because that asshole detective showed up, it didn't happen."

"So what now?"

After forcing down one more bite, Robert pushed the hamburger aside. "I'm going to bed," he said. "We'll figure all of this out in the morning."

Beau jumped up. "I'll go get some ice for your head."

Robert just nodded and stretched out on the bed again, wishing that the room would stop spinning. He was only vaguely aware of Beau's quiet return. The cold bag was placed carefully on his head. It felt good, but he couldn't even say so. Every time he woke up over the next few hours, Robert was aware of Beau's presence nearby in the darkness. Mostly the kid seemed to be watching television, keeping the volume turned very low.

It was probably an indication of just how much trouble Robert was in that he found being watched over like that pretty reassuring.

Finally he woke up and saw some morning sun leaking in through the cheap draperies. Robert stayed very still, staring at the ceiling, as he tried to evaluate his physical condition. Well, he was still alive, but that was about as far as he was willing to go at the moment. It was something.

Beau was sitting on the floor, his head resting on the bed, sound asleep. Robert watched him for a few minutes, then reached out and touched him lightly on the arm.

Beau woke up immediately. "What?" He rubbed his eyes. "Oh, damn, I'm sorry. I didn't mean to fall asleep like that."

"No problem. You're not being paid by the hour."

"How're you feeling, Robbie?"

"Better, thanks."

"Really?"

He shrugged. "How's my head look?"

"There's a lump."

"I'll bet there is." He needed to get into the can, badly, so he accepted Beau's help in getting up from the bed. Once in the bathroom, he avoided looking in the mirror. His whole body felt bruised and stiff. But, crummy as he felt, he knew that there was really no choice. He had to keep moving.

Beau was sitting at the table, eating a cold apple pie when Robert came out. He sat with him, but refused the offer of a share of the pie. His stomach lurched at the thought. He took a deep, careful breath. "Okay," he said. "This is how it is. I'm going to track Boyd down and this time I'll kill him."

Beau was listening, licking at crumbs on his upper lip.

"But things have sort of changed now." He couldn't help giving a short, humorless laugh, even though it hurt like hell. "Hey, things are totally fucked, that's how they are, right, Tonto?"

Beau nodded, but tentatively, as if he didn't think he was going to like what was coming.

"So," Robert said, "you can split." He leaned back in the chair carefully.

"What?" Beau said, forgetting to swallow the last bite of pie.

"I said, you can split. Right now. Before things get any more screwed up than they already are. If that's possible. Take off, kid. Go home. Wherever. Tell the fucking cops whatever you want to or have to in order to save your own ass. I won't stop you."

Beau was staring at him. "I don't want to do that, Robbie. Please. I want to stay with you."

That really wasn't what Robert had expected to hear. He was doing a damned decent thing here and it would be nice to have it appreciated. Instead, he was being looked at like somebody who drowned puppies. "You want to stay with me? Why?"

"Because."

Robert shook his head. "Don't tell me 'because.' That's what a little kid says. 'Because' is not a reason for a man to do something like this."

"Well, maybe I could help. Like last night." His look turned slightly defiant. "I *did* help you last night."

"Yes, you did."

Beau nodded, as if that settled things. "Well, then. I owe you that much."

Robert waved off those words as if they were pesky flies. "Fuck that," he said.

After a moment, Beau pushed his chair back and got up. He walked over to the window, pulled the curtain open a little, and peered out. Then he turned and looked at Robert again. "I guess I sort of love you," he said, sounding combative again. "Like we're brothers or something."

"My brother is dead," Robert said sharply. Almost immediately, he regretted the tone he'd used.

Beau ducked his head for a moment.

"I'm sorry," Robert said. "I shouldn't have said that."

"It's okay. I know he's dead and I'm just . . . well, I'm just a pest you can't get rid of."

"No," Robert said. "That's not true."

"Anyway, my folks are dead, too. You don't have anybody now and neither do I. So maybe we could stay together. Make our own kind of family. You know? Like adoption or something. We could be blood brothers."

Robert didn't say anything right away. Then he shook his head. "Jesus, Beau, haven't you been paying attention to any of this? What do you think is going on?"

Beau walked back to the table, looking at him.

Robert reached out and grabbed Beau's shoulder, shaking him hard. "You think this is some goddamned adventure we're on here? Something out of a freaking paperback book? *Blood brothers?* Huck and Big Jim riding a raft down the fucking Mississippi, maybe?" He stopped, frustrated, and ran a hand through his hair, grimacing at the pain it caused.

Beau pulled away and went to the other side of the room. "I don't know why you're mad at me."

"I'm not," Robert said wearily. "I'm just tired. I'm tired and I don't know what the fuck is going to happen next."

"Please, Robbie, let me stay with you. Whatever is going to happen."

"But that's crazy."

"Yeah, maybe. But I don't care. I just feel good when we're together. Sometimes I'm scared, yeah, but I know you'll take care of me. And I'll help you."

Damn.

Robert didn't know what the hell to do.

Beau just stared at him.

Finally, reluctantly, he nodded. "Okay, Tonto. We'll ride through this together."

"Promise?"

"Sure, I fucking promise."

Beau relaxed visibly. "And I promise, too. I'll hang in, whatever happens."

"Great," Robert muttered.

3

She called again.

Still scared, but at least willing to talk. Only not on the phone, Mr. Sinclair, could they meet? Did he know Joey's on Wilshire?

They could and he did.

The early-lunch crowd was just finishing its first glass of wine when Gar arrived. He took a table near the front and waited, wondering if he would recognize a frightened young woman when she came in. In fact, he did. She was a tall blonde, wearing a big straw hat and dark glasses. Hovering in the entrance, she was obviously scared of something.

Gar caught her eye.

She hesitated, almost bolted from the place, then walked over. "Mr. Sinclair?"

"Yes. And you are—?"

"Just . . . Maureen, that's all."

"Okay, Maureen, sit down."

She did. "I shouldn't be here. If he finds out . . ."

"He won't, at least not from me."

Darryl, their server for the day, ambled by. They both listened to his recitation of the specials. She chose the Exotic Fruit Salad and a glass of French water. Gar picked Joey's Famous Boursin Burger and a beer.

When Darryl had left them, Gar leaned back and stared at her. "Okay, Maureen, what's the story? You know something about Beau Epstein?"

"Yes. At least, I think it was him. His hair . . . the man I'm talking about had cut his hair and changed the color, but I'm pretty sure it was the boy you're looking for."

Gar thought back to the face of the boy he'd seen in the car the night before. Yeah, darken the hair and cut it short and that would be what Beau looked like. "Who is the man?"

Her fingers were knotted on top of the table. "You have to understand, I never thought he'd be involved in something like murder or kidnapping. I just thought . . ."

Darryl brought their drinks.

She squeezed the lime slice and stirred the water with a straw.

"You just thought what?" Gar prompted.

"He was exciting. Different from any man I dated before. I guess maybe there was a sort of aura of danger and maybe that was one of the attractions. And he's very good-looking. Sexy, if you know what I mean."

Gar just nodded.

"I thought maybe he really cared about me. Bobby was always a gentleman. There aren't too many of those around these days."

"Bobby?" Gar said.

"Yes. He came into the restaurant where I work one night and we just talked. Then he came back the next night and asked me out." She picked up one of the whole-wheat rolls and neatly cut it in half. After a moment's debate, she apparently decided against butter and nibbled the roll as it was.

Gar swallowed some more beer and tried to keep his impatience hidden. If she couldn't tell this her own way, she might not tell it at all. "So you and this Bobby are seeing each other?"

"Well, not anymore. After his brother died a few weeks ago, he just dropped me. No calls or anything. I mean, I didn't even know he had a brother, isn't that weird?"

"You know anything about the brother?"

"No. Except that Bobby said he was murdered."

The food arrived. They both started eating and it wasn't until Gar was halfway through the burger that she spoke again.

"So when I didn't hear from him, I got sort of worried, you know? I decided to go by his house and just make sure he was okay. And if he was just trying to dump me, then I had the right to hear it face-to-face, don't you think?"

"Definitely."

"Well, he was okay. Fine, he said. But he was in the middle of cutting this boy's hair. Weird, huh?"

"Did he call the boy by name?"

She nodded. "But not his real name. Called him Tonto. How about that? Tonto."

"Okay, Maureen. Who is this guy?"

She picked through the remaining fruit with her fork. "Robert Turchek."

The name meant nothing to Gar. "Do you know anything else about him?"

"Not really." She looked up. "His address, if that would help."

It would help, yeah, although there was little chance that this guy Turchek would be sitting in his living room waiting for them to show up.

Maureen looked up at him. "I hope you find the boy," she said softly. "But I really hope you don't have to kill Bobby. He's not all bad, you know? Even though I'm scared of him, he's not all bad."

Gar didn't say anything. Turchek must be a real charmer. He could hardly wait to meet the bastard.

4

Beau sat on the bed and stared at the television. The volume was down low again, because Robert was on the phone. He was trying to track down Danny Boyd.

Finally he hung up and came over to the bed. "The son of a bitch has split," he said. "Someone told him it was me on his ass and he took off."

"Where'd he go?"

"New fucking York."

Beau handed Robert the cigarette he'd been smoking. "What are we going to do?"

Robert took a long drag and handed the cigarette back.

"We're going to the Big Apple."

"I've never been there."

"It's big and dirty and noisy. But I like it."

He stretched out next to Beau. "There's one more thing I have to tell you, Tonto, before you sign on for this trip."

"What?"

"It looks like somebody—maybe Marcello in Vegas or maybe half a dozen different bastards—is trying to shut me down."

Beau just looked at him. "What's that mean?"

"Somebody wants me dead, kid."

There wasn't anything Beau could say to that.

20

1

Wally Dixon stretched his feet out on top of the desk and glared at him. "This is something new in your job description?" he said. "Taking on mob hitmen with nothing but your fucking cane?"

"I sincerely hope not," Gar said. "It was not my finest hour."

Wally snorted.

"But don't forget, I did find out the guy's name. Which is more than you people have been able to do."

They were waiting for whatever dope the computers—local, state and/or federal—might kick back on Robert Turchek. So far, the information had been slim. Turchek led, it seemed, a very low-profile kind of life. Most people had never heard of him, and those who had were not inclined to talk, either because of whatever code they happened to live by (most of which codes included strong injunctions against talking to the cops) or because they were obviously scared shitless of Robert Turchek. Having encountered the man once, and heard that quiet, deadly voice, Gar could understand that.

"Instead of just sitting around here with our thumbs up our asses waiting for somebody to tell us something that won't help a damned bit anyway," Gar said finally, "why don't we make a run by Turchek's place?"

They tossed around the notion of getting a warrant to search the house, an idea that appealed to nobody, and then came up with a nice compromise. Gar would actually be the one to break and enter, in his search for the boy. Wally, a good cop just doing his duty, was almost obligated to investigate. It was maybe on the edge of propriety, but they had always operated that way.

Just to keep things legal (on the surface anyway), they took separate cars to the address the mysterious Maureen had provided.

The small stucco bungalow was something of a surprise; it didn't look like the kind of place a hotshot paid killer would live in. It just looked like a nice quiet home. Wally walked around the tiny front yard, which could have used some landscaping, pretending not to notice as Gar jimmied the lock on the front door.

If they had expected to find an arsenal or maybe even a couple of bodies stacked in the hallway, they were disappointed. "A very tidy fellow," Wally commented as they surveyed the living room. Nothing was out of place—magazines were neatly stacked on the coffee table with an opened copy of *Mad* on top, videotapes were alphabetized, and even the blanket and pillow that seemed to indicate someone had been using the couch as a bed lately were folded and tucked in the corner.

"Wonder if he does windows," Gar said.

"He may have to," Wally said as they walked into the kitchen. "From the rumors on the street, his bosses are not too happy these days. No names, of course, but it's a good bet Turchek is the one everybody's whispering about."

Gar nodded. "I got that impression in Vegas, talking to Marcello. Those guys don't like it when an employee strays from the straight and narrow."

"Turchek must have more balls than me," Wally said. "I wouldn't want those boys mad at me."

"Maureen says he's full of charm. And very sexy."

"Oh, good. That should make him real popular when he's doing life inside."

Gar stepped out the back door onto a small patio. He glanced around, then peeked inside the trash can. "Looks like Maureen was right about the haircut," he said. "Hair clippings. And a bottle of hair dye, dark brown."

He went back inside. There were no dirty dishes sitting in the sink, no overflowing wastebaskets. "This is not very interesting," he said. "I was sort of hoping to uncover all the secrets of this guy. So far, all we've uncovered is the fact that he makes both of us—and our women—look like pikers in the domestic department."

Wally didn't disagree.

The bedroom was no more illuminating. All the drawers held just what you would expect them to—clean underwear, socks, shirts, all folded, of course, and organized. The closet was the same; Turchek was a snappy dresser. Of course. Gar was beginning to think that he wouldn't like this guy much even if he *weren't* a killer.

Only one corner of the bedroom didn't fit the pattern. A chair sitting there was piled with clothes, all of which looked new, some worn only once or twice. Gar fingered one of the brightly colored T-shirts. "Well, at least he dresses his hostage well," he said.

Dixon was on his hands and knees going through the neatly aligned shoes on the closet floor. "Hostage?" he said in a muffled voice. "Is that what you think the Epstein kid is?"

"Until it's proven otherwise, yes."

Dixon stuck his head out briefly. "How many hostages get to go on shopping sprees at the Gap?" he said, indicating the pile of new clothes. "I have three kids, remember? There must be over three hundred dollars' worth of clothes there."

Gar shrugged. "Doesn't mean a thing. Remember Patty Hearst? And there have been other cases, hostages identifying with their captors, almost bonding with them. And some of those people weren't lost, lonely kids like Beau Epstein."

Dixon made a rude noise that was probably supposed to be an opinion.

Gar wondered if he'd been that closed-minded when he was a cop. Probably.

"Aha" came Wally's voice from deep inside the closet.

"Aha what?"

He crawled out, holding a metal box in both hands. It was locked, and so Gar was called into service again. It took him only a few moments to get it open. Inside were three loaded handguns just like the ones found at so many murder scenes.

Wally locked the box again and put it right back where it had been. He didn't want to blow any court case later by introducing illegally obtained evidence. Time enough to come back with a warrant later.

There was one room with a closed door, and after they left Turchek's bedroom, Gar opened that door. "Shit," he said. "What happened in here?"

Wally nudged a Louisville slugger with his foot. "Looks like somebody went to town with this."

It was a puzzle that they couldn't solve at the moment.

Gar carefully locked the door as they left the house. He hadn't learned anything very helpful, at least in a concrete sense. There was, however, something in the very neatness of the place, the sense of strict order, that made Gar worry a little, especially when contrasted with the destruction of the one small bedroom. The mind, the personality, that could produce both those states was a mind that had to be reckoned with. Turchek, as if he hadn't already realized it, was a powerful adversary. Which seemed a strangely personal way of putting it. As if all of this were just some private war between Robert Turchek and Gar Sinclair. With the prize, apparently, Beau Epstein.

They stood on the porch and he had a cigarette. "Boyd is still the key," Gar said. "We have to find him and that will lead us to Turchek."

"You don't think he'll give that up now?"

Gar thought about that soft voice again. "No. I don't think he'll give it up. Not as long as Boyd is still alive."

"And neither will you, right?"

"No."

"That's what I figured. Gareth Sinclair, Knight in Shining Armor. Riding to the rescue again."

"Fuck you," Gar said, starting down the front steps.

"Watch yourself. And carry more than that damned cane, willya?"

Gar patted the gun under his arm to reassure Wally and kept moving toward his car.

The phone rang while they were having dinner. Mickey looked at him, her brows raised, but Gar shook his head. "I'll get it," he said.

It was Wally.

"Tell me you found Turchek," Gar said hopefully. "You found the bastard, he's sitting in jail, and the kid is safe at home with Grandpa."

"Would that I could," Wally replied. "But that would mean I had done your job for you and I know you'd miss the challenge."

"Fuck the challenge," Gar muttered. "So what is the bad news?"

"Actually, I think this could be called good news. Or, anyway, interesting news."

"Yeah?"

"We don't know where the hell Turchek is, but we do know where Boyd is. Will that help?"

"It should."

"We checked out the airlines and found out that Danny Boyd caught a flight for New York City. He has a sister there."

"Doesn't that violate his parole?"

"Oh, yes. But surprisingly, the powers that be in the department are not willing to send anybody off after him."

"Which is where I come in."

"Well, you did say that to find Turchek we needed to stay on Boyd."

"Okay," Gar said. Wally gave him the sister's name, but he didn't have an address. "I'll be in touch."

He hung up and went back to the table. Mickey was still eating. "I guess I have to go to New York," Gar said glumly, picking up his fork and staring at the pasta on his plate.

"When?"

"Soon as I can get on a flight. I'll call when we're done."

He hated flying.

Not that he was frightened of it, but it was just such a pain. Getting to the airport. Hanging around the airport when your flight was delayed. Getting into one of the damned little seats on the plane. And then finding out that you're squeezed in between a hot-blooded divorcee on one side and a Moonie on the other.

He wasn't looking forward to it.

He started to eat again.

There was a red-eye flight leaving at midnight and he got a reservation over the phone. He threw some things into an overnight bag and then went with Mickey to walk the dog.

"If I don't pull this off," he said, watching Spock run ahead of them, "maybe I should get out of the business."

"Are you serious?" Mickey said.

"I think so. I mean, my track record lately isn't so great."

"You're talking about Tammi McClure, aren't you?"

He nodded.

"Gar, that girl had problems you couldn't be expected to deal with. You're a detective, not a shrink."

"But there must have been something I could do. A young girl that desperate . . ." He shook his head. "There must have been something I could do, but I don't have a goddamned idea what it was. I let her down."

"Are you talking about Tammi McClure or Jessica Sinclair?" Mickey asked quietly.

Gar looked at her sharply. "You going to psycho-analyze me, are you?"

"No, of course not. But I wish you could just stop being so down on yourself. Think about all the kids that you have saved."

"All the ones I save aren't the ones I wake up thinking about in the middle of the night."

"I know."

"I don't want to be waking up for the rest of my life thinking about Beau Epstein."

Mickey didn't say anything.

After a moment, he whistled for the dog and they turned back toward the house. It was time to head for the airport.

2

Robert filled a plastic cup with lukewarm water—whether you turned on the hot or cold tap, all you got was lukewarm water—and washed four more capsules down his throat. He'd lost count of how many of the damned things he'd taken over the last couple of days. Too many, for sure, he knew that. When this latest batch seemed to have settled in his stomach, he leaned forward to peer at his bruise in the cracked, streaked mirror. His eyes looked a little funny, even to him, spacey or something. Maybe he really did have a concussion. The way things had gone lately, that wouldn't come as any big surprise.

Getting out of L.A. had been a nightmare.

They'd left the damaged Saab right where it was

behind the motel and walked several blocks to a cheapo rental place. Robert fell back on contingency plans made a long time ago but which, until now, had never been necessary. Fake ID—charge card and driver's license in the name of William Russell—made it possible for him to get a car. The next stop was one of the banks where he kept a safe-deposit box, again under the name of Russell, to retrieve enough cash to see them through the immediate future. And that was a cheerful phrase, wasn't it? It made him wonder how much of a future they had beyond an immediate one.

LAX was a little tricky.

Because he figured anybody looking for them would be looking for a man and a boy together, they separated temporarily. With cash in hand, they hit different ticket agents and paid for one-way fares to New York. Beau went first, nervously, but the harried woman behind the counter didn't pay any more attention to him than was absolutely necessary. When Beau ducked back to where he was waiting, Robert saw what seat "John Young" was in and got the adjoining seat for William Russell.

Then it was just a matter of waiting the two hours until flight time. Those had to be two of the longest hours in Robert's life.

Once they were finally on the plane, he took several pain pills and passed out, vaguely hearing Beau tell the flight attendant that the bruise on his head was from a recent automobile accident.

He didn't really wake up until they were landing at La Guardia. Usually in New York, he stayed at the Parker-Meridian, but it seemed like a very good idea to avoid all the usual places, so here they were in this pisshole on Eighth Avenue.

He sighed and walked back into the other room.

Beau was standing at the window, drinking a can of
7-UP as he watched the midday traffic below. He
turned around as Robert dropped onto the rock-hard
bed. "How're you feeling?"

"Like hell. Now I think I've got a fever."

Beau walked over and rested the back of his hand
against Robert's cheek. "Yeah. You do feel sort of
hot."

"I'd have to die to feel better, I think." But, as
rotten as he was feeling, there was still work to be
done. He reached for the phone and hauled it onto
the bed with him. It took several moments of careful thought before he could recall the number he
needed. After six rings, a woman answered. She
sounded angry over something. Probably life. "Corley there?" he asked.

"Yeah, hold on." She dropped the receiver with a
crash that made his ears ring even more than they
already were.

Robert rested back against the wall and held out
his hand. Beau gave him the can of soda. He took a
long gulp and then handed it back.

"Yeah?" The man didn't sound any more cheerful
than the woman had.

"This Corley?"

"Who the fuck wants to know?"

"This is Robert. From L.A."

There was a pause. "I remember you," Corley
said then. "Why are you calling me?"

"I just hit town and I need to purchase some
equipment."

"What kind of equipment?"

Robert watched Beau pace the perimeter of the
small square room. "Something good for distance
work." He was worried that by this time there was
no way he'd be able to get as close to Boyd as he

usually did for a job. It didn't really matter, though, because he was sure that Boyd already knew why he was going to die. "Nothing too fancy," he said to Corley. "I'm not a goddamned expert in those things."

Corley gave a nasty little laugh. "Right. You like to get right up close to a guy and then blow his fucking brains out, don't you?"

Robert gave that crack exactly the response it deserved.

Corley turned businesslike again. "When do you need the merchandise?"

"Today sometime. As soon as possible. I need to be able to move fast when the time comes."

Corley whistled softly. "You don't want much, do you?"

"I'll pay."

"You sure as hell will." Corley was quiet for a moment. "Soonest I can get to you is ten tonight."

Robert figured that, since he didn't have any idea in hell where Boyd was yet, ten that night would be fine. "Okay." He gestured to Beau for something to write with.

Beau quickly found a ballpoint pen and some paper in the desk drawer and brought them over to the bed.

Corley gave Robert an address, which he scribbled on the hotel stationery. "Ten tonight, then? Oh, and bring me something small and cheap, too," he added, wishing for the Magnum left back in L.A.

Corley grunted and hung up.

Beau moved the phone back to the nightstand for him. "How are you going to find Boyd, anyway?"

"I'll find him, don't worry. A snake like that only has a few rocks to hide under, even in a city this big."

Beau nodded.

Robert slid down into the pillow and closed his eyes. "You wanna go see the fucking Statue of Liberty or something?" he mumbled. "We could do that maybe, then look for Boyd."

"No," Beau said. "You better just get some sleep."

"Yeah, okay. I'll sleep. We can play fucking tourist after Boyd is taken care of."

"Whatever," Beau said.

A slow blackness was creeping over Robert and he let it come. Some distant part of his mind was vaguely aware of Beau sitting carefully on the other side of the bed and that was the last thing Robert knew.

Beau let Robert sleep for hours. He even dozed a little himself before getting up from the bed and watching the traffic some more. He watched some television, keeping the volume low again. Finally, when his stomach began to growl, he ran down to the deli six floors below for some food.

The deli was crowded and the fat man behind the counter yelled at him to hurry up and decide what he wanted. Beau settled for a ham on rye, kosher dill on the side, with a cream soda. He took the food back upstairs and sat watching Robert as he ate. It was sort of scary to see how pale and sweaty Robert looked. How vulnerable he seemed. *Vulnerable*, that was the word. A good word, and one that Beau had never understood completely until that moment.

He chewed the sandwich, which was very good, slowly and listened to the shallow sound of Robert's breathing.

When it was a few minutes before eight, he

leaned over the bed and touched Robert lightly on the arm. "Hey, Robbie? Robbie?"

Robert's eyes flew open. For just a second his expression was filled with what looked like fear, then he blinked and managed a faint smile. "Hi," he said.

"You're supposed to meet that guy Corley at ten," Beau said.

"Yeah, yeah, right, right. Thanks, Tonto." He sat up, swaying a little.

Beau kept a firm hold on him until he was steady, then Robert walked into the bathroom and bent over the sink to splash tepid water into his face. He cleared his throat a couple of times and spit.

"Robbie," Beau said from the doorway, "if I ask you something, you won't get mad, will you?"

Robert was drying his face on the coarse towel. "I don't have the energy to get mad. What do you want to ask?"

Beau looked at the floor for a moment, wanting to phrase the question just right. "Would it be so terrible, really, to just forget this whole thing? Would it?"

Robert threw the towel into the corner and looked at him. "You want to crap out on me now, Tonto, is that it?"

Damn. Beau bit his lip. Robert had taken the question wrong, just as he'd been afraid would happen. "No," he said quickly. "That's not what I meant at all." He hit the wall with his fist once and then again. "Crap out? How could I do that? If you say we go through with it, then I'm okay with that. All I'm saying is, it might be a good idea to stop now."

Robert just shook his head.

"But you're sick," Beau said desperately.

"I'll be fine." Robert pushed by him and went back into the other room. "I'm going to Brooklyn. You fucking coming with me or what?"

"Yeah, sure, Robbie."

Robert opened the door and waved him through. Beau went without saying anything else.

Corley was already eating when they reached the Chinese restaurant. Before they approached the table, Robert paused to take a deep breath and straighten his shoulders. Then he moved forward briskly, followed by Beau. "Corley," he said in greeting.

The stocky, ruddy-faced man barely glanced up from his bowl of noodles. "I was beginning to think you weren't coming."

"Ever try to get a cab to come to fucking Brooklyn?" Robert said in a surly voice. "Suddenly everybody was going off duty and heading the other fucking way. But I'm here now." Robert sat and nodded Beau into the third chair.

Corley noticed him and evinced just a touch of curiosity. "That your kid?" he said through a mouthful of noodles.

"No" was all the explanation Robert gave him.

A waiter scurried over and poured them tea. Robert decided that maybe one reason he felt so shitty was that he hadn't really eaten since . . . well, he couldn't actually remember the last time. He scanned the menu quickly and decided on cashew chicken. "You want something?" he asked Beau.

"Sweet-and-sour pork, please," Beau said in the polite, quiet voice he always seemed to use when they were in the company of other people.

When the waiter was gone, Corley took a gulp of beer from the bottle and smirked. "You in some kind of trouble, are you, Robert?"

Robert kept his face expressionless. "Trouble? No, of course not. What kind of trouble could I be in?" Except for the FBI and some private cop on my tail, a few so-called friends who want me to disappear, and a killer headache, what kind of trouble? "I just need what I need, Corley, that's all."

"Funny." Corley's chin had a coating of grease from the noodles that trailed out of his mouth with each bite. "That's not what I heard."

Robert poured some more of the hot, slightly bitter tea for himself and then for Beau. "Just what is it you heard?" he asked carefully.

"That you were definitely in trouble. It seems like a lot of people aren't too happy with you at the moment." He smirked again; Corley was a man it was easy to hate. "The golden boy is a little tarnished." His eyes, which were somewhat more intelligent than you might expect, focused on Robert's face. "I even heard that maybe there's a contract out on the number-one contract man himself."

"Don't worry about it," Robert said flatly. He glanced at Beau, who was listening intently. And frowning. Great, spook the kid some more; that was all he needed. He winked at him, and after a second, Beau smiled in response. "Corley, you ever know me not to do what has to be done?"

"Nope. So far, you're pretty much perfect, I'll give you that."

"Fine."

Corley finished his meal, used the sleeve of his shirt as a napkin, then gestured toward a Bloomingdale's shopping bag that sat on the floor by his feet. "The merchandise is in there."

"Okay. Both pieces?"

"Right. And ammo for both."

"Good."

Corley slid a small piece of paper across the table. "This is the price."

Robert unfolded the paper and glanced at the figure written there. "A little steep, isn't it?"

Corley shrugged. "Hey, you wanted it fast. And you said you'd pay."

"Yeah, yeah." Robert took an envelope from his pocket and handed it over to the man. "When you count this, you'll see that you owe me twenty bucks change."

Corley went to the men's room to do his accounting.

"What an asshole," Robert said, shaking his head.

The waiter finally brought their food. Beau stirred his sweet-and-sour pork thoughtfully. "You're very good," he said.

"Very good at what?"

Beau shrugged. "At what you do. Nobody could tell that you feel so shitty. Nobody but me, of course. Corley must think that you're right on top of things."

"I am right on top of things," Robert said. "Don't you forget that. But, anyway, that's the first rule of life. Just like the TV commercial says. Never let 'em see you sweat. You remember that, Tonto."

"I'll remember, Robbie."

Corley came back from the can. He paused only long enough to drop a twenty on the table and then disappeared.

Robert smirked, put the twenty back into his pocket, and picked up his chopsticks. "Eat up," he said. "We have a busy night ahead of us."

3

First things first.

They needed a car.

Robert knew a guy, he said, who would supply them with one, even at this hour. There was no way of knowing what it would be, of course, your basic transportation or maybe a pimpmobile. But beggars couldn't be choosers, right?

Right, Beau agreed quickly. He wasn't going to argue about anything, not now. Robert seemed to be on some kind of roll, filled with energy and power, as if nothing could stop him. If there was something a little frantic about it all, Beau decided to ignore it.

The car salesman, a short, fat black man named Chester, seemed pleased to see Robert and offered him a choice: either an '88 silver Caddy with furry upholstery, or a pale-yellow VW Rabbit. Robert walked around each car a couple of times, kicked a tire or two, and then looked at Beau. "Whattaya say, Tonto?"

Without hesitation, Beau pointed at the Rabbit.

Robert slapped a hand down onto the hood. "This is it, then."

Chester grinned, Robert handed him a roll of bills, and they were on the move again.

Robert whistled softly as he drove the car back into Manhattan. Beau watched him warily. "Where are we going now, Robbie?"

Robert grinned. There was a circle of red on each cheek; otherwise, his face was pale. "Now we're off to see the man who will probably be able to tell us where Boyd is," he said with remarkable good cheer. "If he really is in town and planning any action, Uncle Pat will know. A dope like Boyd doesn't make a move in the Big Apple without checking it with good old Uncle Pat."

Beau watched an old woman pushing a shopping cart cross the street in front of them. "I have a feeling I'm not going to like this Uncle Pat guy," he said glumly.

Robert laughed softly and touched Beau's knee. "'S okay. Nobody likes Uncle Pat," he said. "Besides you won't actually be seeing him at all. He doesn't care much about outsiders. You better—"

"—wait in the fucking car," Beau finished wearily. "I know, I know."

The Irish social club was nearly deserted by this time. The members that were left were mostly old men sitting around playing cards. Robert sent a message in with the surly doorman and waited in the cloakroom for Uncle Pat to come out.

In about ten minutes, he did. "Mr. Turchek," he said, looking not the slightest bit avuncular. "This is a real surprise."

"Yeah, I know," Robert said. "I'm at the top of everybody's most-fucking 'Wanted' list. But nobody's got me yet, so I'm still tending to business."

Uncle Pat gave a hoarse bark that was supposed to be a laugh. "You know," he said, "I maybe should call my bookie and put a few bucks down on you."

Robert shrugged.

"So what do you want?" Uncle Pat said.

"Danny Boyd. I heard he's in town."

"Is that what you heard?"

"Hey, Boyd is the man who killed my brother. Are you saying I shouldn't be after him?"

"I'm not saying nothing like that. You got a right." Uncle Pat sighed and shook his head. "I only don't

understand how an honorable thing like avenging a
beloved brother gets to be so messy. This is very
untidy."

Robert gave him the same response he'd given
Marcello. "Life just gets complicated."

"Uh-hmmm." Uncle Pat looked at him thoughtfully.
"You know, there are people, important people, who
wouldn't be happy to hear that I helped you."

Robert met his gaze innocently. "Does that really
worry you, Uncle Pat?"

Another bark filled the cloakroom. "You always
were too damned smart, Robert Turchek." He produced a calfskin notebook and a silver fountain pen.
Carefully he printed something onto the page, tore
the page out, folded it, and handed it to Robert. "I
have not *told* you anything," he said. "Remember
that."

"I'll remember. Thank you, sir."

"Take my advice, Mr. Turchek, and be very careful. I always liked you. It would be a shame for a
young man like you to meet with a fatal accident."

Robert nodded.

He left the social club, stepping back out onto the
dark sidewalk. Someone grabbed his arm. Robert
pulled the newly acquired hand-gun out of his
pocket and spun around, all in the same move. His
finger was actually twitching on the trigger before
he realized who it was standing there.

"Jesus fucking Christ, Beau," he said in a shaky
voice. "I almost fucking killed you."

Beau was still gripping his arm. "There's a man,"
he whispered. "In the alley. I think maybe he's
waiting for you."

"What are you talking about?" Robert said, whispering now too.

Beau took a deep breath. "I was waiting in the car,

like you said, but it was hot and I wanted a cigarette. So I got out and walked around a little bit. Okay? And then this car showed up, going real slow. It stopped back there and a man got out." Beau paused for another breath. "I didn't like his looks, Robbie, so I watched him. I followed him."

"That was dumb."

Beau shrugged it off. "He's on the other side of the building. Just standing there, smoking and watching."

"He didn't see you?"

"Nope."

"Okay. You hang tough right here until I come back for you."

Beau nodded.

Robert kept the gun in his hand and slipped around the building the opposite of the way he'd arrived. He moved like a cat burglar through the darkness, until he could see the silhouette of the man who was waiting to kill him.

The bastard was holding a glowing cigarette in one hand, a long-barreled gun in the other, and he was staring at the empty Rabbit as if he were expecting the Second Coming to happen right there.

Well, he was going to meet his Maker before very many more minutes had passed, so maybe he wasn't so far off.

Robert bent and untied his shoes, slipped them off, and moved silently in his stockinged feet.

There was no time for the ambitious assassin to react, even if he knew what was happening. The barrel of the gun was against the back of his head and the bullet hit his brain at almost the same instant.

Robert put the gun away.

Beau was pacing the hotel room again.

Robert ignored him, staring instead at a detailed

street map of the city, trying to find the address Uncle Pat had written down. He had less than twenty-four hours to set this up, and he had the feeling that this was his last chance to get Danny Boyd. He couldn't afford to fuck it up again.

Beau stopped suddenly and looked at him. "I guess I sort of saved your life tonight," he said.

"Yeah, right," Robert said, still studying the map.

Beau just stood there for a moment, then he sighed. "I'm going to bed."

"Good idea."

He undressed silently, crawled into the bed, and pulled the sheet up over his head, blocking out the light.

After a moment, Robert folded the map. He switched off the lamp, stripped to his shorts by the outside light coming in through the window, and got into his bed. "By the way," he said then, "thanks."

"Don't mention it," Beau replied.

There was a pause and then they both started to laugh.

21

1

Gar had to do a little hard-core detective work to find LaVerne Boyd Ratigliano.

He checked the phone book, found a listing for an L.B. Ratigliano, and took a chance. This was the way things happened for TV dicks, with only an hour (less commercial time) to solve a case, but he didn't often get so lucky.

The address in the phone book proved to be a small wood-frame house in an Italian section of Brooklyn. He parked his rented car in front of the house and got out. A child's red wagon blocked the sidewalk and a small yipping dog protested his approach from the front window.

Before he could even ring the bell, the door was yanked open. A tired-looking young woman in blue jeans and a T-shirt, with a baby balanced on one hip, was standing there glaring at him. "You're a cop, right? And you want to ask me questions about my brother Danny. Am I right?"

"I would like to talk to you about Danny, yes," Gar said, neatly evading the issue of whether or not he was a cop. "Your brother's life could depend upon it."

"Right," she said sarcastically. "Well, you might as well come in." She kicked the door open with one foot.

Gar stepped into the hallway and was immediately charged by the little white dog. The dog skidded to a stop and began to sniff vigorously at his pant leg. "Yes, that's right," Gar said, bending to pat him. "I have a dog, too."

"Get outta here," LaVerne said, and the dog took off.

They walked into a small cluttered living room that smelled of sour milk and wet diapers. LaVerne dropped onto a worn stuffed chair and waved at the couch.

Gar cleared a space in the clean, unfolded laundry and several days' worth of newspapers. He sat and propped the cane next to his leg. "About Danny," he said.

"Ah, yeah, about Danny. Let me tell you about that SOB. He just keeps getting into trouble. I thought maybe spending all that time in prison would help, but I guess it hasn't." The baby let out a sudden shriek and she shoved a none-too-clean pacifier into its mouth. "For years I worried about Danny, I really did. But it didn't do him any good and it did me all kinds of bad. Now I've got problems of my own. Two kids and a no-good husband doing time for dealing. So I've got no more time to worry about Danny anymore. Understand?"

Gar nodded. "I can understand how you feel." Since there was an overflowing ashtray on the coffee table, he figured she wouldn't object if he smoked, so he lit up. "You do know, then, that he's in town?"

"Oh, sure. This was the first place he came. But I wouldn't have him here. Not with kids around. Danny's a bad influence."

Gar decided that if he was ever going to get past the soap opera, he had to be blunt. "I think a hitman may be in town to kill Danny," he said flatly.

She stared at him. "You're kidding, right?"

"No. This is not a joke. And whatever you think about Danny, he is your brother. You don't want to see him dead, do you?"

She shook her head slowly.

"Then I need your help. Do you know where I can find him?"

"No. He was just sort of moving around."

"Will he be coming back here, do you think?"

She shrugged. "God, I don't know."

Gar cursed to himself. "Okay," he said. "How about any friends?"

"Danny was away a long time. I don't know whether he has any friends left."

"Just one name," Gar said, almost pleading.

She thought for a moment, then her face cleared. "Try Billy McNeer," she said. "They used to run around together."

"You have an address for this McNeer?"

It took some time searching, during which time Gar and the baby sat staring at one another. The baby's eyes looked wiser than its mother's. LaVerne finally produced a page torn from a child's writing tablet, upon which she had scribbled an address.

Gar thanked her.

She just shrugged and walked him to the door. "Danny told me he'd have some money for me soon," she said suddenly. "That can only mean he's up to something. And when Danny does anything around here, McNeer is always in on it. They're real close."

Gar nodded and left her standing in the doorway.

This case was starting to remind him of those dolls—they were Russian, right?—where inside each doll was one even smaller, until you were left with a teeny final carved figure. To find Beau, he had to find Turchek. To find Turchek, he had to find Boyd. And now, to find Boyd, he apparently had to find Billy McNeer.

It made him tired just to think about it. He took a pain pill before driving away from LaVerne Boyd Ratigliano's house. So now he would go sit in front of McNeer's house. And hope that bastard Boyd would show up before too many hours passed.

2

The team of Boyd and McNeer was really pathetic.

Robert tossed a cigarette butt out the car window and watched the two men who were standing half a block away. To have Boyd this close and not do anything about it was making him feel very itchy.

"What are they doing anyway?" Beau asked finally.

Robert glanced at him. "Why, that's a couple of really dangerous outlaws, Tonto, and they're planning a major heist. Tonight they're going to hit that pharmacy. Uncle Pat gave them permission to do that. And then good old Unc told me. Or, he didn't *tell* me, exactly, but anyway that's what's going on. They're casing the joint and I'd be willing to bet that's exactly what they call it. 'Say, Billy, let's go case the joint.' I can hear Boyd saying that over breakfast." Robert shook his head. "Christ, I love it."

Robert lit another cigarette. He was so damned keyed up that he was afraid of making a dumb mistake. Calm down, he told himself. Chill out.

Beau finished slurping the last of his Coke out of the paper cup. "So what's our plan?" he asked then.

Robert started the car. There was no use wasting more time watching these assholes. He knew damned well where they would be at midnight. "Our plan is to kill Danny Boyd," he said. "And maybe Billy McNeer, just for being so fucking stupid."

"Lemme have a cigarette to smoke while you're gone," Beau said.

Robert glanced at him. "You're hooked on the damned things already, aren't you?"

Beau only shrugged and took the two cigarettes Robert held out to him.

They were parked around the corner from Dawson's Pharmacy in a quiet cul-de-sac. It was almost time for the two stooges, Boyd and McNeer, to show up, which meant that it was time for Robert to get into position. He was feeling good, except for the headache. Maybe things had been a little fucked up lately, but now he was back on track. Robert Turchek was cooking.

Beau had been pretty quiet all evening. Now he looked directly at Robert. "You sure this is the thing to do?" he asked.

"Will you fucking quit asking me that? Why don't you worry about your part in this? Can you handle it?"

"I told you a million times I used to drive the jeep

we had back home. I think I can get this fucking thing around the corner to meet you."

They both seemed to realize at the same moment that it was just nerves making them so short-tempered. Beau smiled and patted Robert on the arm. "Go do it," he said. "And be careful."

"Right."

Robert got out of the car, carrying both the guns he'd bought from Corley. Hopefully, he would be able to get close enough to use the pistol. Boyd sure wouldn't be expecting him to turn up here. Of course, there was also McNeer to deal with.

Well, that turned out to be even easier than he had expected. McNeer's task, apparently, was to watch Boyd's ass. He did a piss-poor job of it, sitting behind the wheel of a great big old Lincoln and staring at the back door of the pharmacy.

Robert walked up to the driver's side of the car, stuck the pistol into the window and pulled the trigger.

So much for Boyd's backup.

The lock on the door of the pharmacy had been taped open, so all Robert had to do was slip inside and stand in the dark hallway.

Boyd, if he had heard the shot that killed his partner—and how could he have not?—must have decided that it was a car backfiring. So he was still inside, ripping off pills as fast as his dirty little hands could move.

Robert took a deep breath. In only moments, the man who had killed Andy would be dead. The pressure to avenge his brother's death would be off him and he could start thinking about other things. Like how to straighten up his life.

But now he had to kill Danny Boyd.

* * *

When Gar heard the shot from behind the pharmacy, he swore under his breath and stepped into the phone booth. Automatically, his finger hit 911. "Shots fired," he said, then gave the address and hung up.

Now he would find out about the response time of New York's boys in blue.

But he didn't have time to wait.

So far, at least, his plan was working perfectly. After spending almost four hours staking out McNeer's place, Billy finally showed up. And Danny Boyd was with him. Then it took more hours before they left the apartment again. Gar could tell they were up to something, just by the overly careful way McNeer drove through the dark streets.

They were ripping off drugs from Dawson's Pharmacy. Gar figured that the chances of Turchek's showing up were pretty good and the sound of the shot seemed to prove him right. For the rest of his plan to work, however, he had to find Beau. And the cops had to show up.

While he was waiting for them, Gar walked a wide circle around the pharmacy, looking for a parked car. There were several, but the ones he checked were all empty. He could just hear the faraway sound of a siren by the time he hit the small dead-end street that ran along one side of the pharmacy.

He saw the VW Rabbit and the dark shape of someone sitting behind the wheel. There wasn't any time to think about it or wait any longer. He walked as quickly as he could to the car and yanked the driver's door open.

Beau Epstein looked at him, startled. Then he swore and started crawling toward the passenger door. Gar grabbed one kicking leg and held on. "Stop it, Beau," he said.

"Lemme go, you motherfucker," Beau yelled. "Lemme go." His free foot connected with Gar's stomach, and he was loose. The passenger door opened and Beau hit the ground running. He got about three steps from the car before Gar came around the front of the car, stuck his cane out, and tripped him flat. Beau fell heavily and Gar was on him in a minute.

They both heard a shot, then another, and then one more from inside the pharmacy. Beau froze for one instant, but then began to struggle again. He kicked and hit Gar, yelling obscenities in both English and Spanish. Gar couldn't really do anything except use his superior size and weight to try and subdue him.

At last, two squad cars roared up, lights and sirens in full operation. Cops jumped out, guns in hand.

"Don't shoot," Gar said, breathing hard from the continuing struggle. "I'm a licensed investigator. This is a runaway juvenile. The shots came from inside the pharmacy there."

One cop stayed where he was, while the others went to check it out.

"Beau," Gar said. "I'm here to help you. Don't be afraid. It's all over now."

Helpless now and finally quiet, Beau stared up at Gar. There were tears on his face. "Lemme go," he whispered. "Please. Just be a good guy. I have to go."

Gar shook his head. "Like I said, kid, it's all over. Any second now the cops will have Turchek in custody. You don't have to be afraid anymore."

Beau didn't say anything as tears continued to roll down his cheeks and into the dirt.

3

Four hours later, Turchek still hadn't been seen and Beau still hadn't said anything. Somehow Turchek had managed to slip out of the pharmacy and evade the cops. All that was left were two more bodies: Billy McNeer in his car and Danny Boyd, shot three times, just inside the pharmacy door. None of the cops seemed particularly broken up about the sudden deaths of the two.

As for Beau, he just sat in the corner of the squad room, alternately gnawing on a hangnail and twisting the fringe on his leather vest, and ignoring everyone.

Gar spent most of those four hours talking hard and fast to the captain in charge, explaining what was going on and also explaining why he should be allowed to take that poor kid home. It didn't hurt that a picture of Beau, labeled MISSING, was hanging on the squad-room wall. Or that Saul Epstein was his grandfather. It was very much a plus that three members of Congress and one cabinet member had been called during those hours as well.

Strings were pulled. The powerful triumphed, as they always did. This time, Gar didn't care. He was pulling for money and power to do their stuff and finally they did. Finally he and Beau Epstein walked out of the police station. Gar kept a friendly but firm hand on Beau's shoulder as they left. Not that it seemed to matter. All the fight seemed to have gone out of him and he was now just a scared, sad kid, who kept wiping his nose on his shirt sleeve.

There were no seats available on a flight to Los

Angeles until that night, so they checked into a hotel near La Guardia. Once they were safely inside the room, Gar relaxed a little. "Maybe I'll dial up some room service," he said cheerfully. "Whattaya say, Beau?"

Beau sat on one of the beds and looked at him with red-rimmed eyes. "I say, fuck you," he said in a dull voice. "Fuck you."

"Okay. I'll get us some breakfast. Eggs, maybe. And pancakes. Everybody likes that."

Beau just shook his head.

Gar picked up the phone.

Robert bent over the toilet and threw up again.

When there didn't seem to be anything left in his stomach at all, he wiped his mouth and left the bathroom. This hotel was even crummier than the one they'd been in last night. He couldn't go back there, of course, because maybe Beau would tell the cops about it. Not on purpose, of course, but they could probably get it out of him. After all, he was only a kid, and not used to being grilled by the fucking pigs.

Tonto had sure put up a hell of a fight, though, hadn't he? Robert felt a sort of crazy pride at the way Beau had handled himself.

He'd watched most of it from the darkness at the far end of the cul-de-sac. What else could he have done, against all those cops? Probably in the long run, it was the best thing for Beau anyway. What kind of a future would he have hanging around with a man on the run?

At least, Boyd was dead. That much had gone right. Robert didn't understand why he felt so hollow about it, though. Hell, he should be celebrating.

He leaned against the window and stared down at the street below. A drunk was crossing against the light and a cab nearly creamed him in the middle of the intersection. Robert shook his head. Idiot. The world was populated by idiots.

Of course, who the hell was he to talk? Here he was in a shitty hotel room all by himself. Every son of a bitch in the world was trying to kill him. He didn't have a job anymore, probably. His brother was dead. And now Beau wasn't even around anymore. This whole thing really sucked.

His life really sucked.

22

1

There were more cops to deal with in Los Angeles, of course. Like Wally Dixon, for one, who was even nice enough to meet them at LAX and drive them downtown personally. He had a few questions, naturally. Saul Epstein himself wasn't part of the welcoming team, although one of his lawyers and a Dr. Lieberman were. Gar's presence was politely tolerated by everyone, mostly, he figured, because Beau wouldn't talk to anybody but him. Still, he was trying to be very careful not to do or say anything that would make him persona non grata.

When they actually got into the interrogation room, it was a little crowded. The original group had been joined by a police stenographer and a clerk from Saul Epstein's law firm. Somehow, through a strange metamorphosis that Gar didn't really understand, it had become Us—meaning Beau Epstein and him—against Them. Meaning everybody else. The two of them sat side by side at one end of the table, confronting a wall of faces that seemed uniformly unfriendly. Even the lawyer and the shrink, ostensibly there to help, seemed to be a part of the Them contingent.

He was not quite sure when, in Beau's mind, he himself had turned from enemy into, if not exactly ally, at least no longer quite a foe. The breakthrough had come during the long flight across the country, when Beau had turned to Gar and politely asked, "Can I have a cigarette, please?" Gar gave him one, lit it for him, and they started talking. Gar was in the middle of an article about Disneyland in the airline magazine and Beau went into a long and detailed description of the day he'd spent there. With Robert Turchek.

"Nobody who was really bad would do that, would he?" Beau said at last. "I mean, it was just my fucking birthday. He didn't have to care."

"Right," Gar said. He didn't want to say anything to get Beau upset again.

That one word of mild agreement seemed to satisfy him. So now Beau was talking. But only to him. He still hadn't said a word to anybody else.

They had already been gathered around this table for nearly two hours and everybody's patience was wearing a little thin. Wally took a gulp of stone-cold coffee, grimaced, and looked at Beau. His eyes were as chilly as the decaf. "Turchek ever give you an idea where he might run for cover when things went bad?"

Beau, who was examining a hangnail on his thumb with complete interest, only shrugged.

Wally turned his glare onto Gar.

After a moment, Gar leaned over and spoke softly into Beau's ear. "Come on, kid, wouldn't you like to get the hell out of this room?"

Beau finally glanced at him. Then he quit playing

with his thumb and stared at Dixon. "I don't know where Robert Turchek is," he said quietly. "That's the truth, whether you want to believe it or not. I just don't know." His face turned fierce for just a moment. "I wish to hell I did." Then he seemed to wilt again and looked very young. "Can't I go to my grandfather's house now, please? I'm really tired."

Wally gave up. "Go home, Beau," he said. "We'll talk again in a few days."

The lawyer and the shrink had been designated to take charge of Beau at this point and deliver him to the old man. Beau shot Gar a look that seemed filled with despair. Gar pulled him aside in the hallway. "You going to be okay?" he asked.

Beau nodded. He was wearing sunglasses and a Batman baseball cap. "I'm fine," he said.

Gar didn't think he was, but this didn't seem to be the time or the place to argue the matter. Instead, he took out one of his business cards. "You stay in touch, okay? Give me a call if you have any problems. Or even if you just want to talk."

Beau took the card, looked at it with only mild interest, then tucked it into his pocket. "He's not bad, you know," he said again. "Robbie's a friend of mine, and I know him."

"I guess it probably seems that way to you right now," Gar said.

"See, the thing is . . ." Beau stopped, thought for a moment, then continued. "The thing is, I know he did some bad things. Killing people. But most of them sort of deserved it. Like the ones who killed my parents. Boyd killed Andy, Robert's brother, you know. But no matter what else he did, Robbie is my friend. He took care of me when I needed help." Beau raised the sunglasses. His eyes were urgent. "You understand that, don't you?"

Gar just nodded. "You better go. I'll see you soon."

"Will you?" Beau dropped the glasses back into place and glanced down the hall to where Lieberman and the lawyer were waiting impatiently. "I sort of feel like I'm going to disappear into some black hole and will never be seen again."

"I'll see you soon," Gar repeated, giving Beau a firm pat on the back.

Beau flashed him a sort of hopeless thumbs-up gesture and then walked away. Just before he reached the end of the hallway, Gar saw him pause to take a deep breath and straighten his shoulders. A moment later, he was gone.

Wally came over to where Gar was standing. "What do you think?"

"Well, I think he's telling the truth about not knowing where Turchek is," Gar replied. "They never talked about what he'd do if it all went bad, because he never thought it would." He paused. "I also think that even if Beau *did* know exactly where Turchek was, he'd never tell us." He leaned more heavily on the cane. "I'm so damned tired. You're not going to charge him, are you?"

Wally looked disgusted. "With what? Being a fucking hostage? Suffering duress or whatever? I may not believe that and I don't even think you do completely, but that's the cover story. And Saul Epstein has a whole lot of pull." He shrugged. "Unfortunately for me, Beau never walked into a bank carrying a gun like what's-her-name did. He's away clean."

"Good," Gar said.

"Well, maybe." Dixon sounded grumpy. Cops got that way when there wasn't anybody to charge with anything.

Gar gave him a weary smile and limped away.

* * *

Beau was politely refusing to come out of his room.

He'd been in there for three days now. Harold or Ruth brought him his meals, and Saul came by once or twice a day to talk. They never seemed to have much to say to each other, so those visits didn't last long. Saul was suddenly into reminiscence, talking about Jonathan a lot. Beau didn't see the point. Was he supposed to be more like his father? Or less? Since he couldn't decide how everybody wanted him to act, he thought it was easier just to stay in the room.

He was standing in front of the mirror, combing his hair and wishing it would grow back faster so he could look like himself again, when there was a knock on the door. He put the comb down and turned around. "Come in."

His grandfather opened the door, but despite the invitation, Saul didn't come all the way into the room, choosing instead to remain on the threshold. "I've tried to be patient with you," he said. "But now I think we've had about enough of this foolishness. You will come downstairs for dinner this evening. Dr. Lieberman will be joining us. Seven o'clock."

Suddenly Beau was tired of the bedroom and his own company. "Okay," he said. "Seven o'clock."

Saul looked a little surprised, but he didn't say so. He started to close the door again, then paused. "You will also please dress appropriately."

"Yes, sir," Beau said.

Saul seemed pleased as he left.

Beau thought about it all for a moment. Then he went to the closet to take out a clean shirt and a sport jacket. Instead of putting them on immediately, however, he began to search through the desk drawers. Finally, he found a large safety pin. Just the thing. Standing in front of the mirror again, he positioned the point of the pin and then, without giving himself time to think about it, plunged it through his lobe. It hurt a little more than he'd thought it might, but actually the sharpness of the physical pain, the *clarity* of it, was sort of a relief from the kind of hurt he'd been feeling lately. He used a Kleenex to wipe away a little blood that trickled out, and studied the effect.

He was pleased.

Now he would get ready for dinner with Saul and the shrink.

2

The bus had been crowded since Las Vegas.

Robert was sitting next to some kid who was studying film at USC. She seemed to think that the trip was a perfect chance to see Real Life, which meant striking up a conversation with an interesting stranger on a Greyhound bus. Robert was it.

He answered in monosyllables, which didn't discourage the fledgling female Spielberg at all. Robert wished he had a gun. More acutely, he wished that it were somebody else sitting next to him.

It was nearly 2 A.M. by the time the bus pulled into the station in downtown Los Angeles. Robert grabbed his duffel and managed to be the first off. As he walked through the waiting room, he had to fight the feeling that everybody in the place was watching him. Nobody here knew who the hell he was, and most of the people who knew him probably didn't think he was dumb enough to be back in town.

Nobody would be able to recognize him, anyway. He was wearing an old army camouflage jacket, baggy jeans, and a cowboy hat. He hadn't shaved in a week, his hair was too long, and just to complete the picture, he'd lost about fifteen pounds unbelievably quickly.

The weight loss wasn't intentional; he just didn't seem to have much of an appetite lately. The damned headaches still came and went with regularity, and he was continuing to pop pain pills as if they were jelly beans.

Once he was away from the bus station, he found a twenty-four-hour coffee shop and went in. The only other customers were three hookers sitting in a booth at the back. Robert took a stool at the counter and stared at the waitress until she put down the *National Enquirer* and walked over. "Coffee and a burger," he said, not bothering to look at the menu.

She nodded and disappeared into the kitchen.

Robert took a quarter out of his pocket and started for the telephone. Suddenly he remembered what time it was. Too damned late to call anybody now. He sat down again.

So here he was, back home again.

A dumb move, yeah, but given the circumstances, what choice did he have? The things that he had to do here would take, maybe, three days. There were several safety-deposit boxes to empty out. He wanted to see Andy's grave one more time, to be sure that the headstone he'd ordered was in place. A few other loose ends to tie up. And, of course, he had to get in touch with Beau.

That last item was the trickiest.

Probably Beau would have wised up by this time and would tell him to go fuck himself. And that was all right, Robert figured. He just didn't want to leave things the way they were. The two of them should at least be able to have a proper good-bye. They owed one another that much.

Then, once all of these things were taken care of, he'd leave this city, probably forever.

The waitress set his plate down with a crash. The bitch was not very good at dealing with the public. She could kiss her tip good-bye, with an attitude like that.

Robert took a bite of the burger and chewed slowly, not really tasting it. Again, the first two items on the agenda were obtaining a car and a piece. Both necessities of life in this day and age. Especially for a man on the run.

Mickey kept stacking up the messages as they came in.

It seemed that just because he was in a bad mood, the world didn't stop. People kept losing their kids and they kept wanting him to find them. Especially since the word had gotten around about his work on the Epstein case. If he was good enough for old Saul, the reasoning went, he was good enough for almost everybody else, too.

The problem was his. Gar just couldn't make himself care very much.

Mickey stepped out onto the deck and watched him play tug-of-war with Spock. "You and your dog have a lot in common, don't you?" she finally said.

"What's that supposed to mean?"

"He gets a hold on something and he won't let go either."

Gar gave her a dirty look, mostly because he knew she was right.

Mickey shook her head. "You found the boy and brought him home safely, babe. That was the job you were hired to do."

"I know that, damn it."

She walked over and rubbed his arm affectionately. "The police will get Turchek one of these days. And even if they don't, that's not your problem. This isn't the O.K. Corral, and you're not Wyatt Earp."

Gar gave a hard tug to the rope Spock was still pulling on. "Mick, I know what you're saying is right. But I can't get over the feeling that this is all so unresolved. How can I work on another case with this still hanging over me? It wouldn't be fair to anybody."

She gave up with a shrug.

"I saw Beau today," he said after a moment.

"Oh? How is he?"

"He looked fine. We didn't talk." Gar didn't meet her gaze. "He was going into the medical building and didn't even know I was there."

"So what you're saying is, you were spying on him."

He frowned. Trust Mickey to get right to the heart of a thing. "I don't think that 'spying' is the right word, exactly. I was just checking up on him, that's all."

"You act like Turchek is going to come swooping out of the sky and carry him off again."

That wasn't actually so far from what he *was* feeling, but Gar shook his head. "No. But I keep waiting for the other shoe to drop. And I just want to be sure that when it happens, the whole thing doesn't land on top of the boy. I like Beau, damn it, even if he is a pain in the butt." He finally quit playing with the dog. Spock looked a little relieved as he padded off to his bed and curled up. Almost immediately, he was snoring.

Gar got up and headed for the phone. "I think I'll see if he wants to go grab some dinner tonight." He paused, looking at her. "If you don't mind?"

She shook her head. "Actually, it's a good idea. Maybe when you see that he really is okay, you'll be able to relax."

"Thanks. Sorry about this."

Mickey smiled. "Hell, Sinclair, your mother-hen act is one reason why I love you."

He grimaced and went to the phone.

Lieberman was such an asshole.

Beau stretched his Nike-clad feet out across the oriental rug and smiled blandly at the psychiatrist. Nothing but dumb questions. The *same* dumb questions over and over again. Sometimes Beau answered them one way and sometimes he answered them just the opposite way. He was hoping that Lieberman would get sick of the endless sparring match before long. Then they could stop spending an hour together every fucking afternoon.

Lieberman occupied himself with filling another pipe. "Tell me, Beau, do you ever blame your parents for dying? For deserting you?"

That was one of his favorite questions. Today, Beau decided, he just wasn't going to answer anything at all.

"Are you feeling any sense of responsibility for the people who died while you were held hostage? Because you didn't do anything to save them?"

No, he just wasn't going to say anything. Let Lieberman jot *that* down in his damned notebook.

"I notice that you keep playing with that pin in your ear. Why did you feel the need to mutilate yourself in that way? Do you feel as if you deserved to be punished for something you did?"

Beau yawned.

"Were you sexually molested by the man who was holding you hostage, Beau?"

That was a new question, at least. Beau couldn't

even believe that he'd heard it right, in fact. "What did you say?" he asked, forgetting his determination not to speak at all.

"Did Robert Turchek sexually molest you?"

Beau leaned forward in the chair. "Why don't you just shut the fuck up?" he said in a tight voice. "I'm sick and tired of you and your damned questions. I'm tired of it, and I'm leaving."

"Okay, Beau," Lieberman said cheerfully. "We're out of time for today anyway. I'll see you tomorrow."

Well, maybe he would and maybe he wouldn't. Beau was really sick of this crap. He'd rather go to jail, for Chrissake.

He stayed mad all the way down to the lobby, where Harold, as usual, was waiting for him. Somebody was always watching him. Talk about being a fucking *hostage*. Now he had no freedom at all. It was clear that nobody trusted him.

Once Harold had done his duty by delivering him safely back to the house again, Beau went straight to his room. He was sitting on the bed, watching a soap on TV, when his phone rang. It rang so rarely that he jumped a little before reaching out to answer it. "Yeah?"

"Is that any way to greet an old friend?"

Beau knew the voice immediately, of course. Automatically, his gaze went to the door, but it was safely closed. "Robbie," he whispered. "Shit, it's really you."

"It's me. How you doing, Tonto?"

"I'm okay," he lied. "How about you?"

"Oh, I'm hanging in."

"How'd you get my number?"

"Connection at the phone company. Even unlisted numbers can be bought if the price is right."

Beau stretched out on the bed. He was excited and scared at the same time. He realized suddenly that what he felt for Robert was a strange mix of affection and fear. He loved him, yeah, but it was hard to forget that he was a killer. "Where are you?"

"In town."

His heart was pounding. "Can I see you?"

"Not right now."

He couldn't stop the disappointment from filling his voice. "Why not?"

"Well, things are sort of complicated. I just wanted to call and check on you. You're really okay? The cops aren't hassling you or anything?"

"No. Well, I have to see this damned shrink."

"Didn't I always say you were crazy, boy?"

Beau laughed. It felt good.

"Look, I have to run now—"

"Robbie, don't go." Beau stared at the television screen, not seeing the picture at all. "I'm not doing so good, if you want the truth. I really need to see you."

Robert was quiet for a moment, then he sighed. "Here's the deal, Tonto. I have a few things left to do in town here. One more day, probably. Maybe two, depending. Then I'm splitting for good. Probably I'll head south. Cross the border and decide then what to do next."

"Yeah?"

"If you want me to, I'll call you again before I leave. Meanwhile, you think about what you want to do."

Beau licked his lips nervously. "You mean I can come with you if I want to?"

"I mean, think about it, Tonto, that's all. Just think real carefully about it."

"Okay. I will. You'll call, for sure?"

"Yes. I will. Bye."

"Good-bye, Robbie," Beau whispered.

Then he hung up slowly.

3

Gar declined Harold's invitation to wait inside for Beau. It was his experience that no matter how much his clients needed him when they hired him, his charm seemed to disappear once the job was done. Bluntly put, they didn't want him around to remind them that he had ever been necessary.

So instead of going in, he walked back to his car and leaned against the front end. He wasn't quite clear about either his motives for asking the boy to dinner or Beau's reasons for accepting. Maybe, as Mickey had said, he just needed to see that Beau Epstein had, indeed, been saved.

It was only a couple of minutes before the door opened again and Beau came out in a near-run. He was wearing jeans and a clean white shirt with the sleeves rolled up. The Batman cap was still on his head. He also had the sunglasses on, even though it was already getting dark. With anybody else, Gar would have assumed that they were Going Holly-wood. With Beau, he didn't think that was it.

They greeted one another briefly and got into the car.

"You want to lose the shades, please?" Gar asked him before starting the engine. "You don't have to travel incognito anymore."

"Okay," Beau said with rather surprising good cheer.

Then Gar noticed the safety pin. "What's with the ear decoration?"

Beau looked at him challengingly. "You have a problem with it?"

Gar shrugged. "Not me."

"Good. That makes you pretty much a minority of one."

Gar was in no hurry, so he drove out to a seafood place he liked in Malibu. Once they had settled in and ordered, he took a really good look at Beau. The boy didn't meet his gaze and seemed to be wishing that he had his dark glasses on. "So how's life in the real world?"

Beau seemed puzzled by the question. "What's that mean?"

"Well, I was thinking that everything that's happened to you lately must have started to seem almost like a dream by now. Your time with Turchek, I mean."

Beau stirred his lemonade. "Maybe. Except that now you're starting to sound like that dope Lieberman. He talks about my dreams, too. Pretty soon, you'll be talking about sex, right?"

"I don't think so," Gar said mildly.

But Beau seemed angry anyway. "You want to know if Robbie fucked me or something, too? Is that the real reason for this meal?"

Gar stayed calm. "The only reason for this meal is that I wanted to have dinner with you. That's all. Sex is not my idea of a terrific table conversation. Neither your sex life nor mine. Fair enough?"

After a moment, Beau nodded and then relaxed. "Okay. I'm sorry. But Lieberman just yaps on and on about things like that and it makes me mad."

"I can understand that."

Beau smiled faintly. "I'm not telling him a damned thing."

"That's one way to handle it, I guess. How are you getting along with your grandfather these days?"

"Okay."

"That's an improvement, isn't it?"

"I guess. He still thinks he can make me into Jonathan, except this time maybe I'll be a son who won't turn out to be a big disappointment."

Their dinner was served and for a few minutes they both just concentrated on eating. Gar watched Beau pack away the food as if it might disappear before he had enough. "You seem to be in a pretty good mood tonight," he commented.

Beau shrugged. "I'm out of that fucking house and talking to a normal person for a change. That would put anybody in a better mood, right?"

"I guess so, but I thought that maybe it was something else making you so cheery."

Beau was sopping up melted butter with a crust of bread. "Like what?"

"Like maybe you heard from Turchek."

He just kept chewing, his face showing nothing at all. "That's a weird thing to say."

"Is it?"

"Sure. Robbie's probably still in New York. Or maybe he's in China by now; who knows?"

"Maybe." Gar took a swallow of his drink. "Can we cut the crap for a minute, Beau?"

"Yeah?"

"I just want to ask you to be very careful. Turchek is a hunted man. And that makes him even more dangerous. He might try something desperate."

Beau seemed amused. "I'm not scared of him."

"Maybe you should be."

But Beau only smiled.

Gar gave up. "Well, just remember, I'm here. If you need somebody."

For a moment, Beau's blue gaze fixed on him solemnly. Then, slowly, he nodded. "Thank you, Gar," he said quietly. "But I'll be fine."

Gar hoped that was so.

* * *

Robert was getting things together.

He had a car now—another cash-in-hand, no-questions-asked deal—and a gun, same thing. He also had a briefcase filled with money. All three of those things made him feel better. So did the fact that he was clean-shaven, his hair cut, and he was wearing clean clothes. He was himself again.

That wasn't all good, of course.

He was just having a quiet drink at a bar he'd never been in before when somebody slid into the booth.

"Well, look who's back in town," a silky voice said.

He knew without looking who it was. "Hello, Leonard," he said. "What the hell do you want?"

Leonard was one of those slimy little men who hovered on the edge of all the real action in life. Once in a while a man like him would hit the jackpot, but chances were he'd lose it again the next day. Leonard would sell his mother or his virgin daughter if the price was right.

Now he looked a little offended at Robert's tone. "Hey, buddy, you shouldn't be alienating anybody still willing to talk to you, should you?"

Probably he had a point, but Robert wouldn't give it to him anyway. "I'm doing fine," he said.

"Sure you are. Probably that contract out on you is somebody's idea of a joke."

"It's all just a misunderstanding. I'll have everything straightened out soon."

Leonard leaned over the table and smiled. "Well, here's hoping you get it straightened out before the contract gets fulfilled."

Robert didn't say anything, and after a moment Leonard got up and left the bar.

Robert left immediately after. It wasn't a good

idea to hang around there now, because Leonard was probably on his way to sell somebody the location of a wanted man like him.

Instead of going directly back to his motel room, however, he cruised to a slow stop in front of the Epstein mansion. Through the bars of the high black fence, he could see that all the lights were off but one up on the second floor. He figured that maybe it was Beau's room. The kid must be awake.

Robert waited a few minutes, thinking that maybe Beau would come to the window. He could flash his headlights or something, just to say good night.

But nothing like that happened, so he finally drove away and headed for the motel.

Once there, he sat on the lumpy bed for a while and did some serious thinking about the contract that was out on him. It wasn't the first time something like this had happened, of course. In his line of work, it was almost an occupational hazard.

But this was the first time he'd ever felt that the odds were with the other guy. It was not a feeling he liked.

Finally he reached for the phone and slowly dialed a familiar number.

There were places you went when things were really fucked up. It wasn't quite like throwing yourself on the mercy of the court, but there was a similarity. The court of last resort.

When the phone on the other end was answered, Robert took a deep breath and started talking quickly. But it wasn't working. There was only silence on the other end and then, carefully, the connection was broken.

Robert pulled the phone from his ear and stared at it in stunned surprise. Then he hung up.

23

1

Wally Dixon truly didn't want to hear any more about Beau Epstein or Robert Turchek. He was tired of that whole damned case, and besides, there were six new homicides vying for his expert attention. A man could only handle so much, after all, and why the hell didn't Gar find himself some new case that would keep *him* out of trouble instead of making phone calls to a cop who was *really* busy?

When Wally paused to take a breath, Gar finally got his question asked. "Any word on Turchek being back in town?"

Wally sighed. "Rumors, that's all. Nothing solid. But you know how the slimebags love to gossip. If he is in this city, he better be watching his ass every minute."

"More gossip?"

"You got it. Turchek is stirring things up too much. Making the outside world peek a little too closely at things some people prefer not to be peeked at. Besides, they're convinced he's going to take a fall before too long and nobody wants to fall with him. I wouldn't give long odds on Turchek's life span, in other words. And that is all I know and now I have a meeting with the captain. Good-bye."

When the phone call was over, Gar stayed where he was for a time, frowning and doodling on the memo pad, as he wondered whether "spying" was the right word for what he was thinking about doing.

When after ten minutes or so, he decided that he just didn't give a damn about semantics, Gar scribbled a note for Mickey, who was in the darkroom. He grabbed his gun and his cane and set off to play detective.

Or spy.

Or maybe just mother hen.

The next day dragged on forever.

Beau hurried through breakfast as quickly as he could without making Saul suspicious, and then went back upstairs. To read, he said. The truth was, he wanted to stay close to his telephone, even though there was a good chance that Robert wouldn't call for another twenty-four hours.

If then.

And, of course, nothing happened all morning. He didn't even read, just sat staring at the game shows on television.

At lunchtime, he ate a sandwich standing in the middle of the kitchen. Ruth wanted to know if he had ants in his pants or something, but he just smiled and carried a big glass of lemonade back upstairs with him. He told Ruth he wasn't feeling too good and so would she please call Lieberman and cancel his appointment. Saul would be pissed, but to hell with him.

It was almost six o'clock before the phone finally rang. He had the receiver in his hand before the first ring had ended. "Yes?" he said cautiously.

"Hi."

He sighed. "I was afraid you wouldn't really call me back."

Robert was quiet for a moment. "I never lied to you, Tonto."

"I know." Beau scratched his bare ankle. "I haven't told the cops anything, Robbie. Not one fucking thing."

"Good boy. I knew I could count on you."

Robert, at least, trusted him. "So did you get all your business taken care of?"

"All done, yeah."

"And now?"

"Now I'm history around this town. Before the cops or anybody else figure out where the hell I am."

Beau was wishing he had a cigarette. "What about me?"

"You." He heard Robert take a deep breath. "Well, that's your choice."

Beau frowned. Making a choice was hard. "I don't know. I want to come, but . . ."

"But what?"

He cleared his throat. "I'm sort of scared."

Robert didn't say anything right away. "Of me?" he asked finally.

"Of course not," Beau said firmly. "Of things, that's all. Just things."

"Well, that's okay. That's really okay. So it's probably better if you stay right where you are."

Beau blinked back tears. "But I'm scared to do

that, too. I'm just all screwed up, Robbie." He hated the fact that his voice broke like a little kid's.

"Ah, hell, Beau, I'm sorry. I shouldn't have even called you in the first place."

"No, I'm glad you did," Beau said quickly. "I've been waiting. Without really knowing that I was, if that makes any sense." He stared hard at the ceiling and then decided. "I'll come with you," he said.

"You sure?"

"Yes. I'm very sure."

"Okay," Robert said. "We'll talk about it anyway, when I see you."

"Tonight?"

"Yeah. I'm at the Pelican Motel, out on the Pacific Coast Highway. Can you get out here without anybody knowing?"

"Yes. I'll be there as soon as I can."

"Room 108," Robert said. "And, Beau—"

"Yeah?"

"Be careful, okay?"

"Sure." Beau hung up slowly. He had to plan.

Luckily, Saul wasn't coming home for dinner. And Harold was out, too, driving Saul wherever it was the old man was going, so that meant all he had to do was slip away from Ruth. Very easy. By the time anybody knew he was gone, it would be too late for them to do anything. He'd be back with Robert, for good this time.

He felt that same jolt of fear mingled with excitement.

But first, he had to get through dinner. Since it was just the two of them, he ate with Ruth in the kitchen. It was an effort to carry on a normal conversation with her, because his mind was leaping ahead to what was going to happen later, but he tried so she wouldn't suspect anything.

When the seemingly endless meal was finally over, he went right back upstairs. He changed his clothes while he waited. Ruth, he knew, was a creature of habit. She would clean the kitchen carefully and then go to the rooms she and Harold had in the back of the house. Once there, she would be lost in front of the television. He could get away clean.

The hardest part was the waiting.

When he was pretty sure that enough time had passed, Beau crept down the stairs. He paused in the foyer to listen, but heard nothing, and so he went out the front door.

He began to run.

2

It took two buses and a hitched ride with a couple of softball players on their way home after a big win to get him all the way out to the Pelican Motel. He went directly to room 108 and tapped lightly on the door.

"Who's there?" Robert's voice was cautious.

"It's me."

The door opened immediately and he went inside quickly. Robert grabbed him in a tight hug, which he returned. After a long moment, they stepped back and surveyed one another with care. "My Disneyland vest," Beau said. "Remember?"

"Yeah, sure." Robert reached out and flicked the safety pin with a finger. "I like that, you idiot."

Beau grinned. "It drove everybody else crazy."

"I can imagine."

"You look like you're feeling better," Beau said, although that wasn't strictly the truth. Robert's face

looked drawn and tight, even though he was smiling.

"I'm okay. The damned headaches come and go,
but I'm okay. Better now," he added, patting Beau's
shoulder. "Christ, it's good to see you."

"Yeah. I missed you a lot." Beau walked over and
sat down on the bed. "I want to come with you."

"I'm glad. If you're really sure that's what you
want."

Beau nodded. "I'm sure. I'm still sort of scared,
but I'm sure."

"You ought to know that I'm in kind of a tricky
position right now. Somebody still wants me dead.
Next to me might not be the safest place to be."

"I know," Beau said.

"If I can help it," Robert said, "nothing will
happen to you."

"We're both going to be okay," Beau said.

They just grinned at one another for a moment.

The sudden pounding on the door crashed into
the room like a bomb exploding.

"Turchek?" came a voice from the other side of
the door. "This is Gar Sinclair. Why not open the
door now and save everybody a lot of trouble?"

Robert's gaze went from the door back to Beau.

Beau felt cold. "I didn't bring him, Robbie. I
swear to God I didn't. He must've followed me
somehow. I didn't bring him."

Robert patted his shoulder again. "I know that,
Tonto. I know it."

"I'm still sorry, though. It's my fault." Beau fought
to hold back tears. "I'm always bringing you trouble. God, I'm sorry."

Robert knelt in front of him. "Shut up. That's a
stupid way to talk. I don't blame you, understand?"

Beau nodded.

"Turchek," Gar said from outside. "The cops are on their way. It would be better for everybody if this was all wrapped up by the time they arrive."

Beau swore softly and hit the bed with his fist. Then he looked at Robert again. "Gar's not a bad guy, Robbie. He really tried to help me. Maybe if I asked him . . . maybe if I could make him understand. . . ."

"Oh, sure." Robert got up and went to the door. "Hey, Sinclair, you've got the kid believing in you. Says you're a friend of his and probably, if he asks nice, you'll just let us walk out of here. Is Beau reading you right, Sinclair?"

There was only silence in response.

Robert looked at Beau with what seemed to be a certain amount of satisfaction. "So much for your friend the detective, Tonto."

Beau shook his head. "What are we going to do, Robbie?"

"I don't know." After a moment, Robert took a gun out of the desk drawer. "Maybe if we can get out of here before the pigs show up, we still have a chance." He checked the weapon and then looked at Beau again. "Unless you want to leave, Beau. You can walk out right now and I won't stop you. I won't even blame you."

Beau swallowed hard. "No," he said faintly. "Not unless you come, too."

But Robert shook his head. "I remember what Andy went through in prison. I don't think I could do that. Even if they let me live long enough to get to prison."

Beau grabbed his hand. "Please, Robbie. Let's just give up. I'll make my grandfather get you a good lawyer. I'll come to see you in jail. I will. It's better than being dead."

"I don't think so."

Beau tried to stop shaking. "It's better for *me* than you being dead."

Robert closed his eyes for a long moment, then opened them and stared at Beau. "I'm sorry. You have every right to hate me, but I have to do this my way."

"I don't hate you," Beau said dully. "I love you. And I'm not leaving."

"Okay." Robert glanced at the door, then back at him. "Do you trust me?"

"Of course."

"Then just go along with whatever I say and do, okay?"

"I will."

Beau stood. Robert put an arm around Beau's neck and held on firmly. Then he put the barrel of the gun against Beau's head. "Okay?" he said.

Beau just gave a jerky nod.

"Don't be scared."

"I'm not," he whispered. But that was a lie, because he was.

"Good." They walked back to the door. "Open it," Robert ordered him.

Beau reached out a hand and did. They found themselves facing Gar Sinclair, who also had a gun.

"I think the trump card is mine," Robert said mildly.

"The police don't like this kind of thing," Gar replied.

"Fuck it. Either I walk out of here okay or neither one of us does."

Gar looked at Beau. "You okay?"

Beau didn't say anything and then Robert gave an extra squeeze to his neck. It hurt. "Tell him you're okay, Tonto."

"I'm okay," Beau said hoarsely.

Gar was watching Robert. "I don't think you'll kill the boy, Turchek."

"Don't you?" Robert smiled icily. "Try me, if you've got the balls. I don't think you do."

Nobody said anything for several long seconds. Then Gar lowered his gun and stepped back. "Okay. You win. Take him and go."

"Thank you. Maybe you really are an okay guy, like Beau here says. Now put the gun on the ground, please." He did. "Kick it away, Tonto."

Beau raised one foot and kicked the gun across the pavement.

The two of them started moving toward the car. Beau felt Robert's arm loosen just a little. "You're doing great," Robert whispered right into his ear. "Almost there."

The shot came at that moment.

3

Gar's first instinct—he'd been a cop a long time—was to hit the ground. But he didn't. Nobody did or said anything for one perfectly quiet instant. Then, when he realized that the shot had come from somewhere across the road, Gar looked that way. He saw nothing of course. A pro wouldn't be that easy to spot.

He looked back toward Beau. Robert was just starting his fall forward, dragging Beau down with him. Gar forgot the gunman, who was no threat to anybody else, after all, and moved toward them.

In the distance, he could hear the approaching sirens. The cavalry, a little too late.

He reached Beau, who was on the ground now,

half-trapped under Turchek's bloody form. "No," Beau was whispering. "Nononono." It came out as a horrified mantra.

Gar crouched down next to them. "Are you hurt, Beau?"

Beau was busy trying to wipe the blood from Robert's face and didn't even seem to hear him.

Gar gripped his shoulder. "Beau, are you hurt?" he asked again.

"Help him," he whispered. "Please, help Robbie."

The squad cars finally appeared, bathing the scene in flashing blue-white lights.

"I think he's dead," Gar said gently, trying to pull Beau out from under his gruesome burden.

"No, he's not dead," Beau said insistently. "He can't be. Not again. This can't happen again." He was patting Turchek's cheek. "Robbie? Robbie, please."

The cops were still just standing around, looking dumb. Gar glanced at them. "The shot came from over there," he said, pointing. "But I doubt seriously if anybody's still around." They went to look anyway, because at least it was something to do.

Gar turned back to Beau. "Robert never even knew what happened," he said. "He didn't feel anything at all. Come on, Beau, let the cops take care of things now."

Beau stared at him, then looked down again. He bent and placed a kiss on Robert's face. When he raised his head, Gar could see the dark blood staining his lips. Very carefully, he rested the limp body on the ground and then stood. "I'm going to get the bastard," he said in a suddenly cold voice. It was only then that Gar noticed Turchek's gun in

Beau's hand. "I'm going to get the bastard," Beau said again. He turned and started to walk off.

Gar grabbed him. "No," he said. It took several seconds to pry the gun from Beau's bloody fingers. "It's over, Beau."

Beau looked at him. "Everybody I love gets killed," he said. "Isn't that funny?"

24

Gar picked up the ball and threw it again. He would tire of the game much sooner than would the dog, who took off after his toy in completely joyous pursuit. Because he was watching Spock and thinking about other things, Gar didn't realize that anybody had approached until Beau actually spoke.

"Hi, Gar," he said.

Startled, Gar turned around quickly. It had been nearly a month since he'd seen Beau, although they had spoken on the phone every day. By now, he was looking more like the boy Gar had started off hunting: his hair was getting long again and was almost back to its natural blond color. Seeing him now, in the pale-blue sweatshirt and cutoffs, Gar had a quick flash of that other kid, the one with the hurt eyes and bloodstained lips.

"Hi, Beau," he said finally. "I'm glad to see you."

"The lady up at the house told me where you'd be."

"That was Mickey. I mentioned her to you."

"Uh-huh." Beau walked over to him. The safety pin was gone from his ear, replaced by a small diamond stud. "Harold drove me over so I could see you."

"Good." Gar studied him closely for a moment, not knowing what he might see. But on the surface, at least, Beau looked fine. They walked after the dog.

"I had to come to see you to say good-bye," Beau said. "I'm going away to school on Monday. Some damned place up in Oregon."

Gar glanced at him. "Well, maybe the change will be good."

"Maybe." Beau didn't sound very sure about that; mostly he sounded resigned. "I made a deal with Saul. One semester. If I don't like it, I don't have to go back."

"Sounds fair."

"I guess. If he sticks to it." He kicked at the sand. "If I write you a letter, will you answer me?"

"Sure. Of course I will. Or call me, if you want to. Collect even," he said with a smile.

Beau nodded seriously. "Thanks. The thing is, I know that finding people is your job. Just because you were hired to do that, it doesn't make you my friend or anything. You're not, like, obligated."

Gar felt as if he were walking through a very dangerous emotional mine field here. He wasn't quite sure how to deal with Beau Epstein. "You're right that looking for people is my job, Beau. But you better believe that what happened with you went way beyond the usual."

"Yeah, I guess."

"I'd like to be your friend. But I know and you know that friendship has to be earned. Just saying it doesn't make it real."

"I know," Beau said. "I know what being a friend means." His tone was vaguely defensive. Or maybe defiant.

"I guess maybe you do," Gar said carefully.

They walked in silence briefly.

"I'll be back home at Christmas," Beau said.

"Great. We'll get together then. Raise a little hell or something."

"I'd like that." Spock finally brought the ball back and dropped it at Beau's feet. "Can I throw it for him?"

Gar nodded.

Beau picked up the ball and threw it a very long way. As they watched the happy dog run off in pursuit, he said, "Robbie wasn't really going to shoot me, you know. It was all just a game."

"Was it?" Gar said quietly.

"Yes," Beau said fiercely. "He loved me. He wouldn't have hurt me."

Gar didn't see much point in arguing over it now. "Well, probably you're right."

"I am." He was quiet for a time, as if trying to pick just the right words. "We just wanted to get away, that's all."

Gar stopped walking and looked at him. "You understand that I couldn't just let you go, don't you? I had to try and stop you."

It was a long time before Beau replied. "I understand," he said. "At first I didn't, but now I do. Mostly."

"I'm glad of that."

Beau stopped suddenly and looked at him with a steady gaze. "But there's something I want you to understand, too," he said quietly.

"What's that?"

"Robbie was a good friend. I know he made a lot

of mistakes and maybe he did some things that were bad, but to me, he was a good friend. Can *you* understand that, Gar?"

After a moment, Gar nodded. "I think so. I can try to, anyway."

"Thank you. So now you believe me when I say that Robbie wasn't going to shoot me? He wouldn't hurt me, ever."

It was nice to think so anyway.

Beau bent suddenly and picked up a stick. He held it over one shoulder and marched along, looking like a little tin soldier. "This place I'm going," he said, "it's a military school. The same one my father went to."

"Terrific," Gar muttered. Actually, of course, he didn't think it was terrific at all. It sounded like a really stupid idea to him.

Beau seemed to know what he was thinking and his voice was almost amused when he spoke. "Well, the dumb school didn't turn Jonathan into a soldier. He went practically straight from there to Woodstock. I don't exactly think I'm West Point material either." He shrugged. "It seems like poor Saul didn't learn anything the first time around."

"He loves you."

"I guess he does. Some people just don't handle love very well. That's what Jonathan said about Saul once."

"Well, you can survive the school."

"Oh, sure." His shoulders straightened a little. "The secret is, never let them see you sweat."

"Promise me one thing."

"What?"

"If you run away from the school, you'll come here. I don't want to have to go looking for you again."

Beau almost smiled. "Okay." He was quiet again. Then he brought the stick around, sighting down its length as he pretended to track a target in the distance. "I'll probably have to learn how to shoot guns and everything."

Gar couldn't think of anything smart to say in response to that.

Beau looked at him suddenly and really did smile. The cheery expression didn't extend as far as his eyes, however, which were still an icy blue.

Despite the heat of the afternoon, Gar felt an almost physical chill go through him as he met the cold gaze. Beau, still smiling, abruptly brought the stick down and broke it over his leg. It made a loud *crack* that echoed in the silence around them.

"Screw 'em," Beau said.

"That's the attitude," Gar agreed. "Screw the bastards."

Beau grinned again, a real smile this time, warm and not at all scary. Then he took off after the dog.

Gar thought that the boy would probably be okay. It wasn't going to be easy, but if he had one friend sticking by him, Beau could come through this mess in pretty good shape.

That made it sound so simple, of course, and Gar knew it wasn't simple at all.

But it was possible. And, he thought, worthwhile.

Beau found the ball before the dog and raised one hand in a V-for-victory sign, grinning at Gar.

Or maybe it was the old peace sign Beau was making.

The sharp crack of the breaking stick was still echoing in Gar's mind, however. He had a feeling that the sound would be with him for a very long time. Maybe it would even wake him up in the middle of some dark night. But he put that thought aside for the moment and trudged after Beau, who was laughing aloud as he scrambled through the sand with the dog.

For the moment, that was enough. In this life, you took your victories where you found them.